PEHNUT BUTTER AND JELLY SANDWICHES FROM OUTER SPACE!

(A Twenty-First-Century Fairy Tale)

I. S. Noah

Copyright © 2024 I. S. Noah
All rights reserved
First Edition

Fulton Books
Meadville, PA

Published by Fulton Books 2024

ISBN 979-8-88731-691-8 (paperback)
ISBN 979-8-88731-692-5 (digital)

Printed in the United States of America

This book is dedicated to my wife, who I love deeply.

I also want to thank the living and departed who have provided me with feedback and encouragement including my family, friends, teachers, fellow students and pets.

I. S. Noah

CHAPTER 1

Yin and Yang

It was the summer of 2019 in a reality very close to our own.

Violet Wilson threw some granola bars and a compass into her backpack. She had already packed several bottles of water, a two-gallon ziplock bag full of writing supplies and correction tape, a pocket thesaurus, two pads of yellow legal paper, and an enormous book of famous quotes. There would be no internet access deep in the forest where she was going, and she was determined to complete her manifesto today! The introduction still needed work.

Look around you. A few decades from now, the children you see will be called on to lead this great nation. Sadly, that job might be too difficult for us.

Many of the students I know have learned to reject facts in favor of slogans. They give more weight to personal bias than to science and history. This makes progress nearly impossible. As Isaac Asimov said, "There is a cult of ignorance…nurtured by the false notion that democracy means that my ignorance is just as good as your knowledge."

Violet was fed up with her classmates spouting bogus, unjustifiable opinions while calling the facts "fake news." Trying to have an honest discussion with some kids, like Irwin Slater, made her blood boil. She felt like punching that sexist jerk right in the nose when he said, "I've known way more than a few females who have serious mood swings. Therefore, I think it's dangerous and irresponsible to vote for a woman president."

What gall! Violet wasn't a violent person, but she wanted to strike back! A self-satisfied, pigheaded culture was growing like mold in her school, and she was aching to stomp it out.

After weeks of brainstorming, one compelling idea burned in her mind like a hot coal. The best way to battle the "cult of ignorance" was to resurrect the Sky View High School journalism club and student-written newspaper. Both had died over thirty-five years ago.

Her best friend, Pamela Edison, thought it was a great idea. She was glad to help with the proposal, but she also had concerns.

"We'll be laughed out of school if we only get geeks and freshmen to join," she told Violet in a text message.

Pamela had just returned from a summer job working as a junior counselor at Grand Pines Wilderness Camp. It was loaded with students from their school, and she spoke to all of them.

Some kids were enthusiastic about the club. Some were ready to sign up. Others were cynical or even angry about her requesting precious school resources to waste on a "stupid newspaper."

The battle lines had been drawn, and Pamela's insights were the likely key to their success. She insisted that the best place to think and write was the forest, so she called for a hike, as usual.

Violet was itching to put a plan together. The fall semester was hurtling toward them like an asteroid headed for planet Earth, and her friend was already sixteen minutes late!

"She better not be doing her laundry from camp," she mumbled while stuffing <u>A Young Person's Guide to the Constitution</u> into her bag. It was starting to get heavy.

"Oogah! Oogah!"

The alert notified her of an incoming message from her mom.

She scowled and hit the text icon. Her mother's words made her overworked brain boil.

"I need to work late. Please watch your brothers. 😔"

"No way!"

Violet resisted the urge to throw her phone out of a window and pretend she never saw the message. Instead, she hit the callback icon and paced around her room.

"I'm not putting up with this."

"Hello, Vi," her mom sang out through the speaker.

Violet froze, like a burglar surrounded by guard dogs.

"I cannot watch the boys," she said through clenched teeth.

"I called all our sitters, and none of them are available. I need you to do this."

"I can't!" Violet kicked her backpack. It toppled over, and a water bottle rolled out. "Pamela and I are going on a hike."

"So? Take the boys."

"No! We have important school business to deal with. I can't focus if I have to watch those two lunatics."

"They are not lunatics. They're your brothers."

"But they—"

"No buts. In five years, you'll hardly remember your 'important school business.' You'll be in college. Then your brothers will grow up, and hopefully they'll go to college too. And you know who's going to pay for all that?"

Violet had heard this speech before. Her mom, who worked part-time as a real estate agent, was giving her the hard sell. There was no escaping it. The lecture about the responsibilities and challenges of parenthood went on and on. She was actually relieved when her mother got to the point.

"Margaret called in sick, and there's an open house today. I have to stay here and take over." She paused, almost daring her daughter to complain. "You can watch the boys at home or take them on your hike. I'm sorry you have to do this, but I'll pay you $15 an hour."

"I don't care about the money," Violet mumbled.

"Good. I won't force you to take it. I expect your father to be home around five thirty. You can deal with your school business then."

A muted beeping told Violet that her mom had an incoming call.

"I have to go now. Please, keep the boys out of trouble."

Mrs. Wilson hung up.

Violet threw her cell phone into a dresser drawer and slammed it shut. She crossed the room and glared at the piece of furniture.

"This isn't fair! It's involuntary servitude!"

Her rant was cut short by the doorbell. She stomped to the front door and peeked out of the little window on top.

Pamela was standing there with a Grand Pines hat on her head and a Nature Conservancy messenger bag slung over her left shoulder.

Violet opened the door and glared at the floor.

"We can't go on the hike."

"Why not?"

"I have to watch my stupid brothers."

Pamela took her hat off as she entered the house.

"Can't they go play with some friends?"

"No. Brad always causes trouble. He thinks it's funny."

Violet shoved the front door shut. She hadn't noticed the chubby thirteen-year-old standing in a doorway behind her.

"Hi, Pamela," Brad said, with a toothy grin. "Do you wanna cause some trouble with me? We can have lots o' laughs."

The girls rolled their eyes and brushed past Brad. They went straight to Violet's room, closing the door behind them.

Pamela deposited her bag at the foot of the bed and sat down.

"If you have to watch your brothers, you may as well do it in the forest."

Violet rolled onto her bed.

"We won't get any work done."

"Will we get more done by staying here? A hike might wear them out."

"This is so unfair." Violet strangled her pillow.

"Sometimes life is fair. Sometimes it isn't."

"That really doesn't help."

"At Grand Pines, the counselors taught us that every problem is a question of balance. For every yin, there's a yang."

"Too bad yin and yang don't babysit."

"Ha, ha." Pamela stood up. "If we go on the hike, I'll help you watch your brothers."

Violet locked eyes with her friend.

"You'll help watch Brad and Willys? In the forest?"

"Yes. Brad's a pain, but Willys is what, like, five years old?"

"He's six."

"I can handle a six-year-old."

"That's what they all think."

Pamela took it as a challenge. "I was in charge of ten kids at camp. We went on hikes all the time. This is no different."

Violet shrugged.

"Fine. We can take them on the hike, but I guarantee we won't get any work done."

"We'll see." Pamela stood up defiantly and walked to the room Violet's brothers shared.

Willys was crawling around the floor playing with superhero action figures.

"Oh no! Loki and Dr. Doom teamed up! Who can stop them? Go get help, Spider-Man!"

Pamela dodged the action figure the boy tossed across the room.

"Whoa. I didn't know Spider-Man could fly like that."

"He was swingin' on his webs."

Pamela sat next to him and picked up a toy jeep with Captain America inside.

"Superheroes are cool," she said.

"Yeah, specially the Avengers." He got up and ran around the room with his Iron Man figure while making jet sounds.

"Do you think Captain America would like to go on a hike in the forest?"

"Probly." The little boy came back and held up another superhero. "He'd take Wolverine to cut firewood. Chop! Chop!"

Pamela put the jeep down.

"I like the forest."

"Me too." Willys picked up a Hulk action figure. "You call that choppin' wood? Watch this! Rah!" He pounded the Hulk against the floor and imagined him reducing a piece of lumber to splinters.

"Hey! Would you like to go on a hike with Violet and me?"

"Really?"

"Really."

"Yes!" Willys pumped his fist.

He ran to his closet and got his plastic baseball bat and a pair of cowboy boots.

"I can protect us from wild animals."

Pamela smiled at the rambunctious little boy.

"Those critters won't mess with you."

"They better not. I bet I can run faster than Violet too." He pulled his boots on. "You wanna race?"

Pamela tousled the boy's hair.

"Not now. I still need to convince your brother to come with us."

"Why? He doesn't like goin' on hikes."

"Your mom won't like it if we leave him alone."

"I guess." Willys frowned. "What if he won't go?"

"Don't worry. I know a trick or two. I'm really good at getting kids to participate in camp activities." Pamela smiled and ran her fingers through her hair. "Do you know where he is?"

Brad was on the couch in the den, playing a video game featuring robot dinosaurs.

Pamela walked into the room and glanced at the television.

"New game?" she asked.

"No, just an old favorite."

She stood behind the couch and leaned close to him.

He could feel her breath on his neck. It annoyed him.

"Even the best games can't beat reality," she said.

"Reality sucks most of the time."

"I'm just saying. A virtual milkshake can't beat a real one."

"You wanna make milkshakes? We have ice cream." Brad liked the idea of milkshakes, but he continued playing his game.

Pamela sashayed to the other side of the couch and sat next to him.

"I make great shakes. My dad taught me how. I'll make one for you if you go on a hike with me."

"With you?" Brad paused the game and looked up at Pamela.

"With me, Violet, and Willys."

"No, thanks. I don't like hikes, ticks, or mosquitoes." He was going to continue his game, but Pamela squeezed his shoulder.

"Come on. We're taking a trail that leads to a hot spring. Even the college kids don't know about it. If you don't come, you'll regret it. It's a beautiful day for a hike."

Brad shrugged and pushed her hand off his shoulder.

"Not if I get poison oak."

"I know all about poison oak and poison ivy. I'll warn you if I see any. It's going to be totally cool."

"I thought you were going to a hot spring. Those aren't cool."

"Come on. What do you have to lose? A little physical activity might actually be fun."

"You wanna have fun?" He raised one eyebrow and grinned. "You don't need to go on a hike. We can have fun right here."

Pamela scowled. She knocked the game controller out of the boy's hands and stormed out of the room.

"Hey!"

Brad smirked. He enjoyed getting people riled up, especially his sister and her friends.

He popped open the can of root beer next to him on the coffee table and drank deeply.

When he got up to retrieve his controller, Violet tromped into the room.

"I'm not going on your stupid hike."

"Mom's paying me $15 an hour. I'll give you five."

"Slave wages," he snorted as he sat on the couch and prepared to resume his game.

Violet blocked his view of the television.

"Fine! I'll give you half."

"Oh boy! Seven fifty an hour! Should I invest in the stock market?"

"Please." Violet begged with her hands clenched together.

"I'm about to kill Megasaurus. Why would I give that up for a stupid hike?"

Violet's shoulders slumped. She looked defeated.

"Okay," she said. "I guess you can go to Aunt Pearl's house."

Brad's eyes shot daggers at her.

"I'm not going there. She tried to make me eat liver dumplings the last time."

"She makes those from scratch. I heard you told her kids they were worse than rat poison."

"They thought it was funny."

"She's still really mad about that."

"So what?" He put the controller down and crossed his arms. "Besides, they don't even have an internet connection. It's like they're living in the stone age."

"You'll survive a few hours without the internet. Do you really want me to call her?"

She already knew the answer.

Brad might whine and resist for a while, but the hike was back on.

CHAPTER 2

A Dangerous Part of the Forest

"The moose's name was Fred. He liked to drink his juice in bed."

Violet repeated the verse of the camp song Pamela was teaching them. She found it mildly irritating, but it kept Willys occupied, so she was willing to sing along.

Do mooses really have beds?" the little boy asked with suspicion written across his face.

"No." Pamela put her hand on his shoulder. "Those are just the words to a silly song."

Brad lagged behind as Pamela led the way up the shady little trail. It followed a sun-dappled creek that twisted through a narrow canyon deep into the forest outside Bend, Oregon.

As the others sang, he considered ways of getting revenge on Violet. He had secretly folded a pillowcase and jammed it into a pocket of his baggy jeans.

I bet I can fit at least twenty lizards in there, if I can catch 'em. Or a snake. I could sneak it into Violet's backpack. That would teach her. I can't believe she'd threaten me with Aunt Pearl. This time, it's the forest. She could make me go to a hair salon next! If I had my BB rifle, I'd pierce her nose with it.

Brad tried to bring his toy weapon on the hike, claiming he needed it to fend off rabid animals, but the girls wouldn't allow it. Violet let him bring an aluminum baseball bat instead. So far, he'd used it to squash two slugs.

Brad took his frustration out on the tree trunks. He struck one after another with his bat.

It didn't take Willys long to join his brother in abusing the local flora with his plastic club. It made the little boy feel powerful and manly. He imagined himself as a bearded lumberjack, roaming the wilderness, searching for the best trees to chop down.

This one's too big. Too much mossy stuff. Too small. Too full of bugs. Yuck! Too leafy. Ah. This one's perfect.

"Timber!" He launched a vicious assault on the innocent twig.

"Stop it!" Violet barked.

"I just wanna chop down this tree." Willys hacked away at the supple sapling.

Violet marched over to her little brother.

"Do I have to take your bat away?"

"Like you took my BB rifle?" Brad smacked another tree trunk. A shower of leaves fell down on his head.

"You really don't get it." Pamela sat down on the smooth stones lining the banks of the creek. "Kids get killed playing with toy guns."

"Wow, and I thought you didn't care." Brad smirked.

Willys finished off the doomed plant by stomping it to the ground.

"If I was a real lumberjack, you couldn't stop me."

"You're not a lumberjack, Willys." Violet pulled him away from the ruined plant.

"Why do you want to chop down trees, anyway?" Pamela took a water bottle out of her bag. "They fight climate change and give shelter to the birds."

"Trees kill people," Brad said as he walloped another one.

"No, they don't," Pamela fired back.

"Really? You mean, you never heard of a tree falling on someone? Besides, people need wood."

Violet turned to face him.

"Not true. I saw a documentary that proved bamboo and hemp could replace most wood products."

"Sounds like fake news to me." Brad grinned.

Violet's teeth clenched and her eyes bulged.

Brad backed away from her, clutching his bat as if preparing to fend off an angry miniature poodle.

"Can I please chop down one more tree?" Willys frowned. "People need wood."

Something inside Violet snapped. She ripped the bat out of her little brother's hands and spun around to confront Brad.

He bolted like a frightened jackrabbit.

"Coward!" Pamela yelled.

Violet watched Brad run around a bend in the trail and disappear.

"We're not termites! We don't need wood!" She held the bat out to Willys.

"All right. I won't chop down no more trees." He took the bat. "Until I'm a real lumberjack."

"Let's hope that never happens," Pamela said. "Trees are more valuable than lumber."

"You know, that would be a great subject for our first editorial." Violet sat down next to her.

"I think the newspaper should have a name before we start writing editorials."

"Why do you wanna make a newspaper?" Willys scrunched up his face as if smelling something rotten.

"To provide people with information," Violet told him. "Lots of people only accept part of the truth, and as Benjamin Franklin said, 'Half a truth is often a great lie.'"

"You should write that down." Pamela reached into her bag and pulled out a stubby pencil and a little notepad with a cartoon polar bear on it.

Violet smiled and took the pad and pencil. She rested against her heavy pack and slid her shoulders out of the straps.

Willys looked at her. "You always make fun of the newspapers in the market."

"Those are tabloids. They make up stories and act like they're real." Violet scribbled a few notes on the pad.

"Our paper won't be like that." Pamela unscrewed the cap of her water bottle. "We'll stop gossip and lies instead of spreading them."

"So if a girl at school goes around saying I eat boogers, your paper would say Willys doesn't eat boogers. Henry Marshall does. Right?"

"I don't think we'd want to accuse Henry of something like that," Pamela said before taking a drink.

"Why not? He really eats boogers. I seen it!"

Violet stopped writing and looked at her brother.

"Eating boogers is not a good topic for a newspaper."

"Kids at my school talk about boogers all the time."

"That's why kids in your school don't write newspapers," Violet said.

"I bet they could write a really good one if they wanted to." Willys pouted and hit the creek with his bat, making a little splash. "Anyway, Superman works for a newspaper, so I guess they're okay." He hit the creek again. "I need to pee."

"Pick a tree," Violet said.

Willys hit the creek one more time and scampered off.

Violet handed the pad and pencil to Pamela and asked, "What do you think of <u>Sky View News</u>?"

"Not a popular choice." Pamela returned the writing implements to her bag.

"<u>Sky Views</u>?" Violet suggested.

"That makes it sound like it's all opinions."

"Well, do you have any suggestions?"

Brad crept back, unseen by the girls. He hid behind a tree and shouted, "Has Mount St. Violet cooled down yet?"

"No!" she yelled back. "I still might erupt!"

Brad peeked out from his hiding place. Violet was no longer in possession of a weapon, so he slowly approached the girls holding his bat in front of him.

"You know I have a bat."

"I'll make you wish you never brought it." Violet grabbed the straps of her pack and rose to face her brother. The heavy bag made a good shield and a formidable weapon.

Brad froze in his tracks, about twenty yards away.

"I'll stay over here."

"You better."

"Good doggy. Stay, doggy! Stay!" Pamela teased.

"You want me to be your doggy? Huh? I bet you'd just love me to lick your face."

"That is so disgusting." Pamela took a big gulp of water, as if to wash the thought away.

Violet sat next to her and tried to ignore Brad, who stood leaning against a tree.

"Did the kids at camp have any ideas for the paper's name?"

"Mostly bad ones like <u>Sky View Nizzle for Shizzle</u>."

Violet chuckled. "Who came up with that?"

"Sammy. He also suggested <u>Don't Let Your Teachers Read This</u>. He thinks it would be an attention grabber."

"He might be right."

"What makes you think you can write a newspaper anyway?" Brad snorted.

"We'll learn," Pamela said. "That's why we're starting a journalism club."

"I like to learn stuff." Brad smiled like a Cheshire cat. "I'll be in ninth grade this year. Maybe I should join your club."

The idea horrified Violet, but Pamela didn't even blink.

"There's a waiting list for freshmen," she lied. "I left it at home."

"In that case, I'll sign up at school." Brad sat down with his back against the tree. "You have to post a sign-up sheet, don't you?"

Pamela picked up a small rock and threw it at him. It bounced harmlessly at his feet.

"Hey! You're lucky that didn't hit me."

"Why?" Pamela threw another rock. "You gonna tell your mommy?"

"I told you this hike would be a disaster," Violet grumbled.

"Rah!" Willys returned, chasing a butterfly with his bat. He was in constant danger of tripping over rocks and tree roots.

"Leave the butterflies alone." Violet scowled at him. "And zip up your pants!"

"But they keep followin' me!" Willys flailed at one of his alleged stalkers.

"They like you," Pamela said. "It's good luck."

"I don't care!" Willys turned his attention away from the bothersome insects long enough to win a struggle with his zipper.

While he was distracted, a butterfly landed on his right shoulder. He swatted it off and chased after it.

"Leave me alone!"

"Don't make me take your bat away," Violet warned.

Willys frowned and gave up his pursuit. He stomped away from the girls, looking for a place to mope further up the trail. "Why are you always tryin' to take my bat?"

"That's how girls are." Brad leaned back with his hands behind his head. "First, they take our guns. Then they take our bats. Then if we're attacked and can't defend ourselves, they act like it's our fault!"

"Oh, please," Violet groaned.

"Don't worry," Pamela said. "I'll protect you from all the scary squirrels and butterflies."

"You think it's funny?" Brad stared at her. "Rattlesnakes and mountain lions eat squirrels. Food attracts predators. It's the law of the jungle."

As if on cue, a loud grunting sound startled them.

Something large was moving through the dense shrubbery only inches from a wide-eyed Willys.

The boy's eyes narrowed to slits.

"You don't scare me," he said as he lifted his plastic bat.

CHAPTER 3

The Cave

"No!" Violet shouted as her little brother furiously bashed the shrubs.

She wanted to rush to his rescue, but her legs wouldn't move. Terrible images of an enormous mountain lion tearing Willys to shreds filled her mind with dread.

This was her fault. She could hear her mother wailing, "How did you let this happen? He was only a baby."

Brad jogged toward the ruckus with his own bat held high over his right shoulder. He was prepared to flee if anything larger than a raccoon emerged from the bushes.

Pamela grabbed the whistle she wore on a chord around her neck and blew it as loud and long as she could. It was part of her junior counselor training.

They were all surprised when a voice called out from the thicket.

"Stop! You stop this instant!"

A tall, gaunt, balding man emerged from the foliage, shielding himself with his left arm. His right hand held long pointy tweezers. He wore thick glasses, disposable gloves, army boots, and camouflage clothing partially covered by a white lab coat.

"Dr. Harrison?" Violet felt shocked and relieved at the same time. She dashed to restrain a confused Willys. "I am so sorry."

"What the heck is a doctor doing out here?" Brad slapped the barrel of his bat against his palm repeatedly.

"I am a scientist." Harrison adjusted his glasses.

"He teaches science at Sky View," Pamela sneered.

"I spent over twenty years at NASA, young lady. Not that there's anything wrong with being a science teacher."

"Were you following us?" Brad asked.

"No." The accusation offended the doctor. "I'm conducting field research."

"On what? Pine cones?" Brad kicked a pine cone toward him.

"I happen to be on the trail of a North American Sasquatch, the species commonly called bigfoot."

"I know what a Suscratch is." Willys snarled.

"Good, then you should be concerned about this." The doctor held the strand of reddish-brown hair held in his tweezers down to Willys's eye level. "It's proof that these powerful creatures have been in the woods around us. You children shouldn't be here." He turned away and strode to an enormous backpack resting against a tree.

"I'm not afraid of bigfoot!" Willys fought against Violet's grip. "Let me clobber him!"

"Yeah! Clobber him, Willys! He's a bigfoot!" Brad cavorted behind them. "If you can catch him, you'll be famous!"

Pamela bent down and held the belligerent little boy by his shoulders.

"He is not a bigfoot, Willys! He's a teacher. His name is Dr. Henderson."

"Harrison!" The doctor shot a chastising glance in her direction. He put the tweezers in a plastic bag, which he placed in a pocket on his pack.

"I'm sorry if my brother hurt you," Violet said. "He thought you were an animal."

"We are all part of the animal kingdom. You girls should know that much." Dr. Harrison gave Willys a stern look as he removed his gloves. "Fortunately, your attack did not harm me, but you have to learn to curb your aggression." He put the gloves in a lab coat pocket and hoisted his pack onto his back.

"Where are *you* going?" Brad asked.

"Wherever the trail leads." The doctor scowled. "This is a dangerous part of the forest. You children should go home. I'm telling you this for your own good."

Violet nodded in agreement. "Sure. I wouldn't want to run into a bigfoot."

"Certainly not," the odd educator said with a genuine look of concern. "One of the creatures has been here recently. You should leave now." He turned and walked down the trail.

"Thanks for the warning, Dr. Henderson!" Pamela shouted as she watched him walk down the trail. "That man is nuttier than a pecan pie."

"Or maybe he just wants the hot spring to himself." Violet released Willys and took his bat.

"Hey! There's wild animals out here. I need that!" Willys pouted. A tear rolled down his cheek.

Pamela removed the chord from her neck and offered the whistle to him.

"Here. Loud noises scare animals."

"I'm not afraid of animals or bigfeet." Willys wiped his eyes and took the whistle.

"I'm not afraid of bigfoot either." Pamela put the chord around his neck. "Everyone knows it's just a dumb old myth."

"No, it's not!" Brad protested.

"Yes, it is," Pamela and Violet said, in unison.

Brad gave the girls a smug look.

"Then why are people always seeing them around here?"

"Because people like to make up stories," Pamela answered.

"If it was real, someone would have found real evidence by now." Violet jammed Willys's bat halfway into her pack.

"You want real evidence?" Brad glared at her. "Fine. I'll find it. I'll be MVP of your club. They'll wanna make me president."

"In your dreams," Violet said.

"In your face." Brad strutted away from the creek. "Come on, Willys! Let's go find a bigfoot."

Willys chased after him.

"If we find him, can I use your bat?"

17

"Sure, but I get to use it first."

As the boys wandered off, Pamela looked at her friend.

"Aren't you afraid they'll get lost or something?"

"No," Violet answered.

"I'd never allow this at Grand Pines."

"We're not at Grand Pines! Brad can take care of himself, and he took Willys, so maybe we can actually get some work done."

"If you say so." Pamela reached into her bag and pulled out a manila envelope full of random notes and messages about the journalism club. She tried to focus on the work at hand, but her thoughts were troubled.

Violet's right. This isn't camp. They're her brothers and it's her responsibility. Still, ignoring my training just feels wrong.

*****

Brad smiled as he led his little brother through a meadow full of tall grass and purple lupine.

I can't believe Violet's making this so easy. What a dope.

He knew that if they didn't return in about thirty minutes, his sister would panic and come looking for them. It would be a cinch to convince Willys that it was a game of hide-and-seek. Revenge would be sweet.

Meanwhile, Brad searched for small animals or large bugs to capture.

Willys searched for bigfoot tracks. He was determined to be the best tracker ever. He looked under every rock and bush, even if they seemed much too small to hide a bigfoot.

I hope I find a baby bigfoot. I'll rule at show and tell if I can bring one back to school.

"Try to think like a bigfoot," Brad said as the boys scoured their surroundings. "If people were chasing you, where would you hide?"

"I wouldn't hide. I'd build a fortress."

"If you spot Fort Susquatch, let me know."

"I still don't see no tracks."

"Good trackers use all their senses." Brad stopped and put his finger to his lips. He whispered, "Look for tracks, but listen for bigfoot too."

"What about smell?" Willys whispered back. "Should I look for bigfoot poop?"

"Yeah. Let me know if you find any poop."

They emerged from the meadow and approached a hill covered with fir trees, boulders, and thick underbrush.

"Bigfoot could have some pretty good hiding places up there," Brad said.

He noticed several hefty banana slugs under a big oak tree and pulled the pillowcase from his pocket. He picked them up one at a time and put them into his makeshift critter carrier.

"What are those?" Willys asked.

"Slugs. Bigfoot eats 'em. We can use them for bait."

"There's some more!" Willys raced to a trio of slugs. He picked them up and dropped them into his brother's bag. "There's another one!" He gathered the slimy insects for several minutes, while Brad lounged in the shade of the big oak tree.

The collection had swelled to over three dozen by the time Brad stood and said, "I think that's enough."

Slime was starting to ooze through the fabric as he tied a knot in the pillowcase.

"Here." He handed the bag to Willys. "I need both hands to cut a trail."

"All right." Willys took the sack.

Brad followed an old animal trail up the hill. He used his bat to hack away at the surrounding shrubbery to make room for his chubby body. On the way, he found several large sticky spiderwebs full of dead insects and pine needles, but he didn't find any spiders big enough to collect.

Halfway up the hill, he spotted a large brown lizard asleep on a rock. "Give me the bag," he whispered.

"More slugs?"

"No. It's a lizard. Bigfoot likes eating them even more than slugs."

Willys gave him the bag.

Brad untied the knot and slowly creeped up on the unsuspecting reptile. He lunged forward and caught the lizard in the bag, but it made a tremendous effort to escape.

"Whoa!" He juggled the bag to keep the creature from climbing out. "Calm down! Eat some slugs!" Brad pushed it to the bottom of his bag and struggled to tie a knot without setting it free or injuring it.

While the battle of the lizard was being waged, Willys wandered past Brad and followed the animal trail up the hill. He climbed over rocks and crawled under prickly bushes, leaving his brother far behind. The trail opened up at a flat grassy area in front of a sea of ferns.

"Bigfoot might be hiding in these plants!" Willys shouted before diving into the foliage.

"Watch out for spiders!" Brad shouted back. "Tell me if you see any!"

Willys swam through the tall ferns and emerged at an outcropping of stone wedged into the hillside. It was partially hidden behind an evergreen huckleberry plant, laden with big purple berries. He plucked one and popped it into his mouth.

"Mmm."

While picking more berries, he saw something behind the plant. There was a large horizontal crack in the rock face. He dropped the fruit and scampered around the bush to inspect the opening. It was deep and about eight feet wide. The bottom was flat, but the top of the crack arced up on both sides to a height of about three feet in the middle.

"Hey, Brad! There's a cave over here! It might be bigfoot's house!"

Brad, who had stopped to add a hairy caterpillar to his bag, picked up his pace.

"Where are you?" he shouted.

"Up here!" Willys saw something in the cave. He stuck his head in to get a closer look.

Brad beat a path up the animal trail and waded through the ferns as quickly as he could. He was just in time to see his brother's feet disappearing into the stony crevice.

"Be careful, Willys! You don't know what's in there." Brad peered into the opening. His wriggling brother blocked his view, but he could see a dim blue pulsing light inside.

"Hey. What's that light coming from?"

"It might be bigfoot's night-light. It's pretty big. He must be a scaredy-cat."

"What else is in there?"

"I don't know. You got a flashlight?"

"No. We're on a day hike."

"Maybe Violet has one." Willys examined the object with his hands. "It's round."

"Can you move it?"

Willys tried pushing and pulling the mystery object, but it didn't budge.

"It's too heavy." He crawled out of the tiny cave.

"I bet I could pull it out if I had a rope," Brad said.

"Maybe Violet has a rope."

"She doesn't have a rope or a flashlight!"

"Well, you're bigger than me. Why don't you pull it out?"

The challenge caught Brad by surprise. He didn't like cramped spaces, but he didn't want to look like a coward.

He stuck his bat in the cave and waved it around.

"Are you sure there's no snakes in there?"

Willys nodded.

Brad handed his bat to his brother and crawled into the cave. He couldn't get a good hold on the object hidden inside. He was barely able to move it at all. The cave was too small to crawl around or see clearly, so he used his sense of touch to understand what they had found. Willys was right about it being round. It felt like metal, and the four-foot-wide disk was suspended about ten inches above the cave's rock floor. Something had to be holding it up.

Brad climbed onto the metal dish. It wobbled a little under his weight. He examined the pulsing blue bowl of light in the middle of the thing. Then he crawled past the light to the back of the disk. He thought that he might be able to get off and push it out from behind, but the gap between the disk and the cave's back wall was too small. "Dead end," he mumbled. Brad crawled backward until he was able to get off the front end of the thing.

What's holding this thing up? he thought as he ran his hands along the rim of the big disk. *I hope there's nothing dangerous down there.*

Despite his reservations, he stuck his arms beneath the plate to explore the space. The disk felt smooth and metallic on the bottom as it did on top. There were no legs holding it up, but there was something near the middle of the disk. *It feels round, like another bowl.* He pictured the object in his mind.

Wait a second. They're not bowls. They're two halves of a globe!

Brad crawled out of the cave.

"Do you think bigfoot lives here?" Willys held out his brother's bat.

"No, I don't." Brad took the bat from him and took a deep breath. "Looks like we found a flying saucer."

CHAPTER 4

The Flying Saucer

"Can you make it fly out?" Willys asked excitedly.

"No, we have to pull it out." Brad brushed imaginary spiderwebs out of his short hair. "It would be easier if I could get a grip on it."

He felt like he was trying to reach the next level of a video game. There had to be a way to claim this strange treasure. Brad made a mental inventory of all their "assets."

Clothes, shoes, belts, bat, bag of slugs, and one lizard. He imagined tying a string to the lizard's leg and making it scurry about under the saucer until it looped around the central globe. If he had a rope, he could tie it to the other end of the string and pull it around the saucer's bottom hemisphere. *Might work, but we don't have a rope or string.* He sat on a big oval boulder a few yards from the cave.

"I wish Spider-Man was here. He could use his webs to pull it out. Fwip! Fwap!" Willys pretended to shoot webs from his hands.

"Yeah, and Magneto could make it float out, but he's not real. This is a real problem." Brad tapped his bat against the boulder as he pondered the situation.

Willys peered into the dark cave.

"How'd it get there, anyway?" He hitched up his pants and walked over to Brad. "I bet I could pull it out if it had a handle or something."

"That's it!" Brad stood up and unbuckled his belt. "I need your belt too."

"Why?"

Willys loved his belt. Its buckle featured a cowboy riding a bronco.

"I need it to pull the saucer out." Brad held out his hand.

"All right."

Willys took his belt off and surrendered it.

Brad tightened it around the neck of his bat and secured his own belt around the bat's barrel.

"This might work," he muttered, and he crawled back into the cave.

The chubby boy squirmed over the top of the saucer. He wriggled to the left of the dome when he reached it and continued until he came to the far end of the big disk.

"Cross your fingers!" he shouted.

While holding onto the ends of the belts, he dropped the bat to the cave's rock floor. He then crawled back toward the mouth of the cave, using the belts to drag his bat along under the saucer. As he crawled around the top of the globe, he felt the bat snag on the bottom of it, exactly as he planned.

Brad crawled to the front of the saucer, and as he got off, he pulled the belts entirely underneath it. Now they served as handles. Brad tried to pull the heavy saucer out, but the limited space made it impossible to get any leverage. Progress was slow.

"Is it working?" Willys shouted into the cave.

"The handles work, but it's still hard." Brad stopped for a rest.

"I'll help!" Willys reached into the cave and tugged on his brother's feet.

"Stop it!" Brad bellowed.

He left his improvised apparatus in place and crawled out of the cave.

Willys backed away from him.

"I was just tryin' to help."

"I'm not mad at you." Brad held his hands up. "In fact, you gave me an idea. If we work together, I think we can pull that thing out."

"Really?" Willys nervously shifted his weight from one foot to the other.

"Yeah, but you have to go back in the cave."

"Okay!" Willys ran toward the cave.

"Hold on!" Brad caught him by the shoulders. "You need to find the belts under the saucer. Wrap them around your hands, and I'll pull you out."

"All right."

"Let me know if the belts start to slip off."

"Okay."

"Tell me when you're ready."

Brad released Willys, who practically dived into the cave.

It was only a matter of seconds until he gave the signal.

"Ready!"

Brad reached into the cave and grabbed his brother by the ankles. He pulled.

There was significant movement.

He pulled again, another two inches.

"It's working!" Brad yelled into the cave.

He pulled again, yielding at least three more inches!

Another tug, and Willys shrieked.

"I need to pee!"

"You peed like ten minutes ago!"

"I need to pee now!" Willys freed his hands from the belts and crawled out of the cave. He ran through the ferns and headed for the nearest tree.

The respite gave Brad time to think.

What are we going to do with this thing after we pull it out? We won't be able to hide it. Even if we cover it with branches and stuff, that blue light will be a dead giveaway. Somebody else might grab it if we don't take it home, and it's way too heavy to carry.

I could build a sled, but I'll need help.

Or I could make a raft and float it down the creek! But I'll still need help. I'll have to tell the girls, unless we just leave it in the cave.

I wonder if we could get Dad to come back here with an ATV. He might not believe Willys and me, but if Violet backs us up.

This sucks. I've got all these bugs and a lizard, but I'm gonna need Violet. I'll have to be nice to her.

When Willys returned, Brad took Pamela's whistle from him.

"Why do you want that?"

"We need the girls' help. Stay here. I'll be back."

"What if bigfoot shows up? Or aliens."

"If anything scares you, hide in the cave."

"I'm not a sissy! That stuff doesn't scare me."

"You should be scared of some things, Willys. Just be careful, okay?"

Brad turned and tramped through the ferns, whistle in hand.

*****

The girls were munching on granola bars and discussing Pamela's research.

"The number one thing kids want is good snacks." Pamela shook her granola bar at Violet. "These won't cut it."

"Seriously? Snacks are more important than racism, sexism, or social justice."

"Yes. At least for kids in our school, they are."

In the distance, a whistle blew.

"Is that your whistle?" Violet asked.

"I didn't become a whistle expert at camp." The whistle sounded again. "It could be."

"You told Willys it scares wild animals."

"It's more likely Brad trying to scare you."

The whistle blew again, louder and longer.

Violet was worried.

"What if they ran into Dr. Harrison again?"

"You have Willys's bat," Pamela pointed out. "I don't think Brad would hurt him."

Violet sighed and rose to her feet.

"I better go check it out."

"Do you have to? I mean, I didn't think letting them wander off was smart, but now—"

"I know. Brad's probably just messing with us, but I don't have a choice. I'm in charge."

Violet took Willys's bat out of her pack and used it to smack a pine cone into the middle of the creek.

"They went this way." She shouldered her pack and sauntered in the direction the boys had gone.

Pamela picked up her messenger bag and followed at a leisurely pace.

The girls strolled through the meadow, trying to follow the whistle. The sound echoed off the hillside making it difficult, and the foliage made it hard to see.

"Brad, where are you?" Violet called out a few times.

The whistle grew louder.

Pamela paused and focused on the sound. "I'm pretty sure we need to go left," she said.

Violet cleared a path through the tall grass with Willys's bat. Yard after yard, she hacked away. Butterflies and a variety of other insects and small birds fled from the disturbance.

There were brief pauses in the whistling, but it did not stop.

"I'd like to shove that whistle down Brad's throat," Violet grumbled.

"We're not even sure it's him," said Pamela.

The whistle played a one-note rendition of the national anthem.

"It's him." Violet stopped. The grass in front of them had been trampled down. "Looks like a chance to practice your junior ranger skills."

Pamela knelt to inspect the alleyway of flattened grass.

"Hmm. I'd say a tubby kid in tennis shoes and a skinny one in cowboy boots left these tracks. They went that way." Pamela pointed to the right.

The girls followed the path of trampled grass across the meadow and found Brad, still blowing the whistle.

Violet marched up to him.

"You better have a great reason for bringing us here."

"Took you long enough," he said. He put the whistle in his shirt pocket. "I think I have an awesome story for your newspaper. We found a flying saucer."

"No kidding. Did bigfoot lead you to it?" Pamela sneered.

"I'm not joking! Willys found a cave, and when he crawled in—"

"You let Willys crawl into a cave?" Violet's eyes burned with anger.

"Do you think he waited for my permission? He just crawled in and found a flying saucer."

The girls both rolled their eyes.

"Look, I'm really sorry we forced you to come on our hike," Violet said. "I know you don't want to be here, so if you want to climb into your flying saucer and go home, I'm okay with it."

Pamela burst out laughing.

Willys emerged from the cave-concealing ferns and shouted, "Hurry up, you guys! The aliens might come back!"

This made Pamela laugh even harder.

"You'll see!" Brad sputtered as he turned and hurried up the hill.

Pamela wiped her eyes with the back of her hand. "There has never been a more obvious prank."

"If they try anything, I'll be ready." Violet brandished Willys's bat and headed up the enlarged animal trail.

Pamela followed her. "At camp, kids were always pulling pranks. It pays to plan ahead."

"I plan to beat the hell out of my brother if he tries anything stupid." Violet used the bat to nudge a slug off the path in front of her.

"Did you see the way Willys disappeared into the ferns up there?" Pamela asked. "They must be pretty tall. The boys could be hiding something foul behind them. It's a perfect setup."

Violet imagined the boys hiding a dead skunk behind the plants, but she knew it was something else. They would already smell a skunk.

Violet pushed another slug off the trail. "Let's try to walk around the ferns. If we can't go around, we'll go through as far as possible from Brad's trail."

"Good idea." Pamela grinned. "If we have to go through the plants, hold the bat in front of you. If they're planning a sneak attack, they might go for the bat instead of you."

"I'll do that," Violet agreed.

Pamela spotted a couple of large yellow slugs just off the path. "This hill is loaded with slugs."

"I've noticed," Violet said.

"Raccoons love to eat slugs."

"So?"

"So maybe they've got a dead raccoon up there."

"Maybe." Violet nudged another slug off the path. "That would be gross."

They soon came to the flat grassy area in front of the ferns. Slightly to their right, a hole in the wall of foliage marked Brad's passage.

"Let's go left," Violet said.

The girls creeped along the edge of the ferns until they came to a barren ledge of rock embedded in the hillside.

Pamela climbed up onto the ledge and looked back toward Brad's trail. "No sign of the boys from up here," she said softly. She took one more look and climbed down.

"If we follow this rock around the plants, we should come out behind them," said Violet. She held the bat in front of her and waded into the ferns. A huckleberry bush obstructed her view of her brothers when they emerged from the foliage, but she could hear them.

"Hold on, Willys!" Brad grunted.

Willys's muffled voice answered, "I still got it, but my nose itches."

The girls creeped around the bush and saw Brad pulling on Willys's feet, which were sticking out of the tiny cave.

"You can scratch your nose after we get that thing out." Brad gave his brother's feet another tug.

"Dead animal, for shizzle," Pamela whispered in Violet's ear.

They both sat down on the oval boulder and watched Brad struggle.

Violet shed her backpack. "Whatever it is, they're having a heck of a time pulling it out. It must be pretty heavy."

Pamela grinned. "I hope it's a dead bigfoot. We'd have to let Brad join the club, but can you imagine how jealous Dr. Henderson would be."

The girls giggled and watched as Willys's knees emerged from the cave.

"Now my ears itch!" Willys complained.

"Just hold on. I'm doing my best." Brad pulled and made another four inches of progress.

Pamela imagined Willys inside the cave, holding onto the vermin-infested corpse of an elk. Fleas and ticks swarmed over the animal and into the little boy's nose and ears. Her face contorted with disgust.

"We should get him out of there."

"I guess." Violet stood and stretched.

"Argh!" Brad grunted as he pulled.

"Do you see that?" Violet pointed to the seat of Willys's pants. A blue light flashed dimly on the denim.

"Hold on!" Brad yanked Willys a bit closer to freedom.

"What the—" Pamela stood. Blue light clearly reflected off the bottom of the boy's white T-shirt.

"That light's not coming from a dead animal," Violet said.

The girls approached the boys from behind.

"I think Willys has been in there long enough." Violet put her hand on Brad's back.

"Then help me!" he gasped.

She grabbed one of Willys's legs, while Brad kept hold of the other.

"On three," Brad said. "One, two, three!"

Working together, they pulled their brother entirely out of the cave along with the front edge of the saucer.

"What the heck?" Violet dropped Willys's leg.

Brad released his other leg and shouted, "I can pull it out now!"

The little boy stood with his eyes wide open.

"We found a spaceship!"

Brad grabbed the belts, planted his feet, and pulled with all his strength.

He slipped and fell smack on his butt.

"Use your muscles!" Willys growled, before racing off to retrieved his unattended bat.

Brad set his feet again, but this time, he managed to pull the saucer completely out of the cave.

The four-foot-wide disk had strange hieroglyphics etched onto its surface. It balanced perfectly on the beach ball-sized bulge in the center.

"I told you!" Brad let go of the belts and stood up.

Willys used his bat to poke at the thing.

"Where'd you come from?"

"Looks like some kind of drone or satellite," said Pamela.

Brad retrieved his bat and the belts from beneath the saucer. He returned Willys's belt and slung his own over his shoulder.

"I think it crashed," he said.

"Right. It crashed into a tiny, little cave," Violet bent down and peered into the dark hole. "Someone obviously hid it in there."

"Why would a person do that?" Pamela put her hand on Violet's back. "Your brother was right. There is an awesome story behind this if we can just figure it out."

Brad knocked on the saucer's dome with his knuckles.

"Hello! Anybody home in there?"

Willys climbed onto the saucer and joined Brad in knocking on the dome.

"Come out, little aliens."

"I left my phone at home," Violet told Pamela. "Do you have yours?"

She nodded and produced her cell phone.

"Come on, guys!" Violet shouted. "We need to take some photos of this thing without you climbing all over it."

"I want to see what's inside. Maybe I can smash the dome." Brad raised his bat over his head.

"No!" Pamela screamed. "Don't break it! That thing looks valuable."

"We just wanna open it." Willys continued knocking on the dome. "Hello in there. We got a present for you."

Violet's expression softened. "You should have proof that you guys found this thing. If you let Pamela take photos, we'll have solid evidence."

"You'll be the star of our first school paper." Pamela smiled.

"You might even get in a real newspaper," Violet added.

"Or television. I can take video." Pamela circled the saucer, viewing it through her phone screen.

"You can try to open it later," Violet pointed out.

Brad put his bat down.

"Fine. Come on, Willys. Once we have photos, no one can say we made this up."

As Brad got off the little spaceship, Willys snagged the chord hanging from his shirt pocket. He pulled the whistle out and looked at it.

"Maybe this scares aliens too."

He held the whistle next to the dome and blew.

The saucer transformed the sound waves into a powerful vibration. It knocked the children off their feet.

Brad dropped his bat and his belt, but Willys somehow stuck to the vibrating disk.

The light emanating from it changed from blue to green to yellow. The hieroglyphics lit up and shifted into entirely different symbols. The silver disk rotated clockwise then counterclockwise. It moved slowly at first, but soon, it was spinning like a top and making a wobbly ascent into the air.

Like the cowboy on his belt buckle, Willys refused to end his ride.

The other children got to their feet and stood stupefied as the saucer rose higher and higher.

"Three, two, one. Blast off!" Willys shouted.

CHAPTER 5

The Sandwich

Violet rushed to the rising saucer. She jumped up and tried to grab her brother's feet, but he was already over seven feet in the air.

"Let go, Willys! I'll catch you," she screamed.

"No! I wanna go to outer space!"

Brad scrambled to Violet's side.

"You'll die without a space suit!"

Willys stuck to the saucer like a wad of chewing gum. It stopped spinning, but it shook and tilted in every direction, pulsing with energy.

"The force is in me!" Willys said in a jittery voice.

An instant later, the saucer turned upside down and he was dumped feetfirst into the ferns.

Violet yanked him out of the plants and away from the soaring disk.

Pamela recorded a video of the saucer flipping over at increasing speed. Soon, it was spinning so fast, it looked like a ball of lightning. Bolts of energy danced all around it.

A stray spark singed the ground inches from Brad's feet. He stamped out the little flame and rushed to get water bottles from Violet's backpack.

"If one of these trees catches fire, we're in big trouble," Pamela zoomed in on the crackling disk as birds fled the trees near it. It was over thirty feet in the air.

"I got gypped." Willys sat and pouted. "I'll never get to outer space now."

"It's slowing down," Pamela said as the saucer's ascent decelerated along with its spinning and sparking.

Violet grabbed a water bottle from her brother and helped with fire control.

Green light flashed from the hovering silver disk as it slowly, gently floated to the ground. Pamela circled the saucer, recording it from every angle. Violet joined her as Brad doused the rest of the hot spots.

"Let's try again!" Willys raced toward the whistle, which had fallen to the ground.

"No!" Brad dropped the water bottle and tackled him.

"Let me go!"

Violet stomped over to the boys.

"You're not going on another spaceship ride, Willys."

"Why not?"

"Because I say so and Mom left *me* in charge."

"That thing almost started a fire," Pamela said. "You don't want to burn down the forest, do you?"

"I wanna see outer space."

"You're not seeing it today." Violet picked up the whistle and handed it to Pamela.

The light from the saucer grew brighter. It started shaking again. The children backed away, as if it was a basket full of rattlesnakes.

The light on top cycled from green to blue to yellow quicker and quicker. Then it turned blood red.

"It's a bomb!" Brad let go of Willys and sprinted down the hill.

The light became unbearably intense. The kids shielded their eyes with their hands and arms.

There was a blinding flash and then nothing.

The light was gone. The saucer was at rest, but the dome was melting away like a hollow ice cube under a heat lamp. It was completely gone in seconds. There was a small square compartment inside.

PEANUT BUTTER AND JELLY SANDWICHES FROM OUTER SPACE!

Violet grabbed the collar of Willys's T-shirt. "You're not going anywhere near that thing."

"There's a slice of bread inside," Pamela said as she walked around the little spaceship. "I think it's a sandwich."

Willys broke loose and sprinted to the saucer.

"The aliens must think we're hungry."

Violet grabbed him around his waist.

"Maybe it's a science experiment," Pamela said. "You know, like seeing if a tuna sandwich stays fresh in the vacuum of space."

"It's tuna?" Willys scrunched up his face. "I hate tuna."

Violet lifted Willys to her shoulder like a baby she was trying to burp.

"Maybe it's a prototype for a drone delivery service."

"Not likely." Pamela shook her head. "It would have somebody's logo all over it."

"Then maybe there's more to that sandwich than meets the eye." Violet circled the ship with her brother in her arms. "It could have a microchip in it or something."

"What if it's a spy drone?" Pamela grabbed Violet's arm. "The chip in the sandwich could have surveillance files. If the spy gets caught, she's supposed to eat it."

"That might be it." Violet smiled. "This story could be huge."

"But doesn't that mean there's a spy in the forest?" Pamela felt a shiver go down her spine. She dashed over to Brad's bat and picked it up.

Brad chose that unfortunate moment to return. He bent down to pick up his belt and asked, "What happened?"

Pamela spun around with the bat raised high and screamed. "Aah!"

"Aah!" Brad raised his arms as a shield and fell over backward.

When Pamela realized who it was, she lowered the bat and offered him a helping hand.

He refused it.

"What is wrong with you?" He rose to his feet and snatched the bat from her.

"The spaceship opened up," Willys told him. "The aliens sent us a sandwich."

"What?" Brad walked to the saucer and leaned over its edge to take a closer look.

"Don't touch it!" Violet warned. "It could be poison or radioactive."

"Like Spider-Man?" Willys asked.

"No, like Chernobyl," Pamela answered.

"Who's that? Is he an X-Man?" The little boy wiggled like a wet cat in Violet's arms.

"It's not a person. It's a Russian town with a busted nuclear power plant." Brad inspected the sandwich. "It's definitely wheat bread. I think it's peanut butter and jelly."

Willys clapped his hands.

"That's my favorite!"

Violet carried him to her pack, away from the ship.

"Promise me you won't touch that sandwich, Willys!"

"You promise!" he said.

Violet looked back at Brad and Pamela.

"Don't let him anywhere near it."

They both nodded in agreement.

Violet put Willys down and reached into her pack. She removed a pad of paper, a roll of tape, and a thick marker.

Willys peered into her pack.

"Are you writing a thank-you note for the sandwich?"

"No. This is what they call journalism." She scrawled the date in large numbers on a sheet of paper. "What time is it?"

Pamela looked at her phone. "Three thirty-two."

Violet added the time to the paper and taped it to the saucer.

"I hope that sandwich doesn't mind close-ups." Pamela put her phone in photo mode and took several shots of the saucer and the sandwich. Then she took more pictures of the boys and Violet with the little spaceship. Finally, she took some selfies with it as well.

"This thing gives me the creeps," she said when she finished the photo shoot. "Can we go somewhere else?"

PEANUT BUTTER AND JELLY SANDWICHES FROM OUTER SPACE!

Brad shook his head. "Birds or squirrels might chew on the sandwich. It could start an alien plague or something."

"I'll fix that." Violet reached into her backpack and emptied the big plastic bag of writing supplies into the pack. She carried it to the saucer and held it over the round opening where the dome had been. "Perfect fit."

Brad handed her the roll of tape.

"You better tape it down good. We don't want any insects getting in either."

Violet taped the bag down, making sure to leave no openings. "Satisfied?"

Brad inspected the bag and tape. "I guess it's good for now."

Willys picked up his bat and Brad's pillowcase as the girls got their things.

They hiked down the hill together and settled in the shade of the big oak tree.

"A plastic bag and some tape won't save that sandwich from raccoons." Brad kicked some dry leaves off a patch of grass and sat down.

"We should show it to Dr. Harrison," Violet said.

"I don't like him." Willys sat next to the tree and crossed his arms.

Violet set her pack down in front of the tree.

"He might know what it is. He did work for NASA."

"The man's weird, but he knows his science," Pamela said. She adjusted her Grand Pines cap and lay down, using her bag as a pillow. "If we find him, I hope he believes us."

"Well, does he have a sandwich?" Willys asked. "I'm hungry."

Violet got a granola bar out of her pack and handed it to him.

"I want one too!" Brad whined.

She threw one at him.

He caught it and wolfed it down in three bites. "I don't trust Dr. Bigfoot either," he said while chomping on the last piece of his snack.

Pamela sat up and crossed her legs, assuming a lotus position. "We need advice from a higher source. Luckily, I learned to contact the forest spirits at camp." She closed her eyes, rolled her head in circles, and repeatedly chanted the phrase "Om, Foo, Lin, Yawl."

She stopped in mid chant and sat bolt upright, her eyes opened wide. "Oh, great spirit, what should we do? Stay with the saucer or find Dr. Harrison? Please, send us a sign." She closed her eyes again and shook her body in a fake convulsion. Speaking in her deepest tone, she said, "Bananas, ice cream, nuts, chocolate sauce, whipped cream, and a cherry."

"That's a banana split!" Willys licked his lips.

"It's a sign!" Pamela opened her eyes. "We should split up."

"Good idea." Violet smirked. "Willys, you better stay here. Dr. Harrison might run and hide if he sees you again."

"Fine." Pamela stood up. "You and Brad look for Dr. Harrison. Willys and I will stay here to keep an eye on the saucer."

"No way!" Brad crossed his arms. "Me and Willys found it! We should be the ones to watch it!"

"The great spirit doesn't trust you two with that sandwich, and neither do I," Violet said.

Brad crossed his chubby legs and imitated Pamela's lotus pose. "Well, I can contact spirits too!" He rolled his head in circles. "I am the great, great, great spirit, and I say don't follow the chocolate ice cream, marshmallows, and nuts. Hey! That's rocky road. He wants me to stay here."

Violet sighed. She lay down and rested her head against her pack. "We have to find Dr. Harrison."

"I'm not going," Brad insisted.

"What if I go with you?" Pamela walked over to him and sat by his side. "I know you have a crush on me."

Brad's jaw dropped. "I do not! I already have a girlfriend."

Pamela and Violet exchanged knowing looks.

"I do! She has red hair, and her name is Heather."

Pamela put a hand over her mouth.

Brad's face was turning red, starting with his ears.

"She's older than you too. She's sixteen."

Pamela could no longer control herself. She fell backward, roaring with laughter.

Violet shook her head.

Brad lay down with his hands behind his head.

"Go ahead and laugh. Some girls like bad boys."

Willys sat with his chin resting on his fists. He didn't understand what Pamela found so funny, and he wasn't interested in Brad's yucky girlfriend. The talk of banana splits and rocky road ice cream had fanned the flames of his hunger. The only things on his mind were the sandwich from outer space and his growling stomach.

Aliens wouldn't send a sandwich to Earth if they didn't want someone to eat it. They're probly watching us right now. I bet they know it's my favorite. Why else would they send peanut butter and jelly on wheat bread?

Brad sat up and looked at Violet.

"Maybe we can stand it on its edge and roll it."

"Great idea." Violet nodded. "I'm sure you want to show it to Heather. We can roll it to her house."

Pamela burst out laughing again.

Brad glared at Violet.

Willys licked the last crumbs off his granola bar wrapper and dropped it on the ground. *That sandwich isn't poisoned. Why would aliens poison a little kid like me?*

"I don't wanna tell that screwball doctor about this, anyway," Brad said. "So what if he worked for NASA? I don't trust him. I'd rather tell Dad than someone I don't know."

"Too bad your daddy's not here." Pamela shrugged her shoulders.

"Call him," Brad demanded.

"There's no reception out here, but if you want to try, go ahead." Pamela pulled her phone from her pocket and handed it to him.

Brad took the phone and punched in his father's work number. The screen read, "No service." He tried again and again with the same results.

"We're wasting time," Violet complained.

"That last call almost went through," Brad said.

"No, it didn't." Pamela held her hand out. "Give it back. The battery's low."

"One more try." Brad started to punch in the number again, but Pamela grabbed the phone. "Hey!"

Willys felt his stomach grumbling. His mind was made up. He grabbed his plastic bat and lay on his back. He fidgeted and squirmed away from the other children, an inch at a time. They were too busy arguing over the phone to notice. When he was out of their sight, he stood, hunched over, and tiptoed away.

He pretended to be a soldier behind enemy lines, careful to stay out of sight. When there was no cover, Willys crawled along the ground. He crept through the tall grass and hid behind trees, bushes, and boulders, keeping one eye on the enemy camp and one eye on his objective.

He was more than halfway to the saucer, crawling over rocks and pine cones, when a small brown snake wriggled down the slope a few feet in front of him. "You better stay away from me," he whispered as the snake slithered by. His hands gripped the handle of his bat, and his jaw tightened as he fought the urge to pulverize the little reptile. "You're lucky I'm on a mission," he told the snake as it disappeared beneath a fallen branch.

Operation Sandwich proceeded with no further incident.

Willys arrived at the saucer undetected by his opponents. He climbed onto the disk and tore off the plastic bag his sister had so carefully taped down.

He reached into the saucer and picked up the sandwich.

I should 'zamine this before I eat it.

The outside looked okay. There were no signs of mold, and the bread was soft and supple. He pulled the sandwich apart. The peanut butter was smooth and creamy.

"Yes! Strawberry! I knew they made this for me," he said softly.

He put the two halves of the sandwich back together and licked some of the peanut butter and jelly oozing down one side.

"Those aliens sure know how to make a good sandwich, except for one thing."

Willys tore off the crust and opened his mouth to take his first bite.

CHAPTER 6

The Oath

Pamela had won the tug-of-war over her cell phone, but Brad was still reluctant to search for Dr. Harrison.

"I think we should keep the saucer a secret for now," he said.

"Well, we can't just leave it here." Pamela returned the phone to her pocket.

Brad struck the ground with his bat. "I can make a wood frame. We'll roll it home like a wheel."

"If we do that, everyone in Bend will know about it," Violet told him. "Not much of a secret."

Brad rolled onto his back and looked up at the sky. "I see your point." He mulled over their options. None of them were good.

"Ew." Violet brushed away a slug that was starting to crawl up her leg. She looked next to her and saw a trail of the big yellow bugs flowing from the pillowcase. There was a hole in it, and the lizard was already halfway out. She shrieked and sprang to her feet.

"What's wrong?" Pamela asked.

Violet pointed to the bag.

"Crap." Brad thought his bag was still near the cave. He rushed to pick it up, but it was too late. The lizard got out and ran straight toward his sister.

She screamed as the scaly brown creature ran over one of her feet and into the meadow.

Brad swallowed the beginnings of a smile and tried to act sincerely apologetic.

"Sorry, Willys must have brought it down here. Why'd you do that, Willys?" He looked for his brother but didn't see him anywhere. "Willys?"

Three pair of eyes searched everywhere for the little boy.

"I can't take much more of this." Violet looked down and shook her head. She stayed behind as Brad and Pamela raced up the hill yelling her brother's name. She walked around the tree as if in a trance, calling, "Willys. Come out, Willys."

I bet he had to pee again. He didn't go back to the saucer. He's got to be around here somewhere.

"Willys. Please come back."

She tried to push away the images flooding her mind: Willys lost in the forest, Willys drowning in the creek, Willys laying in a hospital bed, poisoned by the mystery sandwich, Willys with radiation sickness, and Willys in a coffin.

This is all my fault. I should have kept my eyes on him.

From a distance, Pamela's voice rang out, "Willys, put that down!"

Violet's mind froze. She could see. She could hear. She could smell, but her brain seemed disconnected from all her senses. It was like falling into a deep, dark hole.

*****

Willys sat on the edge of the saucer, holding a piece of the sandwich. The crust rested beside him. His hands, face, and clothes were smeared with peanut butter and jelly.

"Gimme that!" Brad took the sandwich remnant from his brother.

Using the discarded plastic bag, Pamela picked up the crust like it was dog poo. She held the bag open, and Brad dropped in the piece he'd retrieved.

"That was good." Willys licked his fingers.

"It was really dumb." Brad used Willys's shirt to wipe the goo off his hands.

"You have no idea what was in that sandwich." Pamela zipped the bag closed.

"Creamy peanut butter and strawberry jelly. I looked."

Pamela held up the bag. "You can't see viruses or radioactivity."

"It was good." Willys wiped his mouth with his shirt and burped.

Brad looked him over. "If it's from outer space, you might be infected with alien spores or something."

"Just 'cause it's from outer space doesn't mean it's bad. Green Lantern got his power ring from outer space." Willys picked up his bat.

"That's true. Lots of superheroes got powers from alien gemstones and stuff. I guess it could happen."

"Sandwich powers? I don't think so." Pamela sneered.

"Maybe I can shoot jelly out of my fingers!" Willy held his arms out and tensed every muscle in his upper body. "Argh!"

Pamela shook her head. "Come on. Your sister's worried sick about you."

She and Brad trudged back to the clearing with Willys skipping between them, like a happy little mountain goat.

Violet was standing under the big oak tree with tears rolling down her cheeks.

She wiped her eyes as they approached.

Pamela held out the plastic bag containing the remnants of the sandwich.

"How's your tummy?" Violet looked at her little brother and struggled to hold back a new wave of tears.

"Fine." Willys wiped his mouth. "That sandwich was really good."

Violet knelt down and hugged him.

Brad picked up his bat. "The sandwich might give him powers. We should test him."

"We need to get him home!" Violet snarled.

"What about the spaceship?" Willys asked.

"We don't have time for that." Violet picked him up.

"Why not?" he complained.

"We need to get you near a hospital in case you get sick."

"I'm not sick!"

"She's right," Brad told him. "But I still think we should test you for powers."

"He's not going to get powers," Violet said.

"How do you know?" Willys asked.

"Yeah, what makes you so sure?" Brad shrugged.

Pamela put her hand on Violet's shoulder. "Let Brad test him on the way home."

Violet heaved a heavy sigh and put Willys down.

"Let's get started." Brad held out his aluminum baseball bat. "See if you can bend this."

Willys took the bat. He held it with both hands and tried to bend it. When that didn't work, he held it between his legs and yanked on the handle with the same results.

"No super strength," Brad concluded.

"Maybe I can fly." Willys jumped as high as he could, hoping to defeat gravity. He made several wholehearted attempts, but gravity won every time.

Pamela pulled Violet aside.

"Looks like your brother's okay. He's really lucky." Pamela held out the remains of the sandwich. "What do you want to do with this?"

"We should probably have it tested." Violet took the bag from her. She looked at the crusty remnants and shook her head.

Pamela fidgeted with a thread dangling from her pant leg. "There were no wires or anything going into it. I don't think there was a microchip. Do you?"

"I don't know." Violet put the bag in her pack.

By now, Willys had failed Brad's tests for both telescopic and microscopic vision.

"Let's see if you can read minds." Brad put his hand on Willys's shoulder. "Tell me what I'm thinking."

Willys closed his eyes and scrunched up his face. He massaged his temples with the fingers of both hands, searching for a message or an image. After several seconds, his eyes opened wide.

"The Hulk!"

Brad sighed. "No. I was thinking of spaghetti and meatballs."

"Let's go." Violet shouldered her backpack.

"Okay." Brad started putting his belt on. "Let's test you for super speed. I'll race you down the trail."

Willys took off running, while his brother fumbled with his belt and his bat.

"Hey! That's not fair!" Brad hurried after Willys.

"He seems fine. It doesn't help to worry." Pamela picked up her messenger bag.

Violet forced a smile, and the girls headed down the trail the boys were racing on.

*****

"No super speed," Brad panted. The girls had caught up with them in under ten minutes. "Let's check for X-ray vision."

"I don't want X-ray vision."

"Why not? You could see through walls and stuff."

"What good is that?" Willys frowned.

"Maybe you can be extra sticky like peanut butter," Pamela joked.

"Yeah!" Willys tried to make fallen leaves and pebbles stick to his hands. "Look! It's working!"

"That's 'cause you still have peanut butter on your hands," Brad said. "If you're extra sticky, you should be able to climb a tree like a spider." He found a large tree with no low branches for the test.

Willys did his best, but he only managed to pull off a piece of bark and fall down.

"No enhanced stickiness or climbing abilities," Brad declared.

Pamela took the phone out of her pocket.

"I should write this all down, what time Willys ate the sandwich and all Brad's stupid tests." She started typing on her phone.

"We can't write about this in our paper," Violet told her. "People might think I let my brother poison himself."

"I'm not poisoned!" Willys scowled.

Pamela looked up from her phone. "I'd never do that, but when you visit the doctor, he might want details."

"Besides," Brad said, "we didn't let Willys do anything. He snuck away from us."

"It doesn't matter. I'm responsible." Violet let her head hang low, her eyes fixed on the ground at her feet.

Willys failed Brad's tests for heat vision, fire-breathing, ice projection, super hearing, super smelling, super loud voice, magnetic powers, electrical powers, telekinesis, teleportation, mind control, invisibility, invulnerability, superfast spinning, digging power, enhanced math skills, spelling skills, and even riddle-solving skills.

Brad scratched his back with his bat. "Maybe your powers are activated by a magical word like *SHABAKAZOW!*"

"Maybe the aliens think I'm too little for powers." Willys pouted.

"That saucer might not be from outer space." Pamela put her phone away. "You might have eaten some rich kid's science project."

"It's a spaceship!" Willys pouted, teary eyed. "If this was a comic book, I'd already have powers. Maybe I was supposed to eat the whole sandwich."

"That's not going to happen." Violet scowled at him.

"I want superpowers!"

"Don't worry." Brad patted him on the back and gave Violet a concerned look. "Some powers take time to develop."

The words sent shivers down his sister's spine.

"You need to see a doctor," she said.

"I don't wanna."

"When are you going to tell your parents?" Pamela asked.

Brad raised his eyebrows.

"Whoa! Let's think this through."

"We can't keep it a secret." Violet glared at him.

He dragged his bat along the ground. "If there's nothing wrong with Willys, why should we rush to tell Mom and Dad? I think we should give it a day or two."

"Two days," Pamela said. "Do you know how far an infection can spread in two days?"

"Wow. That's comforting." Violet shook her head.

"Maybe I can control the weather." Willys scrunched up his face and tightened his fists. "Snow. Snow. Snow."

"The sooner you tell your parents, the better," Pamela told Violet. "Willys will have a checkup, and we can all stop worrying."

"They'll probably tell the police about the saucer." Brad smacked a stray rock with his bat. "We'll never see it again. It'll be like Roswell. Why can't we tell them tomorrow? If Willys gets sick, we'll tell them everything, but if he gets powers, we might want to keep it a secret."

"Hey, maybe I can turn into animals." Willys scrunched up his face again. "Elephant. Elephant. Elephant."

Violet looked at Willys. "He isn't going to get powers."

"I'll keep an eye on him, just in case," Brad said.

"If I get powers, I don't wanna tell no doctors." Willys scowled. "They might wanna 'speriment on me."

"Good grief." Violet sighed.

They were back at the trailhead.

Pamela gave Violet a hug.

"I better go home."

"Wait a minute." Brad blocked her path. "You have to promise you won't tell anyone about this."

"Why not?"

"It might get back to our parents," he said. "We'll be in more trouble if they learn about this from someone else."

"He's right," Violet mumbled.

Willys joined Brad's one-man blockade of Pamela.

"We can't tell! We all have to promise."

"I swear to keep the spaceship a secret, unless Willys gets sick." Brad held out his hand.

"I swear I won't tell about the spaceship." Willys put his hand on top of Brad's.

"Until tomorrow." Violet put her hand on top.

"I don't like this." Pamela shook her head.

The Wilson siblings all glared at her.

"Fine!" She put her hand on top and said, "I swear I'll give you a chance to tell your parents about it first."

The oath made, Pamela headed for her home and the Wilsons headed for theirs.

CHAPTER 7

Dinner Is Served

When Violet, Brad, and Willys got home, their dad was waiting for them.

"I got pizza!" he said.

"That's good, Dad." Brad walked straight to the hallway, right past the pizzas.

"Did you get one with veggies?" Violet's stomach was churning from both hunger and anxiety. She lifted the lid of a pizza box to take a peek.

Willys came in last.

Mr. Wilson stuck his arm out to keep him from marching by.

"Whoa there, little man." He examined his son's face and T-shirt. "What kind of junk has your sister been feeding you?"

Violet dropped the lid of the box. "I only gave him a granola bar!"

"This isn't from a granola bar." Her father pointed to the stains on Willys's shirt.

Violet's pulse quickened.

"I had a sandwich too," Willys said. "It was real good."

Brad turned around in the hallway. His eyes nearly popped out of his head.

"What kind of sandwich?" Mr. Wilson asked.

"Peanut butter and jelly on whole wheat."

"Ah, so that's what this is." He pulled off Willys's T-shirt. "Let's take care of this before your mother gets home."

Violet grabbed Willys's shoulders from behind.

"You should get cleaned up for dinner." She steered him to his bedroom, and Brad followed, closing the door behind him.

"Why did you tell Dad about the sandwich?" Brad spoke in a furious whisper. "We swore not to tell!"

"I didn't swear about the sandwich. I swore about the spaceship."

"You are such an idiot!" Brad tried to keep his voice down.

"No, you're not. That was brilliant." Violet patted Willys on the back. "Now Dad knows about the sandwich, but he doesn't suspect anything. If you get sick, we're already covered. Have a problem with that, Brad?"

"Yeah. You have a problem, Brad?" Willys challenged.

Brad pushed his forehead against his brother's. Their noses were almost touching.

"Don't tell anyone else."

Violet pulled Brad back.

"We have to tell Mom and Dad the same story." She looked in Willy's eyes. "If Mom asks about the sandwich, you have to tell her."

"I guess you're right." Brad was impressed by his sister's skill in covering this up. "We could say Pamela gave it to him."

"That's a lie!" Willys scowled at him.

"This is useless." Brad sat on the bottom bunk bed and held his head with both hands.

Violet held Willys's shoulders.

"If Mom and Dad know where that sandwich came from, they'll take you straight to the doctor. Is that what you want?"

"No."

"So what will you tell them if they ask where you got it?"

"I ain't tellin'!"

Brad threw his arms in the air. "See, he can't keep a secret."

"That's a lie, you liar!" Willys roared.

Brad and Violet shushed him.

"We better get ready for dinner." Violet said in a worried whisper.

Willys crossed his arms. "I'm not hungry."

"You still need to wash that jelly off your face." Brad got off the bed and pushed him out of the room, down the hall, and into the bathroom.

Violet carried her backpack to her room and closed the door. She took out the bag of sandwich scraps and looked at it.

I should put this someplace where Willys can't find it.

She went to her closet and put the bag inside an empty shoebox, which she hid high on a shelf behind other shoeboxes.

It made her feel a little better, like she had regained a tiny bit of control.

*****

Meanwhile at Pamela's house, Mrs. Edison was serving blackened salmon and brown rice with an organic avocado beet salad.

Mr. Edison always came home for a healthy, home-cooked meal before returning for the night shift at his business, Edison's Genius Grill and Ice Cream Creations.

"How did your meeting with Violet go?" Mrs. Edison passed the dill sauce to Pamela.

"Not good. She had to watch her brothers." Pamela spooned some sauce on her fish.

"You could have left them with your Aunt Molly," her mom said. "She can always use some help at the B and B."

"Violet's brothers aren't very helpful."

"I hope you're not about to bad-mouth Brad." Her dad took the dill sauce. "He's one of my best customers."

"Did you cancel the hike?" her mom asked.

"No, but we hardly got any work done."

"Well, that's too bad." Mrs. Edison ground pepper over her salad. "I know it was important to you."

"It was." Pamela played with the food on her plate. "Hey, Dad, I've been meaning to ask you something."

"What is it, baby girl?"

"Well, starting our club won't be easy."

"You need money?"

"Sure, money helps, but what we really need is snacks. Kids love your ice cream, so—"

"Done deal."

"Thanks, Daddy!"

"I can do sliders too."

"That would be incredible!" Pamela's face lit up.

Mrs. Edison kissed her husband on the cheek.

"I'll deliver them to your club meetings," she said. "They're much better hot."

"I should tell Violet." Pamela pulled out her cell phone.

"Put that thing away," Mr. Edison said.

"You know the rules." Mrs. Edison took a bite of salad.

"No cell phones at the dinner table." Pamela pocketed her phone and picked up her fork.

*****

Violet picked up a slice of veggie pizza and put it on her plate.

Brad was devouring his second slice of pepperoni pizza and telling their dad about Willys's assault on Dr. Harrison.

"He beat the heck out of him, but the geezer wasn't hurt."

"He said he was a bigfoot." Willys took a gulp from a can of cola.

"No, he didn't." Violet sprinkled parmesan cheese on her slice. "He said he was on the trail of a bigfoot."

Their dad shook his head.

"He seems like a real crackpot, but that's no excuse for what you did, Willys. I don't want you hitting anybody or anything with your bat, unless it's in self-defense. Is that clear?"

"He was making weird noises."

"That doesn't matter. You could have hurt the man."

"Fine," Willys said, sadly. "I won't hit nothin' with my bat." He pouted for a long while. "Can I still hit baseballs?"

"Of course, you can hit baseballs or softballs, just nothing that's alive. Okay?"

"Okay." Willys perked up. He liked playing baseball.

"It never would have happened if you let me bring my BB gun." Brad spoke with a mouthful of pizza. "I would have fired a warning shot, and Dr. Harry and the Hendersons would have stood up before Willys could clobber him."

Mr. Wilson's eyes narrowed. He looked at Violet.

"You stopped him from bringing his BB gun on the hike?"

"Yes, I did."

"Thank you." He nodded to Violet before turning his attention to Brad. "Didn't I tell you never to play with that gun anywhere but our backyard?"

"I don't remember that."

"Well, I'm saying it now! Don't forget it."

"Yes, sir!" Brad saluted.

Before their dad could react, the front door flew open and Mrs. Wilson stepped in, holding a bottle of champagne.

"I sold the house!"

Mr. Wilson gave Brad a look that said their conversation wasn't over. Then he rose from the table and greeted his wife with a hug.

"Congratulations!"

"Marsha called in sick, so I'm getting the whole commission." She kissed her husband and practically skipped into the room, waving the champagne. "A young family from San Francisco is buying it. They offered fifty thousand over asking!"

"Fantastic." Mr. Wilson followed her into the kitchen.

"You do the honors." Mrs. Wilson handed him the bottle and went to get glasses.

"I see you got the good stuff." He popped out the cork and filled the two wineglasses his wife had placed on the kitchen counter.

"An older couple was interested too. We nearly had a bidding war." Mrs. Wilson picked up a glass of champagne and took the bottle from her husband.

"Cheers," he said as he picked up the other glass.

"Cheers." Mrs. Wilson smiled, and they clinked glasses before taking their place at the dinner table.

"It's going to be my biggest sale this year." Mrs. Wilson helped herself to a big slice of pizza.

Violet felt poisoned by her mother's cheerful mood. She wanted to deflate it.

"Willys attacked a teacher from my school today."

"What?" Her mom acted as if she hadn't really understood what Violet had said.

"He wasn't hurt, thank God." Mr. Wilson took a sip of champagne.

"But he was really angry." Violet was outraged by her mom's nonchalance.

"Oh." Mrs. Wilson sprinkled some pepper flakes onto her pizza. "What was Willys doing at your school?"

"It happened in the forest." Brad took a big gulp from a can of root beer.

"I couldn't see him. He was hiding in the bushes." Willys grabbed a slice of veggie pizza and sprinkled cheese and pepper flakes on it.

"Why was your teacher hiding in the forest?" Mrs. Wilson bit into her pizza.

"He's not my teacher." Violet slapped the table with both palms.

"He was looking for bigfoot." Brad grabbed another slice.

His mother looked skeptical.

"It's true," Mr. Wilson told her. "I sold him a truck last month. He measured the bed to make sure a Sasquatch would fit in it. I thought he was kidding, but apparently, he wasn't."

Mrs. Wilson shook her head.

"He claims he saw bigfoot during a camping trip," her husband continued. "It was probably a bear, but he quit a job at NASA to hunt for it."

"Some people have no sense." Mrs. Wilson sipped her champagne and smiled. "Did I tell you they're paying for the house in cash? No mortgage. No holdups."

"Can't beat that." Mr. Wilson took a big gulp of the bubbly.

"That's wonderful." Violet took another slice of pizza. "Can I eat this in my room?"

"You mean 'May I eat this in my room?'" Her mom took another sip of champagne.

Violet fought the urge to throw the pizza in her face.

"May I eat this in my room, please?"

"Yes, you may." Mrs. Wilson put her glass down and took another bite of pizza. "Mmm."

Violet picked up her plate and left the dining room.

*****

Pamela's dad wiped his mouth with his napkin and got up from the table.

"Time to go back to work," he said.

"Bye, Daddy." Pamela rose from her seat and gave him a hug, while her mom cleared the plates from the table.

"I'll see you later, Mr. Edison." His wife smiled and winked at him.

"Yes, you will." He smiled back.

He took his Portland Trail Blazers cap off the coat rack and put it on.

"Thanks again, Daddy." Pamela walked to the front door with him.

"Anything for my baby girl." He kissed her forehead and stepped outside.

Pamela watched him walk to his car and drive away.

She locked the door and walked to the kitchen to help her mom with the dishes.

"Want me to load the dishwasher?"

"No, I'm almost done, but you can dry the things in the rack and put them away."

Pamela picked up a dish towel and went to work on a skillet.

"Mom, can I tell you something?"

"Of course." Her mom loaded the last dish and closed the dishwasher.

"Well, I always thought it would be nice to have a little brother or sister."

"That's not likely to happen." Mrs. Edison dried her hands on her apron.

"Good. The hike today changed my mind. A dozen hyper kids full of candy would be easier to handle than Violet's brothers."

"Are they really that bad?"

"Well, I'm glad I'm not in her shoes. I guess I can see how being an only child has its benefits."

Her mom smiled.

"Well, having a smart daughter like you is all I could ever ask for." She kissed her daughter on the cheek and went about preparing a pot of flavored green tea.

Pamela finished drying the dishes and went to her room to text Violet.

"How's Willys?"

"He's fine," Violet answered. "He ate a huge slice of pizza."

"That's good," Pamela texted. "My dad said he'd donate food for our club meetings!"

"Great!" Violet replied.

"Ice cream and sliders, the best snacks of any club at Sky View. ☺"

"If not for my mom, 😼 we'd probably have our mission statement done too."

Pamela grinned at the emoji. "We can work on that tomorrow," she wrote.

"I don't know. If I tell my parents what happened, who knows what they'll do."

Was Violet trying to back out? Pamela scowled at her phone.

"YOU HAVE TO TELL THEM THE TRUTH!"

She was about to call her friend to continue the conversation on FaceTime when her mom knocked on the door and opened it. She stood in the doorway with a wild look in her eyes.

"You need to come see the news. It's incredible." She held out her hand.

Pamela had never seen this kind of expression on her mom's face before. She left her phone on the bed and took her hand.

CHAPTER 8

The Breaking News

Violet replied to Pamela's text but got no response.

"Are you still there?" she texted.

No reply.

Something was definitely wrong. Violet took a deep breath and started unpacking her backpack.

She was sorting through the items that had once occupied the large plastic bag when Pamela finally wrote back.

"OMG! Turn on your TV."

Violet thought it was an odd request, but she texted, "OK," and walked to the living room. She picked up the remote and turned on the television.

A very serious-looking reporter appeared on the screen. She was standing in a field speaking into a handheld microphone. "SPECIAL REPORT" was written in a red rectangle above her.

"Government officials have declared a state of emergency. Police have cordoned off the area, and helicopters are constantly circling overhead."

Mr. Wilson walked into the room and looked at the TV.

"What's that about?"

"I don't know." Violet sat on the couch.

Her dad sat next to her.

"The president has issued a proclamation of our peaceful intentions and greeted the aliens on Twitter, but there has been no response," said the reporter. "Military personnel are on their way to take control."

Mrs. Wilson came in with a full glass of champagne. She snuggled up to her husband.

"Crowds have gathered on both sides of the Columbia River near Government Island despite official requests that people stay away from the area." The camera cut to a crowd of cheering people.

"Looks like Woodstock." Mrs. Wilson grinned at her own lame joke.

"This is momentous. The importance of this event cannot be overstated. Things will never be the same. Local resident, Dave Pinsky, captured the arrival on his cell phone. He shot the footage you are about to see."

On the screen, what appeared to be a spinning metallic sphere hovered over the Columbia River. As it descended, its size became apparent. It was as big as a football stadium! The huge ball slowly stopped spinning as it neared the water, revealing its true shape.

It was a saucer with a huge sphere in the middle, a gigantic twin of the little spaceship in the forest!

"Must be a remake of *War of the Worlds*." Her dad changed the channel. The same footage of the saucer was on that channel.

He changed the channel again and again and again, but every one had breaking news about the alien spacecraft.

"Hey, if the aliens are real, maybe they're in the market for some real estate." Mr. Wilson grinned and winked at his wife.

"This might be their vacation," she said. "You could sell them a used minivan."

They both chuckled at the joke.

Violet was entranced by the images on the TV. She didn't even notice when her phone started chiming.

"Aren't you going to answer that?" her mom asked.

"What?" Violet looked at her phone screen. "Oh."

Pamela had texted, "Did you see it?"

"Yes," she wrote back.

Violet left the couch. She tried to hide her feelings as she sauntered to her brothers' room.

PEANUT BUTTER AND JELLY SANDWICHES FROM OUTER SPACE!

Brad was searching online for obscure powers his brother might acquire.

Willys was lying facedown, motionless on his bed.

"Willys, are you okay?" Violet rushed to him.

He moved his head to one side.

"I'm trying to ooze like jelly, but it's not workin'."

"Hey, I never thought about plant-based powers." Brad swiveled around in his chair. "Maybe you can make plants shrivel up and die or sprout and grow."

"Cool." Willys sat up and abandoned his attempt to ooze.

"Forget about superpowers," Violet told them. "We have a real problem."

"Let me guess." Brad closed his laptop. "Pamela told her parents."

"No. She didn't." Violet glared at him. "For your information, there's another flying saucer all over the news, a really big one."

"Where?" he said in a skeptical tone.

"Over the Columbia River. It's on every TV channel."

Brad's expression changed as the news sank in.

Even Willys was worried.

"I hope they don't want their sandwich back."

"No one knows what they want, but it looks like we'll find out pretty soon." Violet left to watch the news.

Her brothers followed close behind.

An Army general was on the television. He was accompanied by a huge force of heavily armed soldiers in jeeps and tanks. They took up positions around the saucer as the world watched. A reporter's deep voice narrated the scene playing out on-screen.

"General Hazard's men have set up a wooden platform and a mobile communication system. He's taking the microphone."

"Welcome," said the General. "The president of our great country has asked me to offer you the hand of peace."

"If we want peace, why did we send soldiers and tanks?" Violet asked.

"That's how the government works," her dad said. "They want this weird story to seem realistic."

"If they wanted realism, they should have left out the flying saucer." His wife chuckled.

"Our nation's great leader has requested that I read the following statement. Ahem." The general picked up a single sheet of paper. "We greet you, alien beings, in peace and in friendship. We are sincere and honest about peace as always, and it is in this spirit that I greet you. I am honored that of all the countries on our planet, you chose to visit ours. Your choice is proof that America is great again, and it is our greatness that I am most proud of."

"Something's happening," the reporter said. "The ship's dome is pulsing with green light. The general has stopped speaking, and the light has changed to blue. Now it's yellow. It's turned green again. The light is pulsing quicker and brighter. The colors are changing in a cycle. It's getting faster and faster, like a psychedelic strobe light."

The Wilson children exchanged glances. The light show was familiar to them.

"The general and his soldiers are retreating from the platform."

The camera focused on a group of soldiers pulling back, weapons aimed at the saucer.

"The light has turned red. It's getting very bright!"

The children expected a bright flash. They weren't disappointed.

"Oh my goodness. That was intense. No one seems to have been hurt, but I'm having trouble seeing." The reporter paused to rub his eyes. "The saucer is no longer producing light of any color. A long strip of metal seems to be melting away from it and forming a ramp."

The camera scanned the still-morphing silver ribbon and the narrow opening in the saucer caused by its creation.

"Something is emerging from the spaceship. It's a small black box on wheels. I don't see any censors or weapons, just wheels."

"I wonder what kind of horsepower that thing has." Mr. Wilson grinned and took a sip from his wife's glass.

"As the box rolls down the ramp, I see our tanks rolling toward the spacecraft. This could be a pivotal moment in human history. The box has stopped. It's at the end of the ramp, a few yards from the river's edge. I think… Yes. It's opening up! A T-shaped metallic gadget is sprouting from it."

Soldiers aimed their weapons at the device and waited for orders. A bulge grew like an inflating balloon where the contraption's horizontal and vertical bars met.

While the soldiers' attention was focused on the black box, a large bird flew out of the spaceship. The crowd pointed and gaped. The television cameras zoomed in on it.

"A creature resembling a blue Macaw has flown out of the saucer. It's wearing a little silver helmet."

The crowd cheered as the bird flew in a huge figure eight above the saucer.

"This is ridiculous." Mrs. Wilson drained her glass and left to refill it.

"The parrot has gone into a dive. It's heading for the ramp."

The bird landed gracefully on the crossbar of the T-shaped device, and the crowd exploded in applause.

The bulge on the crossbar pulsed with green light.

"Incredible as it seems, we may be moments away from witnessing man's first contact with an alien life-form," the reporter said.

"I hope it's not angry about us eating chicken," Mr. Wilson joked.

"General Hazard and several of his men are returning to the platform."

The camera cut from the general, to the soldiers, to the crowd, to the helmeted parrot and back again.

General Hazard stepped up to the microphone and said, "Welcome."

"Greetings, Earth people." The parrot's voice boomed like thunder, amplified by the device below it. "I was hatched on planet Earth, just as you were."

Mr. Wilson chuckled.

"The owners of this craft rescued me from a cage on a sinking ship long ago. Since then, I have traveled the galaxy with them. My name is Pirate's Pet 1."

"Does that mean the aliens are space pirates?" Willys squirmed like a worm on a hook.

The parrot hopped to another part of its metallic perch and was instantly speckled by hundreds of red laser gun sights. "My masters, Goobex 1 and Goobex 2, come in peace."

"That's good news." Violet shared a meaningful look with her brothers.

Her mom returned with two glasses of champagne and handed one to her husband.

"Did I miss anything?" she asked.

"No," her husband told her. "The bird claims it's from Earth, but nothing exciting has happened."

"Are you sure there's nothing else on TV?" Mrs. Wilson took the remote from her husband and changed the channel over and over again. The parrot's speech was on every station. "This must have cost a fortune." She sighed and sat down.

Mr. Wilson took the remote from her.

"We can always watch something on Netflix."

"No!" the children protested.

"You really want to watch this?" he asked.

Willys nodded.

"Yes!" Brad said.

Violet grabbed the remote. "When school starts, all the kids will be talking about it."

Mr. Wilson shook his head and drank some more champagne.

"I'd like to speak with your masters," General Hazard told the parrot. "When can I see them?"

"The Goobexes cannot vocalize." The parrot swayed from side to side on his perch. "They are telepathic. Direct communication could damage your mind. For that reason, I will act as their interpreter."

Mrs. Wilson laughed.

"Didn't see that coming." He wrapped one arm over his wife's shoulders.

"Goobex 1 and Goobex 2 are anxious to share their thoughts. There are important matters to be resolved, so it is time for you to meet them." Pirate's Pet 1 puffed out his chest feathers. "People of

PEANUT BUTTER AND JELLY SANDWICHES FROM OUTER SPACE!

planet Earth, I am pleased to introduce the wise and beneficent Goobexes!"

The aliens emerged from the spaceship.

Willys took one look and ran to his room.

"This is incredible," the reporter said. "I can't believe what I'm seeing. The Goobexes are over ten feet tall, and they bear an uncanny resemblance to...well, giant sandwiches."

CHAPTER 9

Truth or Consequences

The Goobexes were conveyed down the ramp by two black boxes on wheels. Each box projected a cone of rotating colored lights that levitated the massive creatures four feet in the air.

The crowd cheered.

The tanks rolled closer.

TV cameras focused on the Goobexes, while reporters did their best to describe them.

"Their epidermis looks like wheat bread, and the sides of the creatures are pulsing with a red jellylike substance supported by thicker stuff that looks a lot like creamy peanut butter. They don't appear to have arms or legs or facial features, but I see two thin horizontal slits where you might expect to see eyes."

Mrs. Wilson grinned at her husband. "I don't think they'll fit in a minivan."

"You're right. A bakery truck would be much better." Mr. Wilson took a sip of champagne. "They may have special needs."

Mr. and Mrs. Wilson chuckled and snuggled a little closer.

A close-up of General Hazard appeared on the TV screen. He was confused, confounded, and conflicted. The picture slowly zoomed out to show the forces at his command.

"The aliens have stopped near the end of the ramp," said the reporter. "The bulge on their interpreter's perch has begun flashing at different intervals in different colors. It reminds me of Morse code."

"I learned Morse code in the Boy Scouts," Mr. Wilson told his wife. "That parrot might be an Eagle Scout."

Mrs. Wilson snorted with laughter. She was a little tipsy.

"It's not funny!" Brad stalked out of the room to join Willys.

Mrs. Wilson watched her son leave.

"I hope the boys aren't taking this seriously."

"Brad's been grumpy all day," said Violet. "I'll go talk to him."

"If this is about that BB rifle—"

"What BB rifle?" Mrs. Wilson elbowed her husband in the ribs. "Ow!"

"What BB rifle?" she repeated.

Violet left her parents and headed to the boys' room.

Willys lay, rolled up in a little ball under the bunk beds. It felt like the only safe place in the universe. He clutched a Spider-Man action figure to his chest and waited. He didn't know what to expect, but he was certain something bad was coming for him.

Brad sat in his chair, using his laptop.

"If you're lookin' up stuff on the aliens, I don't wanna hear it!" Willys heard the door to his room open and close.

"We have to tell!" Violet's voice rang out.

"No!" Willys shouted.

Brad closed his computer and stood up. "The president sent out a tweet saying the aliens might be hostile invaders!"

Willys saw Violet's fleecy slippers approaching the bed.

"I don't think so, but we can't keep this a secret," she said.

"We swore an oath! You liar!" He threw Spider-Man at Violet's ankles but missed.

Brad lay sideways on the floor to look at him.

"We swore an oath before a humongous spaceship landed and a parrot flew out to interpret for giant sandwiches! We have to tell."

"No! I need to get superpowers first." Willys hugged his knees close to his chest and tucked his head down, as if retreating into a protective cocoon.

"I know this is scary," said Brad. "But you always say being scared is for sissies."

"That was before a talking parrot came out of a spaceship with alien sandwiches." A few tears rolled down the boy's cheeks.

"You're being a sissy," Brad told him.

"No, I'm not."

"Yes, you are! If we keep this a secret, the Goobexes might attack or something."

Violet's phone buzzed.

"Pamela wants to know if we're still watching the news." She sat on the bottom bunk with her feet dangling over the side.

Brad rose from his spot on the floor. He returned a few seconds later with a pillow, which he shoved under the bed.

"Here." He bent down on his hands and knees to look at his brother. "I got a feeling you're going to be under there for a while."

"I'll come out when the aliens leave."

"What if they stay?"

"Shut up, Bradley!" Willys positioned the pillow beneath his head.

The text alert sounded again.

Willys watched Violet's feet. They stopped moving completely. He could tell there was another problem. "I wish they'd go home."

"That would be great, wouldn't it?" Brad looked up at their sister. "Are you okay?" She didn't answer. "What's wrong?"

Brad got up off the floor. Willys saw his feet facing Violet's immobile slippers.

"Let me see that. Come on. You are such a drama queen."

Willys couldn't see what was going on, but he guessed that his brother was reading the text message.

"Whoa," Brad said, and he, too, fell silent.

Terror grew inside Willys like an alien fungus.

What kind of news could possibly make Brad shut up?

It had to be bad, really bad.

The little boy burst into tears.

Their mother knocked on the door after she opened it.

"What's going on?" she asked.

PEANUT BUTTER AND JELLY SANDWICHES FROM OUTER SPACE!

"We're playing a game! Go away!" Willys sniffled under the bed.

He saw his parent's feet coming toward him.

Violet could not speak. She felt like she was sinking to the bottom of a murky lake.

"Mom, Dad," Brad said in a calm, respectful tone. "Something really important happened today in the forest. Willys and I found a little flying saucer."

"Liar!" Willys kicked at Brad's feet.

Brad thwarted the attack by moving away from the bed.

"It had a peanut butter and jelly sandwich inside," he continued.

"Wait a second," Mr. Wilson said. "Didn't Willys say—"

"He ate it," Violet managed to croak, despite a huge lump in her throat.

"No, you're not serious." Mrs. Wilson chuckled nervously.

"I was hungry," Willys sobbed.

"This whole thing reeks of a promotional stunt," Mr. Wilson grumbled. "They're setting up a treasure hunt for the missing sandwich."

"How do you fake a giant spaceship?" Brad asked.

"They do it in movies all the time," his dad answered. "They must have spent a fortune to get it on every channel."

Mrs. Wilson got on her hands and knees to look under the bed.

"Come on out, honey. It's dusty under there."

"Not till the aliens go away."

"They're not real." She shook her head gently. "It's only make-believe."

"They are real! I ate their baby."

His mother looked away. She stood up.

A wave of despair washed over Willys. He had guessed the bad news, and nobody said he was wrong. It could only mean one thing. Tears flooded his eyes.

Violet took her phone from Brad and texted Pamela.

"We told my parents, but they think it's a hoax."

"I'll send the video," Pamela answered.

"This is crazy." Mrs. Wilson spoke softly into her husband's ear. "What are we going to do about this?"

"Nothing. It's only a matter of time till they admit some megacorporation set this up. Our kids just stumbled into it."

"Well, we can't just leave Willys under the bed," his wife told him.

"Why not?" He shrugged. "He'll come out when he knows he's safe."

"He might miss second grade," said Brad.

Willys wanted to clobber him, but he wasn't willing to leave his fortress of solitude.

The video from Pamela's phone finished downloading.

"Dad. Pamela recorded this in the forest today. You should see it." Violet handed the phone to him and started playing the video.

The recording began with Willys clinging to the saucer and saying, "The force is in me!" The saucer flipped, dumping him into the ferns. The camera zoomed in on the saucer as its flipping reached a high velocity and energy bolts flashed around it. "If one of these trees catches fire, we're in trouble," Pamela said as the saucer rose higher.

"I used two bottles of water putting out flare-ups from that thing," Brad said as he watched the video at his dad's side.

The saucer's spinning and sparking subsided. It hovered, then floated to the ground. The camera circled it, recording it from every angle before Willys shouted, "Let's try again!" and the recording came to an abrupt end.

"This video is incredible, but I didn't see a sandwich." Mr. Wilson gave the phone back to Violet.

"The top of the saucer melted," she told him. "The sandwich was inside."

"You're a fink, Violet!" Willys sobbed under the bed. "We swore an oath."

"Let me see that." Mrs. Wilson took the phone from her daughter and started the video.

Mr. Wilson's doubts were melting away like the dome of the little spaceship. The story was hard to believe, but there was also Willys's stained T-shirt. "Peanut butter and jelly on whole wheat."

The evidence was piling up. He took Violet's phone and watched the video again.

"Maybe we should contact the government," he said. "Just in case."

"No!" Willys wailed under the bed. "They'll cut me open and 'speriment on me."

Mrs. Wilson gave her husband an anguished look. "I think we should wait."

"Look, Rebecca," he sighed. "If those aliens are real, there are going to be consequences."

"Willys should be our number one concern, not fake aliens!" his wife said.

"I don't think they're fake." Brad opened his laptop and showed them the screen. "There are Native American drawings of square people from the sky thousands of years old."

"That doesn't mean anything." Mrs. Wilson got down on her knees again to talk to Willys. "Everything is going to be all right, honey."

"No, it's not." Willys turned his back to her.

"If this is real, we can't brush it under a rug," Mr. Wilson said. "The government has to prepare for whatever comes next."

"The FBI is asking for information," Brad said.

"No! They'll give me to the aliens." Willys clutched the pillow to his stomach and sobbed. He imagined a Goobex torture chamber equipped with a meat slicer used to turn little boys into deli sandwiches. "You're a rat fink, Brad! I hate you!"

"This isn't Brad's fault," his mom said.

"Yes, it is! He made me look for bigfoot."

Brad felt a twinge of guilt.

"We all warned you not to eat that sandwich, Willys."

"I didn't know it was alive." Willys thought about how he tore the sandwich in half to inspect its filling. The Goobexes would be furious if they knew.

"It's my fault." Violet rested her face in her hands. "I took him on the hike."

"I figured out how to pull the saucer out of the cave," said Brad.

"I let him sneak away." Violet got on the floor with her mother. "We'll tell the aliens that I ate their baby."

"I can't let you do that." Mrs. Wilson stood up. "I put you in charge, so if this is real, I'll take the blame."

"No, Becca." Mr. Wilson looked at his wife with pleading eyes. "The children need you. If it comes down to it, I'll take the rap."

"Are you crazy?" Brad walked to the door. "I guess all those times you said, 'Honesty is the best policy,' you were just lying."

Willys saw Brad's feet leave the room.

"Bradley! Hold on, son."

Their dad's feet left in pursuit.

"Nobody better try to make me come out or I'll bite 'em," he muttered.

CHAPTER 10

The Men in Black

Brad heaved himself onto the living room couch and turned on the TV.

His father was right behind him.

"Your brother needs us." Mr. Wilson turned the TV off. "We need to protect him."

"It's too late for that. He ate an alien. It could be radioactive."

"Good point." Mr. Wilson sat next to his son. "I wonder where we can rent a Geiger counter."

"We don't need a Geiger counter, Dad. We need to take Willys to a doctor, one who knows how to look for alien parasites and stuff."

"I don't think I can find someone like that." Mr. Wilson stuck his hand in his pocket and played with his keys while mulling over his options. "I'll schedule a checkup with Dr. Cohen."

"He won't know what to look for!" Brad held his head with both hands, as if trying to keep his brain from exploding. "The only way to help Willys is to tell the truth!"

"Hmm." Mr. Wilson rested his elbow on the arm of the couch and his chin on his fist.

Brad picked up the remote and pointed it at his father.

"Willys ate a Goobex. Who knows what that's going to do to him? The aliens might be his only hope for survival. We need help, Dad!" Brad turned the TV on and pointed at it. "We can call the FBI right now. They're asking for information."

Mr. Wilson looked at the TV with a furrowed brow. "Why's the FBI involved? The Army's already there."

"What difference does it make? Are you gonna call?"

"No."

Brad slumped over and rested his face in his open hands.

"We can send the video," his dad said.

Brad looked up, and his father offered him the phone.

"You do it. I'm not sure how."

"It should be easy." Brad took the phone and punched the text icon.

Mr. Wilson stood up and loomed over him with crossed arms. "Just write URGENT in capital letters. Include our home phone number and the video, but that's all."

"That sounds kinda creepy."

"We can talk to them when they call back."

Brad sent the one-word message with the video and phone number, and they waited.

His dad sat down and flipped through the TV channels. He stopped on a station with a pretty young blond behind a desk.

"The president has been the eye of a tweetstorm regarding the aliens," she said. "First, he tweeted, 'I do not support separating aliens from their children. Goobex 3 will be found!' Later, he wrote, 'I don't trust the Goobexes. When a planet sends aliens here, they're not sending the best. They're sending aliens that have lots of problems.'"

"US armed forces remain on high alert," said her partner, a gray-haired fellow in a suit. "Next up, the United Nations calls a special session to discuss first contact with the aliens. We'll be right back after these words from our sponsors."

A commercial came on featuring a caveman, and Mr. Wilson changed channels again.

Brad felt terrible.

If I wasn't trying to get even with Violet, Willys never would've found that cave or the saucer. I just couldn't let it go. When the aliens find out what happened, they're bound to want revenge. They might take it out on Willys, the girls, and me! Heck, they might even blame the whole planet! I should've left that stupid saucer in the cave.

Brad's stomach grumbled. He put his hand on his belly and mumbled, "Kids shouldn't have this kind of stress."

The home phone rang.

Mr. Wilson sprang to his feet and answered it. "Hello? Oh. Hi, Frank."

Brad recognized the name. It was Pamela's dad.

"Yes. Our kids told us. Uh-huh. Well, we sent the video to the FBI." He paused. "What do you mean? No. I don't think it was a bad idea. Are you prepared to deal with aliens? I'm not."

Violet marched into the kitchen. She came out with two cans of soda and a single straw.

Brad got up off the couch and intercepted her. "Any luck with Willys?"

"No. He's still under the bed, but if he drinks enough of these."

Brad admired the simplicity of her plan.

"Look, if Pamela wants to cooperate, I'm not sure we can keep her out of this." Mr. Wilson was agitated. He wanted to keep the phone line open for the FBI.

Violet gave Brad a puzzled look.

"I sent the video to the feds," he told her. "Pamela's dad called like five minutes later."

Mr. Wilson rolled his eyes. "I understand how you feel about the government, Frank, but don't you think the aliens are a bigger concern right now? Yes, the FBI could violate our civil rights, but the aliens could vaporize us. Who do you think is more dangerous?"

Violet was transfixed by her father's words.

"I'll take those." Brad held his hands out.

Violet gave him the cans and the straw, and he left.

"So let me get this straight. You want a lawyer to protect us from the government, while the government is trying to protect us from angry aliens. Does that really make sense to you?"

Violet sat on the couch and muted the television.

"Yes, I think the aliens are a threat. If they find out what Willys did, there's no telling how they'll react. Good. I'm glad you agree.

Well, why don't you come over with Ruby and Pamela? We can all be here when the FBI calls. Okay, Frank. Uh-huh. I'll see you soon."

Mr. Wilson hung up and sat next to Violet. She rested her head against his shoulder. Tears welled up in her eyes and spilled onto her cheeks, making her father's shirt sleeve damp.

"I'm sorry, Daddy. I'm the worst babysitter in history."

"No, you're not." He stroked her hair. "I've lost count of how many sitters quit because they couldn't handle your brothers. We should hire lion tamers instead."

Violet chuckled softly and wiped her eyes.

"I should have kept my eyes on Willys."

"Brad and Pamela were there too. He just did what he did."

"He can't help it. He's just a stubborn little kid."

"That's your mother's fault. He's just like her."

Violet smiled at her dad. "You're right."

Using the remote, she found a station airing Pirate's Pet 1's speech and unmuted the TV.

"Goobex 3 left this ship in his personal shuttle," the big parrot said. "He flew to this sector and vanished. The Goobexes beseech your help in locating their missing progeny. Your atmosphere, which is intolerable for many Earth creatures, could be toxic to him within forty-eight hours. It is imperative that he be found."

"This is so messed up," Violet said.

"If Goobex 3 is not located, there will be repercussions. We have scanned transmissions from your communication devices and will keep in touch."

A pair of newsroom reporters appeared on the screen. "And with that, the Goobexes retreated into their spaceship."

"Scientist around the world are wondering about the saucer's energy source and what powers those boxes," the other reporter said. "I just wonder what kind of horsepower they have."

"Hey! That's my joke!" Mr. Wilson pointed an accusing finger at the reporter.

The doorbell rang.

Violet got up and opened the door, expecting to see the Edisons. Instead, two men in black suits were standing in the night air.

They both wore sunglasses.

"Agent Orange, FBI." The bigger man stepped forward and showed his badge. He had a deep voice, broad shoulders and stood over six foot six.

Mr. Wilson rushed to the door.

"Excuse me. How did the FBI get my address?"

"We know your home address, business address, and name, Mr. Wallace Zachary Wilson." The curly-haired agent was much shorter than his partner but taller than Mr. Wilson. He held up his badge. "Agent Goldblatt, FBI."

Mr. Wilson inspected their badges closely.

"FBI." He nodded. "Please, come in."

Orange had to duck his head down to walk through the doorway. He looked all around as if he were recording every detail.

"Nice house."

Goldblatt came in and glared at Mr. Wilson.

"Interesting video."

"He wasn't there when it was recorded," Violet told him. "We were on a hike."

"Really? You found a spaceship on a hike?" Goldblatt exuded smug disbelief.

"I didn't find it. My brothers did. It was in a cave."

"What are the odds?" Goldblatt chortled.

Agent Orange finished inspecting the room and focused on Violet.

"How did they find the cave?" His voice was calm and soothing.

"I don't know. They went off, supposedly hunting for evidence of bigfoot."

"Bigfoot?" Goldblatt was alarmed by mention of the creature.

"We should talk to your sons," Orange told her dad in a soft, confidential tone.

"I'll go get them." Mr. Wilson turned around and headed to the boys' room.

"Where were you when your brothers found the cave?" Orange asked.

"I was sitting by the creek, talking to my friend."

"Where's he?" Goldblatt smirked.

"*She* is on her way here. She took the video my father sent you."

"Is the spaceship still there?" Orange asked.

"As far as I know."

"That's good, Miss Wilson. Very good." Through his sunglasses, Orange looked into Violet's eyes. "Now tell me exactly what happened."

Violet felt an uncontrollable urge to unburden herself by telling him everything.

"The boys went to look for bigfoot, which was fine with me, but Brad started blowing the whistle that Pamela gave Willys because I took his Wiffle bat."

"I hope you're following this," Goldblatt said to his partner.

"Pamela and I followed the whistle, and Brad said he found a spaceship. We thought it was a prank until we pulled it out of the cave."

"How big was it?" Orange asked.

"About four feet across. The part in the middle was about the size of a basketball."

"What happened after you pulled it out?" Goldblatt's voice was gruff.

"I wanted Pamela to take some photos, but the boys were climbing all over it. I convinced Brad to get off, but Willys took the whistle from him and blew it."

Brad strutted into the room with an empty soda can.

"That's when the saucer went crazy," he said.

"You must be Bradley Maxwell Wilson." Goldblatt stared at the chubby boy.

"And you must be two of the men in black." Brad crossed his arms and examined the agents. "What is it you guys keep trying to cover up?"

"There are no men in black. We would know about them. We're from the FBI."

Brad wasn't convinced, but something in Orange's voice made him want to believe.

"I still haven't told you the important part!" Violet glared at the agents.

The doorbell rang.

Goldblatt drew his gun and pointed it at the door.

"Shhh! It could be the Russians."

Violet crept to the door and peeked out the window on top.

"It's the Edisons," she said. "The friend I told you about and her parents."

"Let 'em in." The agent sighed and slid his weapon back into its shoulder holster.

Violet opened the door.

"These are Agents Orange and Goldblatt from the FBI," she said.

"Pleased to meet you." Mrs. Edison walked up to Orange and shook his hand.

"You sure got here quickly." Mr. Edison walked in behind his daughter.

"Already in the area." Goldblatt held his hand out.

Pamela shook it, but Mr. Edison did not.

"This is our daughter, Pamela," he said.

"You shot the video?" Goldblatt held his hand out again. "We need your cell phone."

Pamela pulled the phone from her pocket and handed it to him.

Her dad's eyes darted from one agent to the other. "Are the children in any trouble?"

"Not that I know of," Goldblatt said. "Why? Have they done something wrong?"

The Edisons exchanged tortured glances with Brad and Violet.

Someone had to speak up.

CHAPTER 11

The Amazing Agent Orange

"We didn't mean to do anything. It just happened."

Violet could feel everyone's eyes on her. She could barely spit the words out. She thought about Goldblatt drawing his gun at the sound of a doorbell, and somehow revealing the fate of Goobex 3 seemed like a really bad idea.

Brad saw her freeze up.

"My brother ate the Goobex!" he blurted out. "He thought it was a sandwich."

"Were you trying to hide that from us?" Goldblatt loomed over Violet like a dark cloud.

"No!" She recoiled from him. "I tried to tell you, but you cut me off."

"That's no excuse. If I knew, I would've—"

The agent clearly had no idea what he would've done.

"We need to see your brother immediately," said Agent Orange.

"Sure, but you'll have to get on your hands and knees. He's hiding under our bunk bed." Brad handed Violet the empty soda can. "I'll take you there."

He led the agents down the hall and into his room.

As soon as they left, the tension drained from Mr. Edison's body like air from a punctured pool toy.

"What do you think they'll do to him?" Pamela asked.

Mr. Edison shook his head. "They'll probably want to run a lot of tests. Could be traumatic for the poor kid."

"It'll be worse if they hand him over to the aliens." Violet crushed the empty can and left the room.

Pamela lifted her father's arm off her shoulder and followed Violet into the kitchen.

"Hey. Are you all right?"

"No." Violet threw the empty can into a recycling bin. "It's like the whole world has gone crazy, and it's my fault we've entered *The Twilight Zone*."

"Then it's my fault too." Pamela leaned against the kitchen counter and looked at the floor. "I talked you into bringing your brothers on the hike to begin with."

Knowing that her friend was willing to share the blame made Violet feel a little better.

"I should give them the remains," she said.

Pamela nodded, and the girls left the kitchen together.

Mr. and Mrs. Edison had retreated to the living room. They were sitting on the couch watching the breaking news on TV. Pamela joined them while Violet headed to her room alone.

Outside the closed door to the boys' room, she heard Goldblatt yelling, "We know you're under there! You can't hide from the FBI!"

Violet got the bag of remains and returned to the boys' room. This time, she heard Willys shouting, "Go away! I'll protect myself."

Violet knocked on the door and the chatter ceased.

Her mom peeked out.

"It's Violet!" she said.

"Let her in," Goldblatt replied.

He was holstering his weapon when the door opened.

Violet held up the bag of scraps.

"This is... It's all that's left of Goobex 3."

"You have remains?" Goldblatt snatched the bag from her and examined it.

"There's no time to waste," said Agent Orange. "Your son has to come with us."

"No!" the boy wailed under his bed.

Goldblatt gave the bag of scraps back to Violet and helped his partner move the bunk bed away from the wall.

Willys scooted back under it before they could grab him.

They moved the bed back and forth and all around, but Willys continued to elude them.

"I can keep this up all night," Goldblatt warned.

"So can I!" Willys answered.

Agent Orange put his end of the bed down and snapped his fingers to get Goldblatt's attention. The big man made a short series of hand signals, and his partner nodded.

Goldblatt dropped his side of the bed and quietly herded everyone to one side of the room. The curly-haired agent stood between them and the bunk bed. He turned to his partner and nodded.

Orange strode to the side of the heavy bed and bent down. The Wilsons were all amazed at how easily he flipped it over. Wooden frame, mattresses, box springs, pillows, and blankets went flying across the room.

Willys was totally exposed. He rose from the floor, his red, tear-streaked eyes blinking in the light. He saw the two agents and ran for the safety of his mother's arms.

Goldblatt blocked his way. He grabbed the boy's arm as he tried to run past him.

Willys struggled against the agent's grip.

"Let me go!"

He bit Goldblatt's hand and tore free from his grasp.

"Ow!" the agent yelped.

Willys ran for the door.

Goldblatt spun around and caught him by the armpits. He turned the boy around to face him and jerked him up in the air, almost to the ceiling.

"You can't run away from the FBI," he told Willys.

That's when the second can of soda kicked in.

By the time Goldblatt put the boy down, they were both drenched.

Willys crawled to his mother's knees and clutched them.

"Arrange for transportation," Orange said.

Goldblatt turned toward Violet and reached for the bag of sandwich scraps.

"No!" Orange grabbed his partner's wrist. "You've been contaminated."

Goldblatt's eyes bulged. He rushed out of the room and contemplated rinsing himself off with a garden hose.

"I'm sorry for the mess." Orange took the bag of remains from Violet and put it in his shirt pocket. "We need to continue this investigation at headquarters. I want all of you to come."

"Sure," Mr. Wilson answered.

"What about the Edisons?" Violet asked.

"I want them to come as well."

"I'm not going!" Willys insisted.

"You don't need to worry," Agent Orange said. "I will protect you."

Willys refused to talk to the agent. He wouldn't even look at him.

Mr. Wilson managed to pry him off his mom's legs and take him to the bathroom to get cleaned up.

Mrs. Wilson followed with a change of clothes for him.

They told Willys that no one was going to hurt him, but he just wanted to escape.

*****

Violet, Brad, and Agent Orange joined the Edisons in the living room.

"We encourage anybody with information on Goobex 3 to contact the FBI," said the reporter on TV.

"Here is the number to call," her partner added. "If the line is busy, keep calling."

"Please, turn the television off," said Agent Orange.

Mrs. Edison picked up the remote and hit the off button.

Orange stood between Violet and Brad.

"The Wilsons have agreed to come to our headquarters," he said. "I'd like you to come as well."

Mr. Edison looked at him as if he expected horns to sprout from his forehead.

"If you need to question my daughter, I want it done here."

"Coordinating our response to the Goobexes will be easier if everyone stays together." Orange looked into his eyes. "Your cooperation is very important to us, Mr. Edison. Your family is very important."

"Yes, they are."

"What are you going to tell the Goobexes?" Mrs. Edison asked.

"That is not a decision I can make," he answered.

Goldblatt peeked into the room.

"Transport's on its way," he said and he left.

Agent Orange looked at the Edisons.

"For the sake of everyone in this house, for our country, at least let your daughter come with us."

"Please, Dad. I want to help." The anguished look on Pamela's face was a more potent argument than anything the agent could say.

Mr. Edison rose from the couch. "If my daughter's going to the FBI headquarters, I'm going with her."

"That makes three of us." Mrs. Edison stood and locked arms with him.

"Of course. We encourage your involvement." Orange looked at the people assembled in the room. "You may want to wear something warm. We'll be traveling by helicopter."

"Cool!" Brad ran off to get his coat.

"Now wait a minute." Mr. Edison grimaced. "You want us to go in a helicopter?"

Pamela nodded toward her father and silently mouthed, "He's afraid of heights."

"There is nothing to be afraid of," Orange said. He was an excellent lip-reader.

"Isn't there another way to get there?" Mrs. Edison asked.

"Driving, but it would take much longer. Besides, helicopters are safer than cars."

"But helicopters—" Mr. Edison shook his head.

"Can I be frank?" Agent Orange looked into his eyes and spoke very slowly. "There is no reason to worry. Our helicopters are safer than your car."

Mr. Edison seemed to think it over.

"Fine."

Pamela and her mom were both astonished. It was like watching a live demonstration of the Jedi mind trick.

"Let's get something for you and your parents to wear," Violet said to Pamela.

They left the room.

Brad ran back in wearing a down parka.

"When's the helicopter gonna get here?"

"You'll hear it when it's here." Mr. Edison was on the verge of relapsing into acrophobia.

"It is safer than your car," Orange repeated softly.

Mr. and Mrs. Wilson walked into the room with Willys, who was freshly cleaned and dressed.

"They're sending a helicopter," Brad told them.

"I'm not going," Willys insisted.

"Come on. It'll be cool." His big brother grinned at Agent Orange. "You know, I've flown a lot of helicopters in video games."

"Well, you're not flying this one," said an agitated Mr. Edison.

Orange looked at him and then turned to Brad.

"Why don't you wait outside? Agent Goldblatt can tell you all about helicopters."

"Cool." He left the room but peeked back in a moment later. "Hey, can I bring my BB rifle?"

"No!" Mr. Wilson scowled at him.

"But they probably have a firing range—"

"No!"

Brad left without further argument.

"How long is the flight?" asked Mrs. Edison.

"Less than an hour."

"An hour!" Mr. Edison felt a tide of terror rising in his chest.

Orange put a hand on his shoulder.

"It will be like a short ride on a big bus."

"A bus?"

"A big bus."

Mr. Edison found the idea of riding on a big bus oddly comforting. He started daydreaming about having a party on a bus. Everyone he knew was there. They had drinks, hors d'oeuvres, casino games, roving magicians, and cheerleaders.

The girls came back with coats for everybody. They handed Pamela's mom a purple parka. It was a good fit.

"I'm not sure about this," said Mr. Edison as he held up the raincoat the girls had selected for him. It was way too small. He thought about going home to get a jacket from his own closet. He also thought about going home and locking the door instead of risking an hour-long helicopter flight.

"Everything will be fine." Agent Orange took his own suit coat off and handed it to Mr. Edison. "The cold doesn't bother me."

He took Orange's coat and put it on. It was big on him, but he felt comfortable in it.

Pamela put on the heavy gray hoodie she had picked out.

"Can Violet and I wait outside?"

"Is that okay with you?" Pamela's mom asked Agent Orange.

"Of course. They'll be safe with Agent Goldblatt."

Mr. Wilson tried to get Willys into a Spider-Man sweatshirt, but he wiggled around, making his dad's job harder.

"I'm not gonna go!"

Orange kneeled to the boy's level and asked, "Are you feeling hot or cold?"

"No!"

"That's good. You don't have to worry, Willys. I am here to help you."

Willys squirmed as his dad pulled his shirt on over his head.

How can you help me? I ate an alien! When its parents find out, they'll wanna kill me. What are you gonna do about that? Huh?

Agent Orange could read body language even better than lips. Willys's body was saying, "I am in distress." He chose the perfect words to grab Willys's attention.

"It's my job to keep Americans safe, and I take my job very seriously. We'll hide you until we decide how to deal with the Goobexes."

Willys's anxiety started to thaw. He finally looked at Agent Orange.

"Where can you hide me?"

Orange leaned close to the boy and whispered, "We have a secret base."

Willys inspected the agent. He wasn't sure if he should trust him, but the longer he looked, the more the big man reminded him of Captain America. The only things missing were a shield and a costume.

"You're a brave boy," Orange said. "Your parents should be proud of you."

Willys no longer felt scared and alone. Having the support of Agent Orange felt like having a real superhero on his side. When the unmistakable sound of a helicopter swelled inside the house, Willys looked up at him.

"Can we get in the helicopper first before the other kids?"

"Sure. Let's go."

As Agent Orange led the group out the front door, a large black helicopter landed in the street in front of the house.

"I want the boy and his parents seated first," Orange told Goldblatt. "Make sure they're comfortable."

Goldblatt escorted Willys and his parents into the waiting whirlybird. Brad, Violet, and Pamela followed close behind.

Mrs. Edison clutched her husband's arm and pulled him forward.

"Come on, sugar. Our daughter needs our support."

"Please, don't mention support. I can't imagine what keeps that thing from falling right out of the sky."

"Science," Orange said into his ear. "You don't need to know how it works. It just does. It's like a refrigerator."

"A refrigerator?"

Mr. Edison's mind was suddenly flooded with thoughts about the refrigerator at home. He tried to make a mental list of all its contents. Did he need to get anything from the store? He thought about the big refrigerators and freezers in the market. Then he thought about the freezer at work and started compiling a list of all the different flavors of ice cream he had stored in it over the years. He was so distracted by his thoughts that he was hardly conscious of his surroundings as he climbed into the Black Hawk helicopter with his wife and Agent Orange. He may as well have been sleepwalking.

"Is everyone buckled up?" Orange shouted over the engine's roar.

Mr. and Mrs. Edison fastened their seat belts, and Goldblatt gave him a thumbs-up sign.

"Don't you want to sit down?" Mrs. Edison asked the big man.

"No. I'm used to this. It's like riding a bus."

"A big bus," Mr. Edison mumbled.

Agent Orange signaled the pilot, and the helicopter rose off the ground.

The noise had attracted over a dozen spectators.

Some watched from the safety of their own doorway.

Others gathered in the street to gawk and take photos or videos.

They were clueless about what was happening, but they all wanted to gossip and speculate about why the helicopter had come and where their neighbors had been taken.

CHAPTER 12

So Many Questions

The loud, choppy flight gave Mr. Edison nervous fits, but a few words from Agent Orange always provided instant relief.

Pamela leaned close to her mom and spoke into her ear. "How is he doing that?"

"I wish I knew," her mother said. "Should I ask him?"

Willys was impressed at how the big man stood without stumbling for the entire flight. Was he really some kind of superhero?

"Are we landing at the secret base?" he yelled over the chopper's roar.

"What secret base?" Brad's eyes opened wide with excitement.

Goldblatt whipped his sunglasses off and gave Willys the stink eye.

"How do you know about the base?"

The boy pointed at Agent Orange.

"We are landing at FBI headquarters," Orange said. "We'll go to the base from there."

Goldblatt's jaw dropped. "Since when can you decide who gets to visit the base?"

Orange looked down at him. "I've been authorized to take Willys and Goobex 3's remains directly to the medical unit. I think his parents should go with him. Don't you?"

"Well, what about these people?" Goldblatt flung his arm out toward them.

"You can debrief them at headquarters."

"Does that mean we're not going to the base?" Disappointment was written all over Brad's face.

"Forget the base." Goldblatt sneered at the boy. "You'll never see it unless you're invited by someone really big."

Having reached their destination, the helicopter started circling. It landed on top of a tall building.

Orange helped Mr. and Mrs. Edison get out of the chopper, and the others followed.

Several agents in black suits and sunglasses were waiting for them on the roof.

"Where's the boy?" one agent asked.

"Dr. Baldino wants to see him immediately," said another.

"Which of you needs decontamination?" A man in a hazmat suit pointed to a plastic tent. "We're all set up."

Goldblatt stepped forward and puffed out his chest. "There's no need for that. The field scans came up negative."

"I will take the boy and his parents to Dr. Baldino," said Agent Orange. "The rest of you can help with debriefings."

Orange and Goldblatt escorted their guests to a bank of elevators.

The other agents trailed behind.

An elevator arrived, and Goldblatt got in first, followed by the Wilsons and Edisons. Orange squeezed in last.

The other agents were left on the roof, waiting for another ride down.

The elevator descended for a long time before the doors opened to a room with thick beige carpeting and wallpaper that looked like peach-colored linen. Recessed lighting gave everything a warm glow, but there were no windows anywhere.

Orange led them into a network of hallways decorated with photos of American wildlife and national parks and monuments.

They stopped at a small reception area, giving the agents from the roof time to catch up.

"Mr. Edison, may I have my coat, please?" Orange held out his hand.

"Oh." Pamela's dad rubbed his eyes. "I forgot I was wearing it."

His wife helped him out of the coat, and she handed it to Orange.

"Thank you." The big man put his coat on and turned to the Wilsons. "Violet and Bradley cannot come with us. We have to leave them for now."

Mr. Wilson pulled his oldest son and daughter into a close hug. "Don't be scared. We'll be back together again before you know it."

"That's right." Mrs. Wilson joined the group hug, leaving Willys with Agent Orange. "I won't let anything keep this family apart."

"Maybe we'll see you at the secret base." Willys looked up at Orange and took hold of his hand.

"I sure hope so." Brad extracted himself from the hug and looked at Goldblatt with pleading eyes. "I would love to see it."

Goldblatt sneered down at him. "Until you answer a whole lot of questions, the only thing you'll be seeing is my face."

"Mom! He's threatening me!"

"Don't threaten my brother!" Willys snarled.

Orange kept hold of his hand while he kicked at the empty air between him and Goldblatt. Willys imagined that he had gained super-stretching powers that would allow him to give Goldblatt a good boot.

"Calm down, Willys," Brad said. "You look like a spazz."

"Don't call your brother a spazz." Mrs. Wilson pinched Brad's arm.

"Ow! I didn't call him a spazz!"

"Then what did you call him?" Violet asked.

"Can't you give your brother a break for once?" Mr. Wilson admonished.

"Are you taking his side?" his wife asked, with an angry look on her face.

Goldblatt grinned at the squabbling Wilsons and said, "I hate to break up the party, but Dr. Baldino is waiting."

Mr. and Mrs. Wilson gave their children a last hug and rejoined Willys and Agent Orange.

"Please be seated," the big man said, holding his hand out toward a black leather sofa.

They sat with Willys in the middle.

Orange sat next to Mrs. Wilson and nodded to the agent behind the desk.

At the push of a button, a section of the wall and floor revolved in a half circle, taking the sofa and its occupants to the other side. An identical piece of furniture was left in its place.

"Cool," Brad said. "Do we get to go through any secret passages?"

"No. We're going for a boring walk, but first, you have to sign in." Goldblatt strode to the reception desk. "I need four debrief rooms. Are they ready?"

"Four?" Mr. Edison felt twitchy all over.

"Three for the children and one for you and your wife." Goldblatt handed him a clipboard bearing the visitor sign-in sheet.

"Why do you want to interview us?" Mrs. Edison took the clipboard from her husband.

"We just want to make sure Pamela tells us everything she told you," said Goldblatt.

Mrs. Edison looked at her daughter and sighed. She signed the sheet.

"I'd really like to see a lawyer," Mr. Edison said as he took the clipboard from his wife.

"I keep tellin' you, you don't need one." Goldblatt glared at him.

"We could interview his wife separately," another agent suggested. "She already signed."

"That's dirty pool." Mr. Edison scowled and signed the sheet.

They all signed in, and the agent at reception made a plastic ID bracelet with a computer chip embedded in it for each visitor.

"Number 93492," the receptionist said as he fastened a bracelet to Pamela's right wrist.

"Do you really have to chip us?" she asked.

"It's for your own protection," said Goldblatt. "Suppose you get lost trying to find a bathroom. You might get shot for being in the wrong place if you don't have that chip on you."

"Is that supposed to make us feel safe?" Violet glared at him.

"Your safety is important to us. Your feelings, not so much." Goldblatt took Violet's bracelet from the receptionist. "Number 93493. May I have your right wrist, please?"

When everyone had their bracelet, the curly-haired agent led them through a series of corridors to a long hallway lined on both sides with numbered steel doors.

The children and Pamela's parents were ushered into identical rooms with cold hard concrete walls, floors, and ceilings. They were like a cross between prison cells and bomb shelters. Each room had four metal chairs, a metal table, and fluorescent lighting that flickered occasionally and produced a constant buzz. There were no two-way mirrors, and the doors had no peephole or windows.

None of the agents stayed behind.

"Someone will come to conduct your interview shortly," they told Brad, Violet, Pamela, and the Edisons, but no one came for over forty minutes! This led each of them to ponder the same questions.

"What are they waiting for? Shouldn't they be eager to learn about Goobex 3 and his saucer? How much do they already know about these aliens? What are they doing to poor Willys? Have they told the Goobexes about what happened to their child? Is waiting in isolation a form of torture or are they just waiting for Goldblatt to get decontaminated?"

The questions kept piling up.

*****

Brad felt bored after sitting alone in the concrete bunker for five minutes, so he got up to look around.

The chubby boy climbed onto the metal table to inspect the flickering fluorescent lights and found a hidden microphone.

"Aha!"

Was more surveillance equipment hidden in the room?

Brad felt like he was on an Easter egg hunt. He found two more microphones under the table. He inspected each chair but found nothing there. Next, he examined the walls from top to bottom. In each corner, where the walls met the ceiling, he noticed a dark spot. What were they? Brad dragged one of the chairs to a corner to get a closer look.

Is that a tiny camera lens? Yeah. What else could it be?

He waved at the camera standing tiptoe on the chair. At first, he just smiled, but soon, he was making faces and expressing an array of rude sounds and animal noises.

Brad was shaking his butt at the camera and making fart sounds into his hands when Goldblatt walked in.

"Having fun?" The agent closed the door behind him.

Brad straightened up. "Someone's on the other end of that camera. Right?" He pointed up to the corner. "I thought he should have something to look at."

"You think this is funny?" Goldblatt stood with his fists buried in his hips.

"No." Brad hopped off the chair. "Can we get started now?" He dragged the chair to the metal table and sat down.

Goldblatt followed.

Brad stuck his head under the table. "How's the sound? Should I talk louder?" He sat up and smiled. "What do you wanna know?"

"Tell me everything. From the beginning."

"You mean, like when I was a baby?"

"Don't be a wise guy. We need to know about the spaceship."

"What about it?"

"Well, first of all, how did you find it?"

"Willys found it."

"Where?"

"It was in a cave."

"How did he find the cave?"

"That's a long story."

"I'm listening."

"Well, my sister forced us to go on a stupid hike, so I wanted to get revenge on her. I told her that Willys and I were going to look for bigfoot—"

"Why are you interested in bigfoot?" The subject clearly made Goldblatt tense.

PEANUT BUTTER AND JELLY SANDWICHES FROM OUTER SPACE!

"I don't know. Why are you?" Brad asked.

"I'm not the one being questioned here."

"I'll answer your question if you answer mine."

Goldblatt locked eyes with the boy.

"Fine. You go first."

"Okay. Why am I interested in bigfoot? I'm not. We ran into a nutty science teacher who claimed we were in Sasquatch territory. I just used it as an excuse to get away from my sister." Brad smiled at Goldblatt. "Your turn."

"It has something to do with the Russians."

"Bigfoot is a Russian?"

"Can't talk about that," the agent said in a hushed tone. "It's classified."

*****

Violet was interviewed by Agent Silver, who brought a laptop computer, and Agent Greenberg, who carried an accordion file full of disorganized papers.

"Let's start with where you found the alleged spaceship," Greenberg said as he thumbed through his paperwork.

"My brothers found it. We were in the forest."

"What were you doing in the forest?" Silver didn't bother looking up from his laptop.

"Pamela and I wanted to go on a hike. My mother made me bring my brothers."

"I see." Silver typed several sentences.

His partner pulled some eight-by-ten prints of Pamela's spaceship photos from his file and spread them out in front of Violet.

"Is this what the spaceship looked like when you found it?"

"No. There was a dome on top when we found it."

Silver looked up from his laptop.

"How did you remove it?"

"Willys blew a whistle, and it flew up into the air. When it came down, the dome melted."

"Why did Willys have a whistle?" asked Greenberg.

"He took it from Brad."

"Why did Brad have a whistle?" Silver fired back.

"He must have taken it from Willys after Pamela gave it to him." Greenberg looked puzzled.

"So Pamela gave the whistle to Brad?"

"No, she gave it to Willys."

"Why did she give it to Willys?"

"It was for protection from wild animals. She gave it to him after I took his Wiffle bat."

"I see. Willys is afraid of wild animals." Silver tapped away at the keys of his laptop as if he were writing a novel.

"No. He's not afraid of animals. That's why I had to take his bat away."

"Can we get back to the whistle?" Greenberg pulled more photos from the file as his partner continued typing. "Is it in any of these pictures?"

They spent hours talking about the whistle. "Who gave it to who? Is it metal or plastic? Is it high or low pitched? Does Pamela always wear it around her neck? How big is it? What color is it? Is it tubular or more like a coach's whistle? How big did you say it was again?"

They didn't trust Violet. They asked the same questions over and over, trying to find inconsistencies to prove she was lying, but she wasn't!

*****

When two agents finally entered room ninety-nine, where Pamela was waiting, they introduced themselves as Agents Delmar and Skye.

Skye was a redhead. She carried a black leather doctor's bag.

"For the record, what's your name?" she asked.

"Pamela Edison."

"Are you sure about that?" Delmar gave her a lopsided grin and examined her face. "How do we know Goobex 3 hasn't tampered with your memories?"

"I'm pretty sure that didn't happen," Pamela said.

"Have you experienced any time loss?" Skye asked. "Chunks of time you don't recall?"

"Only in math class."

"How can we be sure the real Pamela Edison wasn't replaced by an android?" Delmar took a small flashlight from his pocket and shined its bright light into Pamela's eyes.

"I'm not an android!" She blocked the beam with her hands.

"Who said that you are?" Skye removed a stethoscope from her bag. "Do you mind?"

"Go ahead, but you guys are making me nervous. My pulse might be fast."

*****

Pamela's parents were debriefed by Agents Colby and Fontina. The agents placed a microphone in the middle of the table and made it clear they were recording everything. They spent over an hour asking the Edisons about their relationship with their daughter before moving on to the events leading up to the alien encounter. It was exhausting.

"When did you first learn about the hike?" Colby asked.

"The girls planned it several days ago," said Mr. Edison.

"It's been at least a week," his wife corrected.

"They want to start a journalism club at their school." Mr. Edison beamed with pride.

"And a school newspaper." Mrs. Edison squeezed his hand. "They were going to talk about it during the hike."

"Why did they bring the boys?" Fontina tapped his pen against the paper pad on which he'd been keeping notes.

"Violet's mother forced her to babysit." Mrs. Edison scowled.

"I see. Tell us about the spaceship," said Colby.

Mr. Edison leaned closer to the microphone.

"The boys found it in a small cave. Brad told the girls, but they didn't believe him until he and Willys pulled the darn thing out."

Mrs. Edison looked at her husband.

"Pamela said Violet helped pull it out."

"Did she? I don't remember that," said Mr. Edison.

"Are you saying I made it up?" Mrs. Edison pulled her hand away from him.

"No! I'm just saying I don't remember. Do you think I remember everything?"

"If I did, why would I remind you about your parents' anniversary every year?"

"Do we have to talk about that here?" Mr. Edison and his wife entered a staring contest.

Colby looked at Fontina. "Maybe we should interview these two separately."

Mr. Edison gave him the look of death and slapped the table with his open palms.

"Why is it so hard to get a lawyer in this place?"

*****

While the others were being interrogated, Willys and his parents waited for the test results in Dr. Baldino's office with Agent Orange.

Willys was enjoying an almond-filled chocolate bar.

The blood test had only hurt a little, and the rest of his examination was totally painless. He thought it was weird that they asked him to poop on a sheet of plastic, but he'd be glad to make a habit of it if he got a candy bar every time he had to go.

The doctor came in shaking his head. He was a short stocky man with bushy eyebrows, wavy gray hair, and a mustache.

"Everything looks normal," he said.

"That's good, isn't it?" asked Mr. Wilson.

"I don't know. I anticipated anything from mild indigestion to elevated brain activity, but we've found no symptoms at all."

"You sound disappointed." Mrs. Wilson glared at him.

"I'm not disappointed. I'm perplexed." The doctor threw his hands in the air. "There's no trace of interstellar radiation or alien DNA in your son's feces."

PEANUT BUTTER AND JELLY SANDWICHES FROM OUTER SPACE!

Willys sucked the remnants of the candy bar off his fingers.

"Do you guys have ginger ale?"

"Dr. Jackson!" Baldino barked.

"Yessir! Ginger ale." Dr. Jackson was a slender young man with pale skin and dark hair. "Is there anything else I can get for you?" he asked Willys.

"Do you have tacos?"

"Tacos?"

"And chocolate gummy bears?"

The young doctor looked at Dr. Baldino, who nodded his approval.

"I'll see what I can do." Dr. Jackson's shoulders slumped as he left the room.

"Hopefully analysis of the alien's remains will tell us more," Dr. Baldino grumbled.

"It is puzzling," said Orange. He turned to the Wilsons. "Until the results come in, you can stay in the waiting room. It has snacks, a large television with cable, and coffee."

"Does it have beer?"

Mr. Wilson was only half joking.

*****

The inquisition dragged on and on.

Delmar and Skye questioned every aspect of Pamela's identity. Could her thoughts and memories have been programmed by someone else? Was she the real Pamela Edison or a clone? Was she even a real human being?

She eventually managed to tell the agents about what happened in the forest, but every detail was viewed through a lens of skepticism based on theories of mind control, super science, voodoo, or mirror dimensions.

She was glad when Agent Goldblatt burst into room ninety-nine with Brad.

"You're done here. They want her in the Situation Room," Goldblatt announced.

"We're going to the secret base!" Brad smiled at Pamela and nodded toward Goldblatt. "He owes me ten bucks."

Delmar handed Pamela a business card.

"Call me if you start losing time outside math class."

Pamela took the card and nodded. She walked out into the hallway with Brad and Agent Goldblatt, tore the card in half, and dropped it on the floor.

The curly-haired agent led the way to room fifty-seven.

Inside, Mr. and Mrs. Edison were still arguing.

"She didn't say Violet covered the hole with tape! She said that Violet taped a plastic bag over the hole!" Mrs. Edison shouted at her husband.

"What's the difference?"

"There is a difference," Agent Colby said.

The door flew open and Goldblatt entered, followed by the children.

"Debrief's over. I'll take these two off your hands."

"Hi, Mom. Hi, Dad." Pamela smiled.

"We're going to the secret base!" said Brad.

Goldblatt looked down at him. "Good agents know which information to keep classified."

"Guess I'm not a good agent."

Mrs. Edison rose from her seat and hugged Pamela.

"Are you okay, baby?"

"I'm fine, Mom."

Mr. Edison joined them. He put his hand on his daughter's shoulder.

"Honey, how high did you say the saucer was when Willys fell off? Eight feet or less?"

"It doesn't matter," said Agent Fontina.

"Agent Goldblatt owes me ten bucks." Brad smiled at Colby.

"Come on. Important people are waiting for us." Goldblatt held the door open, and the group filed out of the concrete cell.

They marched down the hallway and into room nineteen.

Violet was cold, tired, and frustrated. She had been forced to spend the past hour searching for a perfect match to Pamela's whistle online.

"Time's up," Goldblatt said. "This little flower needs to come with me."

"I'm not a flower," the grumpy girl snapped.

"Well, excuse me, Violet." Goldblatt sneered at her.

"We're going to the secret base!" Brad loved mentioning the base. It irritated the agents.

Without saying another word, Silver and Greenberg got up and escorted Violet to the door. They left their files and laptop behind and followed the group as Goldblatt led them through a maze of hallways.

Eventually, they reached a vast empty room with one door on each end.

Mr. Edison's head swiveled to take in the enormity of the room. "What is this place? A hangar for blimps?"

"Everything in here is classified." Goldblatt started the trek across the room.

Pamela looked all around as she and the others followed him. Her eyesight was excellent.

"What's classified?" she asked. "This room's empty."

"Is it?" Goldblatt grinned.

They crossed the room, and Goldblatt placed his hand on a wall-mounted scanner. A green light flashed, and the door slid open.

A pretty young agent sat behind a shiny metal desk on the other side of the doorway.

"Are these the Wilson and Edisons?" she asked as the group gathered in the small room.

"Yes." Goldblatt smiled at her. "Are you new here?"

She ignored the question.

"I need to scan your ID." The agent produced a handheld scanner and came out from behind the desk to register each of their bracelets. When she was done, she looked at Goldblatt. "Bottom floor?"

"That's right, Agent Dollface."

The agent rolled her eyes and returned to her desk. She tapped a few keys on the computer, and a section of the wall slid up into the ceiling, revealing an elevator.

Goldblatt nodded to Silver and Greenberg.

"You two can stay here."

"Yessir," Greenberg said.

Goldblatt herded the group into the elevator and got in with them.

"By the way, sir." Agent Silver stepped forward and held the elevator door open. "Do you know if the whistle has been secured yet?"

"Are you kidding me?" Goldblatt pried his hand off the door and glared at him as it closed. "Why should we care about a stupid whistle?"

CHAPTER 13

The Long Strange Trip to the Situation Room

The elevator doors opened into a large brightly lit tunnel. Its massive concrete walls were painted gray.

Goldblatt got out and turned right. Everyone else trailed behind.

In front of them was a stainless steel subway train resting on its own private track. Dozens of black-clad agents stood next to it.

Mr. Edison shook his head.

"So this is where our tax dollars go."

His wife took hold of his moist hand.

"Where are you taking us?" she asked.

"The Situation Room." Goldblatt nodded to the other agents as he passed them.

Brad's eyes lit up as he inspected the train.

"I can't believe we're taking a secret subway to the secret base. How cool is that?"

He raced past Goldblatt toward the front of the train.

"Hey!"

Goldblatt reached for his gun but pulled his hand back.

"Darn kid. Hold up!"

The agent jogged after the chubby boy, while Violet and the Edisons followed at a more leisurely pace. The other agents formed a loose double line behind them.

Brad boarded the front car of the train before Goldblatt caught up with him.

He gave the agent a puzzled look.

"I thought my parents would be here."

"You'll see them soon enough."

Brad took a seat next to Goldblatt, who remained standing.

Mrs. Edison boarded the train next, followed by her husband.

"How far are we going?" he asked.

"That's classified information." The curly-haired agent looked straight ahead.

Violet sat down next to Pamela.

"Is Willys going to be there?"

"Yes. He's with your parents."

Goldblatt nodded to one of the agents filing onto the train.

The agent pulled a walkie-talkie out of his jacket.

"Three more passengers and we're good to go."

The train began to hum as the last of the agents boarded.

"How fast can this thing go?" Brad asked.

"Really fast. Any more questions?"

Pamela leaned forward and stared at him.

"Yeah. When can I get my phone back?"

Mrs. Edison squeezed her daughter's knee.

"That's not important, honey."

"We'll get you a new phone." Mr. Edison wiped a bead of sweat from his brow.

The train rose slightly and began moving forward on magnetic waves. It was slow at first but rapidly picked up speed.

Brad pressed his face to the window as they accelerated into a smaller, sparsely lit tunnel.

"I heard you guys have undersea bases. I hope we're going to one of those."

Goldblatt chuckled.

"Nobody gets onto those bases. You're more likely to see a bigfoot."

The agent's grin faded when he noticed several of his coworkers glaring at him. He rolled his eyes.

"You know I'm just fooling, right? There ain't no undersea bases."

"That's a double negative," Violet said. "You just told us there *are* undersea bases."

"That's not what I meant! It's an urban myth."

"Like aliens and the men in black?" Brad said, looking up at the agent.

"I am with the FBI." Goldblatt scowled and turned to face the front of the car.

The train sped through the dark tunnel for several minutes with no further conversation, until Brad broke the silence.

"You know, I've seen every episode of *Ancient Aliens* at least twice. I know all about the stuff you're trying to hide."

"*Ancient Aliens.*" Violet shook her head.

Some of the agents exchanged nervous glances.

"You got us all wrong, kid." Goldblatt pointed at Brad. "Your brother ate an alien. We've got nothing to hide from you."

The train began slowing as it approached another brightly lit tunnel.

The walls here were punctuated with signs reading, "Government property. Keep out! Trespassers will be shot and prosecuted!"

Goldblatt held onto a pole as the train glided to a halt.

"This is our stop. Follow me."

He got off before everyone else and strutted away from the train without slowing down.

The others followed him onto a long moving walkway.

"First time I've seen one of these outside an airport," Pamela said.

"This one's different."

Goldblatt fished around in his pocket for a packet of foam earplugs. He inserted them before the walkway descended below the floor.

It entered a small tunnel, brightly lit with flashing red, white, and blue neon, punctuated by LED fireworks displays. An orchestral rendition of the national anthem blared over loudspeakers placed throughout the seemingly endless tube.

Violet covered her ears with both hands and squinted.

This is crazy! It's like some maniac's version of patriotism. Mistry was right when he said, 'Flirting with madness is one thing, but when madness starts flirting back, it's time to call the whole thing off.' This place could give people seizures!

After several minutes, the walkway turned upward and became an escalator that rose nonstop for thirty floors!

Violet's eyes clung to the soft white light at the end of the rising, neon-filled tunnel. The volume of the music swelled to earsplitting levels every time they passed a speaker, but the growing light promised an end to the torture.

When they emerged from the noisy hole, she took a deep breath.

The walkway veered to the right and ended fifty feet later at a quiet reception area. The powder-blue room was dominated by a three-foot-tall, forty-foot-long steel counter with American flags at both ends. Five marines stood behind it.

"Step forward and present your ID," said the marine on the right end of the counter.

Brad eagerly rushed up and let the soldier scan his bracelet.

"Sign in." The next marine pushed a thin book across the counter.

Brad signed on a blank page and drew a smiley face next to it.

He moved to the next marine.

"Put your right hand on the blue square and look at the red dot." The soldier pointed to a red light above a camera on the wall.

Brad put his hand on the blue square and watched it light up. It made a whirring sound.

"Look at the red dot," the soldier repeated.

The boy looked up at the light and smiled.

The camera's flash blinded him for a moment.

The fourth soldier held up a pair of scissors.

"Present your ID."

Brad stumbled forward with his arm held out. He was still seeing stars.

The marine reached across the counter and caught hold of his wrist. His bracelet was cut off and tossed into a shredder.

By the time he approached the last soldier, his vision was clearing. The soldier pulled a laminated card out of a 3D printer and attached a lanyard to it.

"This is your new ID. Wear it at all times."

"Yessir!"

Brad put the lanyard around his neck and looked at the card. One side had his photo and "LEVEL 4 ACCESS" printed on it. There was a twelve-digit number and a computer chip on the other side.

"How do I get level-one access?"

"The president has to put you on a list," said the soldier.

"Oh." Brad shrugged and released his ID card to dangle around his neck.

Violet and the Edisons went through the same process, though no one else drew a smiley face.

When they finished, an agent approached them.

"Your shuttle is here, sir."

"Good. It's time to go mobile." Goldblatt marched out of the room.

Everyone followed him into a broad corridor with tiled walls.

Pamela watched a little blue cart drive by. It wasn't on rails, and there was nobody in it.

"Is this place haunted or something?" she asked.

Goldblatt didn't answer. He walked up to a bright-red electric shuttle, opened the door, and got into the driver's seat.

"Shotgun!" Brad shouted as he scurried to take the front seat next to the agent.

He was impressed by the big computer screen built into the shuttle's strange dashboard, but something was missing.

"Hey! Where's the steering wheel?"

"Don't need one."

Goldblatt crossed his arms and waited for the rest of the group to board the vehicle. He pressed his thumb to the computer screen, and the headlights flashed on. The horn beeped twice, and automatic seat belts secured all the passengers.

The shuttle took off like a race car.

Violet leaned forward and looked over Brad's shoulder.

"How does it know where to take us?"

"Our destination was entered on our mainframe." Goldblatt held his thumb up. "This tells the vehicle all it needs to know."

Ahead of them, a group of people in white lab coats poured out of a set of double doors. They nearly blocked the entire hallway.

The shuttle slowed down and beeped repeatedly. It wove through the crowd like a salmon swimming upstream.

"I wish Dad sold these," Brad told his sister. "Can you imagine being dropped off at school with nobody driving?" He looked at Goldblatt. "Or better yet, we could put a crash test dummy in the driver's seat. That would really drive people nuts!"

"Is that your goal in life? To drive people nuts?" Pamela glared at the back of his head.

"No, it's just a hobby."

"I'd say you're already an expert." Violet kicked the back of her brother's seat.

"Hey!"

Violet kicked the chair again.

"Stop it!"

She kicked his chair three times in a row.

Goldblatt turned around and gave her an angry look.

"Knock it off. This is government property."

Violet crossed her arms and kicked the chair one more time.

"Sorry. Just crossing my legs."

The shuttle made a sharp right turn and entered a long hallway with rows of numbered elevator doors on both sides. It stopped in front of number eighteen.

"Stay here." Goldblatt got out of the shuttle and typed a code on a wall-mounted keypad.

The shuttle lurched forward as the elevator doors opened. It turned toward the opposite side of the hall and then backed up to the elevator.

"I'd feel safer if a someone was driving this thing," Mr. Edison grumbled.

The shuttle stopped to let Goldblatt get back into his seat. It buckled him in and backed completely into the elevator. It was a very tight fit.

The agent pressed his thumb to a scan pad on the inside, and the elevator doors closed.

A strange grinding sound came from the back of the shaft, but the elevator did not move. When the noise stopped, they rolled backward!

"Whoa!" Mr. Edison clutched the back of the seat in front of him.

"Are all the elevators here like this?" Mrs. Edison asked.

"Classified information." Goldblatt grinned wryly.

The elevator rolled back twenty-seven feet. Then it turned left and carried its passengers over one hundred yards in eight seconds flat before stopping abruptly.

"That was crazy!" Brad had a huge smile plastered across his face.

"I think I have whiplash," Mr. Edison complained.

"It's not over yet." Goldblatt put a stick of gum in his mouth and chewed with vigor.

The elevator shook and then shot upward like a missile. When it stopped, everyone inside felt like their ears were stuffed with cotton balls.

Mr. Edison hunched forward with his head in his hands.

"I feel sick. Can I get out of this thing?"

"Do not leave the vehicle! It's easy to get lost in this place."

Goldblatt pulled a motion sickness bag from a dispenser and handed it to Mr. Edison.

The elevator doors opened, and the shuttle zipped into an intense hive of activity. Camouflaged jeeps, trucks, soldiers, people in lab coats, agents in black suits, and men in mechanic's overalls rushed in every direction.

The shuttle weaved between pedestrians and other vehicles in a herky-jerky fashion, like a robotic football player trying to avoid tacklers. It zigged and zagged through the crowded space, coming within inches of solid walls.

They turned down a narrow passageway and sped straight at a big green bus.

"Holy crap!" Brad braced for impact when a collision seemed imminent, but the shuttle made a sharp left at the last second.

It entered a tiny alley barely big enough to drive through. Another sharp left took them to a long downward staircase.

Without even slowing, the shuttle drove bumpety-bump down the stairs.

"Yeehaw!" Brad shouted.

They soon reached an open plaza where a platoon of marines were going through drills.

Brad leaned forward to look up through the windshield.

"Does this place have a roof?"

The agent smirked.

"Does an airplane have wings?"

"I pray we're not getting on an airplane." Mr. Edison leaned forward and rested his head on his forearms.

The shuttle drove up to a humongous wall with a single door in it.

Goldblatt got out and put his right hand on a scan pad.

The door opened.

"What are you waiting for?" he barked.

"Can't we drive in?" Brad asked in a pleading tone.

"No," the agent answered, stone-faced.

Brad felt like he was abandoning a newfound friend as he left the shuttle.

Mr. Edison, on the other hand, couldn't wait to get off, but his legs felt like Jell-O. Pamela and her mom helped him.

Goldblatt held the door open for them.

"Let's pick up the pace."

"We're moving as fast as we can." Mrs. Edison scowled at the agent.

With the help of his wife and his daughter, Mr. Edison lumbered through the doorway and down a few stairs.

Violet and Brad were waiting there in a dimly lit hallway.

A row of recliner chairs rested along one wall of the narrow room.

"Take a seat." Goldblatt gestured toward the chairs.

Mr. Edison plopped into one of them.

"This is more like it. I hope we can stay here for a while."

"You'll have to stay in your chair for twenty-seven minutes," Goldblatt said as everyone sat. "I hope no one has a bladder problem or anything."

He put his hand on a pad atop a pedestal table.

The floor lit up with waves of blue light, while the walls emitted beams of every imaginable color. Banks of sophisticated camera equipment and X-ray machinery sprouted from the ceiling. A mechanical banging sound echoed from somewhere down the hall, and the chugging of a belt-driven engine came from beneath the floor.

With no warning, automatic safety belts locked each of them to their chair.

"Why do we need seat belts?" Mr. Edison said, with a nervous look on his face.

"Don't worry about it." Goldblatt stood over him. "Try to relax, but don't move around too much. The computers hate that."

One by one, the recliners came alive. They rolled slowly down the hallway as if playing a bizarre game of follow-the-leader. Each chair would stop or rotate slowly at specific spots, where robotic machinery inspected their occupants.

"Yow!" Brad was caught by surprise when his chair suddenly reclined. The machinery on the ceiling examined, photographed, and x-rayed him before the chair sat him up and rolled on.

This feels like an alien abduction. I hope they don't try to probe me.

To hide his fear, Brad started making faces at the equipment and squirming around. His chair stopped for another scan, and Brad wiggled his butt as if dancing.

"One, two, cha-cha-cha."

His seat belt tightened automatically. It squeezed the air out of his lungs and bit into his belly. Brad yelped and struggled to loosen the belt, but it wouldn't budge.

This isn't a chair. It's a killer robot!

All the expensive equipment in the room caught Violet's attention.

I bet they could send every kid in Oregon to college for half of what this stuff costs. It's probably "classified information," or I could write a great story about it.

For Mr. Edison, the experience was like an awful ride through a creepy fun house. He almost expected to see a man in a hockey mask threatening him with a chain saw. He kept saying things to himself out loud like, "Oh Lord, what the devil are they doing to us now?"

Pamela and her mom were too worried about him to focus on much else.

Near the end of the ordeal, the chairs reclined in absolute darkness for six minutes while something that sounded like a sledgehammer repeatedly hitting an anvil pounded in their ears. Everyone was relieved when the lights came on and the banging stopped.

The chairs sat them up.

"I need some aspirin," Violet said.

"Me too." Pamela tugged at her seat belt, but it wouldn't release.

"We're almost done," Goldblatt said. "I need all of you to put your hands on your chest, over your ID."

"Why?" Brad asked.

"You'll see." The agent put his hands over his chest and nodded.

Everyone covered their name tag, and the chairs started spinning.

A red laser scanned them from top to bottom as they spun faster and faster.

Mr. Edison felt nauseous. He moved his hands from his chest to his mouth, and his name tag shot up, hitting him in the face several times. He tried to grab it, but it flew off over his head.

A short while later, the chairs stopped and the seat belts released.

Goldblatt picked up Mr. Edison's ID and handed it to him.

"Thank you," Mr. Edison said. He put the lanyard around his neck and rose to his feet.

He felt the room spinning. His legs buckled, and he stumbled forward, grabbing Goldblatt.

The agent stepped away but used his arms to support Pamela's dad.

"Men's room is on the right. Women's room on the left. Use 'em if you need 'em."

Mrs. Edison hooked arms with her husband.

"Do you need help, Franklin?"

"I feel like I've been in a blender." Mr. Edison kissed his wife on the cheek. "I'll be fine."

He let go of his wife's arm and wobbled to the men's room.

Pamela looked at her mother.

"The spin cycle really did a number on your hair, Mom. How's mine?"

"We could all probably use this." Mrs. Edison took a brush out of her purse.

Violet, Pamela, and her mom went to the women's room.

Brad looked up at Goldblatt through narrowed eyes.

"Are we close yet?"

"Two more checkpoints," said the agent.

"Seriously?" Brad's ears were still ringing.

Goldblatt strolled toward the men's room.

"I'm going to check on Mr. Edison. You stay here."

Brad rubbed the place where the seat belt had bruised his stomach. He eyed the recliners with suspicion.

I bet those evil easy chairs are watching me.

He paced back and forth in front of the recliners, but they remained motionless.

They think I'm stupid. They'll just sit there taunting me till I give 'em an excuse to attack.

He walked behind the last chair in the row. He pushed it and jumped back.

The chair didn't respond.

They must think I'm a real sucker.

Brad walked behind the next chair and kicked it hard.

Still, no response.

They won't outsmart me that easy!

He abused the remaining chairs with his fists and feet, but the chairs remained dormant.

"Huh. Stupid chairs."

Brad looked over his shoulder to make sure he wasn't being followed as he walked down the hall, away from the recliners. When they were out of sight, he turned his attention to the cameras, scanners, and other equipment on the walls.

I bet some of this stuff was reverse engineered from alien tech. I wonder who makes it.

He climbed over, under, and on top of machinery searching for labels but found nothing. Finally, Brad spotted a small metal plate on a floor-mounted scanner. He got on his hands and knees to get a closer look.

"General Electric?"

The words seemed to activate a hidden engine. Brad recognized the chugging sound. It meant the recliners were coming.

"No!"

He scrambled to his feet and ran down the U-shaped hallway. Brad's heart was racing by the time he reached the far end of the hall and a door marked "entrance only."

"Help!" he screamed as he struggled to open the door. He pounded on it with his fists, hoping someone on the other side would hear his desperate cries.

"Help!" He heard the recliners approaching and retreated as far from the robotic chairs as he could get. He pressed his chubby body into a corner of the room and covered his face with his hands.

"Help!" he continued screaming over and over.

After a while, he realized the sound of the engine driving the chairs had stopped.

He peeked between his fingers and saw Goldblatt holstering his gun.

The chairs were motionless, in their original positions.

"The chairs were chasing me," he said.

"No, they weren't."

"They're evil robots." Brad lifted his shirt, revealing the seat belt–induced welt and bruising.

Goldblatt snorted.

"I sent the chairs back to their starting position. They weren't chasing you."

"Oh." Brad stood up and stepped out of the corner. "I thought they were."

"I get that." Goldblatt smiled. "You were screaming like a little girl."

Brad glared at him.

"Don't worry, kid. If you forget the ten bucks I owe you, no one has to know about it."

Brad grimaced and stuck out his hand.

"Deal."

The boy and the agent shook hands and walked back down the hallway together.

Violet and the Edisons were waiting at the "exit-only" door.

"What was all the screaming about?" Violet asked.

Goldblatt winked at Brad.

"The kid was climbing some machinery and got his foot stuck."

"Yeah. I slipped and a cable or something must have wrapped around my ankle."

"He's lucky he didn't fall and break something. That equipment's expensive." Goldblatt pushed the exit door open.

"I hope there aren't more spinning chairs or driverless shuttles in there," said Mr. Edison.

Goldblatt smiled. "Nothing like that."

The group filed into a small room furnished with only a trash can.

Goldblatt strutted over to the only other door in the room and pointed to a sign that warned, "NO FOOD BEYOND THIS POINT!"

"You didn't bring any snacks, did you?" He looked directly at Brad.

"No," the boy answered.

"Good. Anyone else?"

Mrs. Edison removed a protein bar from her purse and tossed it into the garbage.

"Low blood sugar," she said.

Goldblatt eyed the rest of the group. He took a deep breath and turned to look into an optical scanner, without removing his sunglasses.

"I hope none of you have allergies."

The door slid open revealing a gauntlet of ten dogs and their handlers, all of whom wore military uniforms.

"These are highly trained sniffer dogs." Goldblatt marched into the room and stood in front of a pug. "Stop in front of each one, and let it sniff you. Their handler will tell you when it's time to move to the next dog."

The pug sniffed the agent for a while and sat down. His handler gave a thumbs-up sign, and Goldblatt moved to the next dog, a Pekingese.

Violet stepped forward and let the pug sniff her.

"Can I pet him?"

The handler shook his head.

"He bites."

Pamela scowled.

"I got bit by a dog when I was little."

Violet got the OK sign and moved on to the Pekingese.

Pamela stepped up to the pug.

"I'm not so little anymore, am I?" She was prepared to kick the dog at the first sign of aggression, but it just sniffed and sat.

Pamela moved on to the Pekingese. It was no larger than the pug, but it was a lot livelier. The little dog circled Pamela, sniffing every inch of her feet and lower legs.

That hair ball better not mistake me for a fire hydrant.

The dog did its job and sat down.

The next dog was a fifty-four-pound basset hound. Its stubby legs made it look harmless.

"Does he bite?"

"No, she doesn't," said the soldier in charge of the dog.

"She better not. I know kung fu."

Pamela struck a cat pose before approaching the short heavy dog. She changed to a crane pose as the dog sniffed her in a disinterested fashion.

"Please stand still," the trainer said.

"No, thank you. That's how I got bit last time."

The hound finished her work despite Pamela's constant shifting. She waddled over to her trainer and sat.

Next up was a beagle with a winning smile and a briskly wagging tail.

"Isn't he adorable?" Violet said as a dachshund started inspecting her.

"Charming," Pamela answered sarcastically.

The beagle circled her clockwise, then counterclockwise, sniffing her from the knees down. It sniffed both of her hands, circled her again, and sat, smiling up at her.

"He likes you. Would you like to give him a treat?" The beagle's trainer held out a dog biscuit.

"No, thanks." Pamela crossed her arms and walked up to the dachshund.

It slowly sniffed all around her and then licked her shoes.

"Gross!"

The trainer sneered at Pamela.

"At least he doesn't drink from toilets."

Pamela scrunched up her face in disgust.

The dachshund sat down.

Pamela looked at the large shaggy Saint Bernard that was next in line.

"Don't worry. She's friendly." The dog's trainer was a big woman in an Army uniform.

Pamela sneered at her.

"You probably say that about every dog, except the pug. I know he bites."

"Who told you that?"

"His trainer."

The soldier shook her head.

"The only thing that dog ever bit was his chew toy."

Pamela looked back at the pug and its trainer.

That jerk! I can't believe I was worried about that little rat dog.

"Woof!" The Saint Bernard seemed to object to the delay Pamela was causing.

She turned her attention back to the big dog.

That thing weighs twice as much as me. My best spin kick wouldn't even slow it down.

"Does she drool?" Pamela asked.

"Occasionally."

"I hate dog drool."

Pamela approached the Saint Bernard slowly as if it were a skunk. She froze from the neck down when it loped over to her.

The shaggy dog circled her, sniffing high and low. Pamela got a bad case of the shivers when it paused to give the seat of her pants some extra attention.

I'd shave my head for a can of bear spray.

"All done," the soldier said a moment later.

Pamela felt like her legs had been petrified. Her knees would barely bend. She shuffled over to the Chihuahua that was next in line.

The little dog bared its teeth and growled at her.

Pamela bent at the waist and snarled back at the cur.

The Chihuahua stepped back and let out a long, high-pitched yowl.

"Off, Brutus!" said his trainer, a thin man in a Navy uniform.

The little dog sat, with his ears at attention.

"If he tries to bite me, I'll kick him over to that Saint Bernard," Pamela warned.

"He doesn't bite. He just likes to act tough. Right, Brutus?"

Brutus barked, and his trainer rubbed his little head.

"Are you ready, miss?"

"If he is, so am I."

Pamela stood with her arms crossed and her head tilted to one side.

She watched the skinny little dog prance around her legs, sniffing at the air around her.

Growl at me again, and I'll show you what acting tough looks like.

An eruption of loud barking made her forget all about the Chihuahua.

Pamela's eyes opened wide at the sight of the next dog in line. He was a huge rottweiler named "Tiny."

The exuberant giant was getting a break to play with his favorite toy, a sixteen-inch-long, hard-plastic egg. The narrow end of the supposedly indestructible toy had been completely chewed off. "Tiny" enjoyed knocking the wobbly egg around and barking at it as if it were a living thing.

Pamela heard the sailor say, "Okay. Brutus gives you the thumbs-up."

"No," she heard herself say. "I mean I was just getting used to him."

The Chihuahua snarled at her, but Pamela didn't even notice. Every nerve in her body told her to turn around and run rather than face that iron-jawed rottweiler.

"Go on," the sailor said. "That rottie is gentle as a lamb."

"That's not what his egg tells me." Pamela's face twisted as she watched the galloping black-and-tan behemoth pushing the egg all over the floor with his muzzle.

"Hey, Mark!" the sailor shouted. "This young lady's scared of your dog."

Pamela felt a tear roll down her cheek as she watched Tiny pick the egg up with his teeth and swing it wildly back and forth.

Tiny's trainer, Sergeant Mark McGurk, strode over to Pamela.

"Are you okay, miss?" he asked.

"No."

Pamela's eyes were glued to Tiny, who jumped up, releasing the egg from his powerful jaws. It flew at least twelve feet in the air, and when it crashed to the ground, the big dog pounced on it. It rolled away and Tiny chased it, yapping with the exuberance of a puppy.

"I know he's big, but Tiny is the gentlest dog I've ever worked with."

The marine's words gave Pamela no comfort.

"Tiny!" The marine clapped his hands.

Pamela cowered behind Sergeant McGurk as the rottweiler abandoned his toy and trotted over to them.

"Sit," the marine commanded.

Tiny sat.

"High-five." The marine held up his right hand, and Tiny put his right paw up against it.

"Lefty." The marine held up his left hand, and Tiny put his left paw against it.

"Good boy." He rubbed the dog's head and shoulders.

What does that prove? I don't care if he plays piano.

"He's drooling," said Pamela.

"That happens when he plays with his egg." The marine poured half a canteen full of water into a collapsible dog bowl.

Tiny lapped up every drop and sat. He was still panting but without drool.

Sergeant McGurk read Pamela's ID necklace with a hand scanner.

"Miss Edison, I've honestly never met a friendlier dog, but I understand that you're nervous. We can do the sniff test right here or we can go to my station. It's only ten yards away." He offered Pamela his arm.

Pamela looked at Sergeant McGurk for the first time. He was tall, handsome, and muscular.

He looks like he could be in the WWE, but why should I trust him?

"I'd prefer to let Tiny do his work at my station. He's used to that." McGurk looked at Pamela with his soft brown eyes.

She took the marine's arm, and they walked the short distance to his station. It consisted of a metal folding chair, a clipboard, and a backpack.

"This should only take a minute," the marine said. "Tiny, go to work."

The big dog sniffed Pamela's shoes for twenty-four seconds.

It was an eternity to Pamela.

Tiny stepped back, satisfied that nothing near her feet represented a threat. He circled her slowly, sniffing the air, as if trying to identify some scent from far away.

Pamela imagined herself tied to a stake and Tiny as a cannibal, doing his victory dance before lighting a fire beneath her.

The big dog circled closer and closer and then he sat by her side.

"Good boy," Sergeant McGurk gushed.

Tiny looked up at Pamela and very gently, took hold of her hand with his mouth.

He's gonna chew my arm off!

Pamela felt the blood drain from her head.

Her bladder emptied as well.

She heard McGurk's voice from far away. "That means he likes you. He wants you to pet him." The words made no sense to her. The room was spinning, and that beast still had her hand in his mouth!

Sergeant McGurk caught Pamela by the armpits as her knees buckled.

"Are you all right?"

Tiny released Pamela's hand and lay down sheepishly, with his head between his paws.

"Sorry about that. It's normal rottie behavior."

"It's not normal! It's not." Pamela recovered her wits and hurried away.

She was confused, angry, embarrassed, and wet.

The trauma left her too numb to worry about the jet-black miniature poodle that came next. She paid no attention to the creature as it did its nose work. The dog finished quickly, and Pamela was sent to the last sniffer.

It was an orange-and-white border collie.

Pamela approached the dog's trainer, who wore an Air Force uniform. He was busy showing off the speedy dog's impressive Frisbee-catching skills.

"Good catch, Harry!"

Pamela's eyes narrowed to slits.

"I hate to spoil your fun, but I'd really like to get this over with."

"No problem, miss." He scanned her ID. "Edison."

The dog dropped the Frisbee at his trainer's feet.

"Good boy, Harry. Now go to work."

Harry focused on Pamela in an instant. He jogged around her, working his way up from her shoes to her knees. When he sniffed the very wet seat of her pants, she clenched her teeth and her fists.

This mutt is asking for it.

Harry moved on to her waist. He circled a few more times and sat.

"You're good to go."

The airman wrote some notes on his clipboard, while Harry retrieved his Frisbee.

Pamela marched over to Agent Goldblatt.

"I need to use the ladies' room."

"Let's wait for the others to clear security."

"I need to go too," Violet said.

Goldblatt sighed.

"All right, but you'll have to go back and use the toilet outside the scan room."

"Fine!" said Pamela.

"Your ID should open the door," he said. "I'll give you five minutes."

The girls marched across the room, and Pamela held her ID over the scanner next to the door. It slid open, and they tromped to the bathroom together.

*****

Pamela's pants were almost dry after twelve minutes under the hand dryer.

Goldblatt was pounding on the door.

"Your five minutes are up!"

"I'll stall for a while." Violet stuck her head out of the door and batted her eyes at the agent.

"Pamela needs a little more time. It's a lady thing."

"Oh, really? I thought it was a rottweiler thing." He snickered.

Violet left the ladies' room and gave the agent a snake-eyed glance.

"You got peed on by a six-year-old, so maybe you can have a little empathy. She'll be out in a minute, anyway."

Goldblatt looked at his watch.

Pamela emerged from the restroom four minutes later.

"I feel much better now."

"Yeah, right," the agent said. "Let's go. People are waiting."

He strutted through the anteroom to the sniffer dog door and held it open for the girls.

Pamela practically hid behind Violet as they entered the room.

With their work done, the dogs were running around as if it was a dog park.

Tiny was playing with the beagle and the Pekingese, while Brutus growled and barked at his heels.

Harry raced in an elongated figure-eight pattern, waiting for somebody to throw a Frisbee or even a tennis ball.

The basset hound dragged Tiny's egg across the room and attempted to hide it in her doggy bed.

The pug and the poodle curled up next to the Saint Bernard, who was napping near her trainer.

"I hate dogs," Pamela said as they passed Sergeant McGurk.

Mrs. Edison rushed to her daughter and hugged her.

"Are you all right, honey?"

"I'm fine, Mom."

"I'm proud of you, PJ," her father said as he joined them. "I know how you feel about dogs. It's exactly how I feel about helicopters and driverless shuttles."

"Let's keep it moving, people. We're almost there." Goldblatt headed to the exit door with Brad close behind.

Violet marched up to the scan pad next to the exit. She scanned her ID, but nothing happened. She scanned it again with the same result.

"Your clearance isn't high enough for this door." The agent put his hand on the pad, and the door slid open.

Goldblatt led the way into a long hallway with shiny white walls. There were no openings on either side, but at the far end stood a single blue elevator door with a bald eagle painted on it.

"What kind of elevator is that?" Mr. Edison felt his stomach churning.

"It's the normal kind." The agent spoke into a microphone. "Agent Goldblatt and five guests to beam up."

The doors opened.

The elevator looked normal on the inside, but Mr. Edison had his doubts.

Goldblatt and Brad stepped in, followed by Violet.

Pamela and her mother linked arms with Mr. Edison and pulled him into the elevator. He closed his eyes and gulped when the doors closed.

The ride was quick and smooth.

Goldblatt smirked at Pamela's dad when they slowed nearly to a stop.

"That wasn't so bad, was it?"

The doors opened, and Mr. Edison stomped out into a large circular room with a high-domed ceiling and a marble floor.

Mrs. Edison rushed after him and hooked one of his arms.

"I know he's a jerk, Frank, but is this the example you want to set for our daughter?" she whispered.

He gave her an annoyed look, but he patted her arm and slowed down.

"That is the Situation Room." Goldblatt pointed to a pair of tall heavy double doors guarded by six armed soldiers.

He strutted to the door ahead of the others and approached the captain of the guards, who was almost as big as Agent Orange.

"Who lives in a pineapple under the sea?" the agent said.

The captain nodded, and a soldier stepped forward to scan the civilians' ID cards.

Brad shook his head. "That's got to be the lamest password ever."

The captain nodded again, and another soldier opened one of the tall doors.

After a long strange trip, they had reached their destination.

CHAPTER 14

The Best Defense

Willys sat on his mother's lap, next to his father. His mouth was a brown smear, thanks to the chocolate-covered gummy bears he ate from a bowl on the long oval table in front of him.

A giant flat-screen television hung on one wall of the room, and on another wall was a large dry-erase board with notes and diagrams written on it. A group of men stood around it as Dr. Baldino spoke to them and pointed to different parts of the board with a laser pointer.

"We can't explain it. The chemical and molecular structure is identical to that of a normal peanut butter and jelly sandwich."

"Hogwash!" said General Hazard, the mustachioed Army chief. "You're looking in the wrong places!"

The doctor stood a little straighter and locked eyes with Hazard.

"You tell me where to look, general. We've tested for cosmic radiation, sub-dimensional energy, extra-dimensional plasma, atomic anomalies, electromagnetic flux, residual radio waves, neutrinos, quarks, and microwaves. Everything about that sandwich seems normal."

"There is nothing normal about the Goobexes," said a pudgy man in a white uniform.

Agent Orange put a hand on his shoulder.

"We all agree about that, Admiral Mimsley."

Violet took a seat next to her mom. She ruffled Willys's hair and smiled at him.

"Are you okay?"

"They x-rayed me, and they tested my blood." He showed her a cotton ball taped to his arm. "Then I pooped on some plastic, and they gave me a chocolate bar and ginger ale."

Brad sat next to them.

"Any alien parasites?"

"No." Willys grabbed another handful of candy.

A thin man in an Air Force uniform held up a surveillance photo of the alien sandwiches.

"I believe the Goobexes are just decoys." He put the photo down and held up another. "This parrot is the real threat."

Agent Orange shook his head.

"You are wrong, General Finch. Pirate's Pet 1 could have flown anywhere in the world without drawing attention. If it was a dangerous alien, it wouldn't have revealed its ship."

"We haven't figured out why it did that," said Finch. "Maybe it's just toying with us."

General Armstrong, of the Marines, took the photo from him and tore it to shreds.

"My men can handle the threat no matter what it is."

The big television flickered for a moment. Then the screen was filled with the image of a bald eagle holding arrows in one talon and an olive branch in the other.

The men stopped arguing and scurried to seat themselves around the table.

The eagle soon faded, and the president appeared on the screen. His blond hair was brushed over a large bald spot, and his artificially tanned skin was the color of cheddar cheese.

"Thank you all for being here. This is a big thing. Very big. This is something that happened that was…some people would say it was an act of God. I don't view it as an act of God. I would view it as something that surprised the whole world. Nobody could have seen this coming. It's a big thing."

"Yes, sir. It is a big thing," General Hazard agreed.

"It's a very big thing, sir," said General Armstrong.

"I have to say it's the largest by far," the president continued. "There's never been anything like this. There never has. Nobody's ever seen it. This is uncharted territory, but we can handle it. I'll handle it. You'll handle it. The great State of Oregon will handle it." He glowered from the big screen. "So which of these kids ate the Goobex?"

Willys raised his hand.

"Really? I would've bet on the fat kid." The orange-skinned head of state made his fat face look even fatter by puffing out his cheeks.

"Did you have time to review my report?" Dr. Baldino waved toward a large pile of papers on the table in front of him.

"I've read a synopsis." The president held up a single sheet of paper. "It's a condensed version. I have a sharp mind. I can process this material without all the mumbo jumbo, and I think I can say I'm not impressed. I hope you've made more progress, Baldino."

"I'm afraid not."

"Not acceptable!" The president pounded his desk. "We need options! Great options! And we need them quickly, rapidly, and I mean fast. When a planet sends their people here, they don't send the good ones. No, they send the worst. The Goobexes could be here to infect us with alien viruses. We cannot trust them! I'm counting on you to defend America."

"The Marines won't let you down, sir." General Armstrong saluted.

"The Army is at your disposal, sir." General Hazard puffed out his chest and saluted.

Admiral Mimsley sucked in his gut. "The Navy has two battleships and an aircraft carrier on the way, sir." He saluted with pride.

"The Air Force is ready for action, sir." General Finch saluted as well. "But I don't think the Goobexes are the real threat."

"I know." The president scowled. "The real threat is the fake media, them and the Democrats."

"No, sir. I think the parrot is our real enemy. How do we know it's really a creature of planet Earth?"

"Hmm. You may be right. How do we know where it was born or hatched?" The president rubbed his chin. "Maybe you're wrong, but maybe you're not. I mean, we've never seen anything like this. Nobody has."

"If you retrieve some feathers or droppings, I'll have them analyzed," Baldino offered.

"See if it left any feathers or droppings, Finch," the president spoke as if it was his idea.

"Yes, sir!" Finch saluted again.

Agent Orange gestured toward the Wilsons.

"These children activated the small spaceship by blowing a whistle."

"I don't want to hear about whistleblowers!" the president yelled. "They're disloyal spies, and you know what we used to do with spies. They're horrible people. Horrible!"

"Yes, sir, but it occurred to me that amplified sound waves may affect the large saucer the way a whistle affected the small one."

"Ah. I see where you're going." The president squinted and rubbed his hands together. Then he pointed his finger. "I want you to do something for us. I want you to make us a sound weapon. Work with Mimsley, and build us a really big sound weapon like nobody's ever seen. I mean something really powerful and very, very big."

"Yes, sir!" Both Orange and Mimsley saluted.

Dr. Baldino looked at Willys.

"Actually, the boy is digesting the little Goobex normally."

"Tell me something I should care about," the president said in a dismissive tone.

"Oh, I think you should care." Baldino grinned. "Apparently, our stomach acid and digestive enzymes can destroy the Goobexes. The stuff dissolves them."

The president's frown turned into a smile.

"Now that's progress! I mean, how about that? We have the best team in the world. It's beautiful, just beautiful. Now get me enough belly juice to drown those creatures. For immediate delivery. Immediate! I mean as fast as we can get it."

"My men will donate their gut juices right away, sir," declared General Armstrong.

General Hazard pounded his fist on the table.

"I have over twice as many men! They'll give up their belly juice and their stomach linings if they have to."

Armstrong glared at him.

"My men would give up their spleens."

"What about the parrot?" General Finch shouted.

"Why don't you try a net?" Willys pantomimed catching a bird with a net.

The president smiled like a happy toad on a lily pad.

"Another beautiful idea! My team is the best! We need an alien-proof net, Finch."

"My men will fabricate one immediately, sir!"

Willys puffed out his chest.

"If I get superpowers, I can help too."

The president's expression soured.

"Have you been testing that boy for superpowers, Baldino?"

"I would never waste time or resources on that," he said.

"Are you sure it's a waste?" The president gestured with his hands. "Maybe it is, but maybe it's not. I mean, superpowers could be a game changer. Maybe not, but I think it could be a game changer."

It took great effort for the doctor to avoid rolling his eyes.

"We'll run tests, if you want us to, sir."

"I want you to," answered the president.

"I already tested him for a bunch of powers," said Brad.

"I wanna try again," Willys objected.

The commander in chief looked at his watch.

"I have to go speak to the fake media. They have not treated us fairly. I'll tell you that. But we'll show them. Believe me. We'll show them."

He faded out, and the presidential seal once again filled the television screen.

Dr. Baldino jumped out of his seat and gathered his papers. He gave the Wilsons an agitated glance.

"Dr. Jackson will be testing your son for special powers."

"Candy makes me strong." Willys gritted his teeth and flexed his pathetic little bicep.

The doctor shook his head.

"Please, wait here. I have to give directions to the medical staff."

"My men will be ready when you are, doctor." General Armstrong stood.

"My men were born ready," said General Hazard.

"I will tell you both when I am ready." Dr. Baldino tucked his files under his arm and left the room.

General Finch rose and rubbed his hands together.

"I'm going to catch that parrot, alien or not."

"Don't you have some turds and feathers to collect first?" Armstrong said on his way out.

"I don't trust the bird, either." General Hazard stood and put a hand on Finch's shoulder. "You build an alien-proof net, and I'll give you a cannon to launch it."

"Do you really need a cannon to catch a parrot?" Pamela asked.

General Hazard gave her a cross look.

"The net was your friend's idea. Besides, this is a military operation now."

Finch and Hazard headed out the door.

"I've been thinking. A submarine's sonar device would be a good start for a sonic weapon," Mimsley said with confidence.

"We already have sonic weapons," Agent Orange told him.

Mimsley was puzzled and a little hurt.

"Why haven't I heard about these weapons?"

"Black budget projects," Orange said in a soothing tone.

"The boss wants you to work together, so you may as well show the admiral our toys." Goldblatt popped one of Willys's candies into his mouth. "I'll stay here and watch the civilians."

"Good." Orange stood and nodded to Willys. "I'll be back."

As Orange and Mimsley headed for the door, a guard opened it and Dr. Jackson came in bearing a tray of tacos, plastic utensils, and paper plates.

"Chef made a whole batch for you!"

"Cool!"

If his mom hadn't been holding him around his waist, Willys would have climbed onto the table to intercept the taco delivery.

"How many do you want?" Jackson asked him.

"Oh, about twenty."

"Willys!" His mom gave him a little squeeze.

"I'm just kidding. Gimme three."

Dr. Jackson put the tray of tacos on the table and served three to Willys.

"I better make sure they're not drugged or anything." Goldblatt took four.

Fortunately, there were enough for all the guests.

While everyone was enjoying the meal, Dr. Jackson kneeled between Mr. and Mrs. Wilson. He spoke to them in a hushed voice.

"Dr. Baldino asked me to test your son for superpowers. Was he serious?"

"The president insisted." Mrs. Wilson sounded boastful.

"I've tested him for lots of powers already," said Brad as he devoured a taco. "I can give you a list."

"That would help," said the doctor. "I've studied science and medicine, but my knowledge of comic books is sadly deficient."

CHAPTER 15

The Big Reveal

Willys was once again tested for all sorts of special abilities.

They started with Brad's list, but Dr. Jackson was pretty good at thinking up new powers. He devised tests for things like the ability to bend sound or control cosmic rays.

Willys believed it was his destiny to develop superpowers, but he had none.

All other preparations for the big meeting with the aliens proceeded at a fevered pace.

General Hazard and General Armstrong ordered hundreds of thousands of troops across the country to donate stomach acid and digestive enzymes. The stuff was flown to an airport near FBI headquarters in fifty-gallon drums. The drums were then transported through the secret subway, and scientists working with Dr. Baldino added artificial enzymes and additional acid. They made enough of the vile goo to fill two big tanker trucks!

Admiral Mimsley's men worked with the men in black to build a sonic weapon. The agents provided several sound bazookas to Navy engineers. They disassembled them and combined the devices into one huge sonic cannon. It was the most powerful weapon of its type ever built. At half power, it could reduce a brick wall to rubble. They hid it inside an ice cream truck.

General Finch did not want to be shown up. His men found no feathers or parrot poop to test, so they assumed Pirate's Pet 1 had incredible alien strength. His team made a super net of bulletproof Kevlar reinforced with remarkably strong resin.

"Good job," Finch said when he saw it. "No alien parrot will escape from this thing. Now when will the cage be ready?"

It was all done in eight hours.

*****

"Incredible job! Incredible," the president said through the big TV in the Situation Room. "You're doing things a lot of people couldn't do."

"Give the command and we'll put our new assets in place, sir," General Hazard spoke with pride.

"We have to be smart about it. Very, very smart." The chubby commander in chief grimaced. "We want to be safe too. We're going to be very, very safe."

"The best defense is a strong offense, sir," said Armstrong.

"The weapons aren't very useful sitting here on the base," Mimsley added.

"I don't know." The president waved his arms in the air. "I mean, I've seen it all. I've heard it all. I understand it all, but I've never seen anything like this. When the Goobexes learn about their kid, maybe they'll understand, but maybe they won't. Maybe they won't understand like you wouldn't believe. I think, we need to be ready in case they don't understand."

"Yes, sir. We do," Finch agreed.

"We're going to be smart about it. We're going to be very, very smart, and we want to be very, very safe." The president pondered the situation briefly. "Is the press still out there?"

"Civilians and the press," Orange told him.

"Get rid of 'em! Clear 'em all out! All of 'em!" the president roared.

"Yes, sir," Armstrong and Hazard said in unison while saluting.

The president smiled. "I don't want the liberal media whining about us mistreating aliens. Besides, we need to keep those people safe. The United States has no higher priority than the safety and well-being of our citizens."

"Do you want the area cleared before we position our assets?" Finch asked.

"No. Put the weapons in place now."

"Yes, sir," said Mimsley and the generals.

"Best team in the world. This was a perfect meeting. Just perfect." He faded from the screen, and the orders were given.

People from around the world had gathered to see the Goobex ship, but the military forced them out of the area with tear gas and rubber bullets. Soldiers rolled out miles of chain-link fencing topped with barbed wire and patrolled the perimeter constantly.

Reporters and camera crews were also forced to leave, but drones and news choppers constantly buzzed overhead. A pair of blimps recorded video from high above.

Despite the president's wishes, the world was watching it all on TV.

He was too.

Hazard and Armstrong positioned their troops around the Goobex saucer.

Orange reviewed plans with the many black-suited agents stationed around it.

Admiral Mimsley gave the sonic cannon a final inspection, and Finch fussed over loading his super net into a cannon.

Finally, everything was in place except the Wilsons and the Edisons.

*****

It was early morning. Most of them were tossing and turning in the Army cots set up in the waiting room outside Dr. Baldino's office.

Willys was sitting up in his bunk, holding a plastic spoon in both hands. He squinted at it and whispered, "Bend. Bend. Bend."

Goldblatt, who was on guard duty, sat snoring in a chair outside the room.

Orange gently shook him by his shoulder.

"What?" Goldblatt reached for his gun. "Oh, it's you. What's going on?"

"Everything is ready. I'm taking our guests topside."

"Good, I need a break." Goldblatt rose from his chair and sauntered down the hall.

"Agent Orange!" Willys dropped the spoon as soon as he saw the big man enter the room. He got out of his bunk and hugged the agent's legs.

"You all need to get up now," Orange spoke in a loud yet calm voice.

Mr. Edison sat up and stretched.

"I sure could use a strong cup of coffee."

"That will have to wait." Orange picked Willys up and held him with one powerful arm. "It's time to meet the Goobexes."

Willys grabbed Orange around his neck and spoke to him nose to nose.

"You're gonna be there with us, right?"

"I'll be with you all the way, but we need to get going."

"Where are you taking us?" Mrs. Wilson rose from her bunk three steps ahead of her husband.

"We are going to the alien ship," Orange answered.

"Why can't they come here?" Brad rolled over and lingered in his bunk.

"How far is it?" asked Violet.

"We are quite close." Orange handed Willys to Mr. Wilson, while Mrs. Wilson rousted Brad from his cot.

"Let's go, Bradley." She sat on his bunk and shook him by his shoulder. "Let's get this over with. Then we can go home and put it all behind us."

Mr. Edison nudged his wife, who was still dozing.

"Wake up, honey. We're going to meet the aliens."

They all followed the agent out of the room to a van driven by a marine.

"Why can't we take one of those driverless shuttles?" Brad asked.

"They don't work outside." Orange waited for everyone to board the van before taking the seat next to the driver.

The huge underground base was eerily empty. They drove past a few people in overalls doing maintenance work, but there were no soldiers or vehicles to be seen.

"Looks like a ghost town," Pamela muttered.

Her mom hugged her shoulder.

They drove up to a scanner near an enormous garage door and stopped. The driver put his thumb on the device, and the door slowly rolled open, revealing the morning sky and a trail leading into a wooded area.

They drove down the bumpy path and stopped at a dock.

Everyone, except the driver, left the van.

"Wow." Brad felt a shiver go through his body when he saw the giant spaceship hovering ominously over the Columbia River on the opposite side of the island.

Their short subway ride had taken them over one hundred miles!

It was a lot to take in.

A patrol boat took them up the river to the other side of the island. They crossed to the opposite bank, nearest the ramp from the alien ship.

Soldiers and black-suited agents were everywhere.

The tanker trucks were positioned near some trees on either side of the ramp, and the ice cream truck was parked between them.

The cannon loaded with Finch's super net was hidden in a dumpster placed near the riverbank. It was less than fifty yards from the bottom of the ramp.

The three Generals and Admiral Mimsley were waiting in a limousine parked near the ice cream truck. When the civilians arrived, it drove up to them and the four men got out.

General Hazard nodded to the group and spoke into a two-way radio. "We have important news for the Goobexes. We want to discuss this in person, face-to-face or whatever."

It took only twenty seconds for Armstrong to grow impatient.

"Do you think they heard us?" he said.

"They told us to communicate by radio," Hazard reminded him.

"Why don't you send a text and ask if they got the message?" Willys asked, innocently.

"We don't have their number. Do you?" Armstrong made no attempt to hide his irritation.

"I'll do it again." Hazard spoke into the radio. "Greetings! We would like to speak with the Goobexes. We have news of Goobex 3. Important news."

Pirate's Pet 1 flew out of the spaceship, and several news drones took up pursuit. The big blue parrot outraced them, flying in a wide circle around the alien craft. He banked sharply and weaved a path through the air that caused two drones to collide and crash. The bird went into a sharp dive, leaving the mechanical flyers far behind, and landed gracefully on the perch at the bottom of the ramp.

"Show-off," Finch mumbled.

The bulge below the perch pulsed with green light.

"Goobex 1 and Goobex 2 send their greetings," said the parrot's amplified voice. "They will be here soon to hear your news face-to-face."

Willys grabbed his mom, and a tear rolled down his cheek.

"I wish I had superpowers," he sobbed.

"Everything will be fine," Agent Orange told him.

"Too bad we don't have giant ants," Brad spoke into his hand to prevent Pirate's Pet 1 from hearing him or reading his lips. "They'd take care of those sandwiches in no time."

"I like the way you think, son." Hazard smiled.

"You shouldn't resort to violence so quickly," said Mrs. Edison. "The Goobexes have been peaceful so far."

"I hope they stay that way." Pamela grabbed her mom's arm and pointed to the giant alien sandwiches who had appeared in the opening of the spaceship.

As before, the Goobexes were conveyed down the ramp by small black boxes on wheels, each emitting a cone of rotating lights that levitated the massive sandwiches four feet in the air.

They positioned themselves on either side of Pirate's Pet 1 who asked, "What news do you have of Goobex 3?"

Agent Orange stepped forward. He stood at the edge of the river, as close as he could get to the Goobexes and their interpreter.

"These children found a small spaceship in the forest," he said calmly. "We believe it is a Goobex craft. There are photos and video of it on this device." He held up Pamela's cell phone.

A beam of light instantly shot out of one of the little black boxes. It latched onto the cell phone and tore it from the agent's hand.

He watched with awe as it floated a few feet in front of them and all the photos stored in the device were projected as giant holograms.

Pamela cringed as several of her most embarrassing selfies appeared as 3D images a hundred times larger than life.

"Can't they skip some of these?" she grumbled.

They found the spaceship photos and were able to zoom in. Their technology allowed them to manipulate the images and enhance details, like the markings on the disk and the little sandwich inside.

"This appears to be Goobex 3's ship, but why is he lying face-down?" the big blue parrot said. "Has he already succumbed to your toxic atmosphere?"

The children gave each other troubled glances.

The aliens then projected the video of the spinning saucer in jumbo 3D.

"There is no doubt. This is Gooby-ooby's ship. Where is he?" Pirate's Pet 1 demanded.

"I ate him," Willys wailed.

"Impossible!" the parrot shrieked! "No Goobex would allow such a thing!"

"Maybe he was already dead or asleep," Brad suggested.

"Goobexes never sleep!" the parrot screeched.

Pirate's Pet 1 could feel the Goobexes' anxiety. He began pacing back and forth across the metallic perch. "Your story makes no sense, but we must be certain. Yes, we must be certain."

The round bulge on the post below the parrot's perch grew larger and larger. When it looked ready to pop, it opened up, releasing thousands of little balls of light that darted around like fireflies. At first, their movements seemed random, but they gradually formed connections with each other and united in the form of a large sphere. It crackled with unknown energies.

"We better get some juice." General Armstrong slinked away with General Hazard as the sphere slowly headed toward them.

"Well, I'm going to get some ice cream," Admiral Mimsley said, with a wink. "Anybody else want some?"

He slowly backed away, before turning and hurrying to the ice cream truck.

"Uh, I think I lost my wallet near that dumpster over there," General Finch said uncomfortably. "I better go find it."

He turned and jogged quickly to the dumpster.

Only Agent Orange remained with the Wilsons and Edisons.

As the crackling globe of light and energy approached them, they could feel electricity in the air, making their hair stand on end.

"What is that thing?" Orange demanded.

"You have no word for it," the big parrot answered. "You may call it an undigester."

Suddenly, the globe shot forward, engulfing Willys. He was torn from his mother's arms and carried to a spot high in the air between the Goobexes.

"I'm sorry," he sobbed. "I didn't mean to hurt nobody. I just accidentally done it."

The globe projected a giant hologram of Willys clutching his knees tightly to his chest. He moaned as he suffered the effects of the alien device.

"I think I'm gonna mess my pants," he groaned.

"Do not fear," the big bird replied. "The undigester does not work like that."

"They're hurting my baby!" Mrs. Wilson shouted. "Do something!" She pounded on Agent Orange's powerful, unyielding chest.

"The aliens are in control for now. We must wait." Orange looked into her eyes. "For the sake of all your children, please try to stay calm."

The giant holograph of Willys suddenly jerked forward, and a flood of holographic vomit filled the sky.

"I wish I could unsee that." Pamela looked down and shielded her eyes with one hand.

The nasty mess moved like a mass of slimy worms. It formed chunks that congealed and piled on top of each other. Mounds of partially digested food flowed like logs in a slow-moving river of putrid puke. In time, the holographic barf separated into three distinct piles. The stuff shifted bit by bit until it stabilized in the form of three tacos.

"I'm glad we didn't have breakfast." Brad scrunched up his face.

Willys lurched forward again, and another stream of vomit exploded from his mouth.

The brown mess was speckled with chunks of many colors. It squirmed and wriggled into one big mound. It pulsed and shifted until it solidified in the form of a pile of chocolate-covered gummy bears.

Violet wanted to look away.

I hate seeing Willys suffer like this, but a good reporter needs to bear witness, even to the ugly stuff.

Willys spewed out another stream of brown material that slowly took the shape of an almond-filled chocolate bar swimming in ginger ale.

"Oh," Willys moaned. "Please stop. I'll never eat chocolate again."

His face turned red, and he disgorged another big stream of nasty chunks.

Some light-colored bits moved like caterpillars shoving other pieces through the air into a triangular shape. Slowly, the puke morphed into a giant slice of veggie pizza.

Pamela peeked. She was repulsed by how tasty it looked.

Willys was exhausted. He had been literally drained. His stomach felt tortured and empty, and yet the poor boy expelled yet another stream of vomit.

The disgusting pool of puke slowly separated into layers of light brown, red, and tan. Slowly but surely, it flowed into a rough square.

PEANUT BUTTER AND JELLY SANDWICHES FROM OUTER SPACE!

Willys sobbed into his knees as it took the shape of a partially eaten peanut butter and jelly sandwich with the crust torn off.

A beam from one of the black boxes locked onto the sandwich and pulled it out of the sphere. It changed colors several times as the sandwich was subjected to various scans.

The truth was clear at last.

The beam died, and the sandwich dropped into the river.

"Why are you doing this?" Pirate's Pet 1 screeched. "You cannot deceive us!"

"We have been completely honest," Agent Orange said defiantly.

"You have not!" the big bird insisted.

"Yes, we have!" Brad shouted. "We found that alien inside the spaceship."

"The children are not lying to you." Mr. Wilson put his hand on Brad's shoulder.

"Irrelevant!" Pirate's Pet 1 paced back and forth on his perch. "It does not matter what they think. Their story is false!"

"It's true," Willys sobbed. "I ate Gooby-ooby."

"You did not!" Pirate's Pet 1 squawked. "You ate a sandwich from planet Earth!"

CHAPTER 16

Putting the Pieces Together

Pamela looked at Violet.

"Why would anyone swap a sandwich for an alien?"

Violet ran through her memories of the hike.

Come on, think like a journalist. Someone swapped the alien for a sandwich, but what was their motive? Are they trying to sell it? Somebody might want to experiment on it, but that would take a real sicko, like Dr. Frankenstein. Or Dr. Harrison? He could have bought the alien from someone else or maybe he found it himself. Either way, that must be why he wanted us to leave the forest.

She grabbed Pamela's arm. "I think it was Dr. Harrison."

The big parrot heard her. It leaped off its perch and flew directly to Mr. Edison's shoulder.

"Who is Dr. Harrison?" the big bird demanded.

"He's a science teacher at our school," Pamela answered. "We saw him in the woods just before we found the spaceship."

Pirate's Pet 1 paced back and forth nervously.

"Oh, Gooby-ooby. What are you up to?"

The energy sphere returned Willys to the shore, and Mrs. Wilson rushed to him.

"Take me to your leader!" the bird demanded.

"We cannot do that," Orange said sternly.

Four lines of men in overalls emerged from behind the tanker trucks. They rushed toward the ramp, carrying four big firehoses.

Orange seemed to sense the imminent assault. He turned and saw the men advancing. He shouted into his radio.

"Stand down!"

The men continued running forward.

"Now!" Armstrong and Hazard shouted together.

The hoses opened up, and digestive juices rained down. The little black boxes and the area around the Goobexes were drenched, but the goo went straight through the aliens.

They were holograms.

There was a loud bang.

The Wilsons, Edisons, and Pirate's Pet 1 were all knocked over by the force of the heavy Kevlar net fired from the hidden cannon. Only Agent Orange remained standing.

The black boxes rolled up the ramp.

Mimsley took it as his cue to deploy the sonic weapon.

A loud deep hum shook the ground. It grew stronger and stronger. The device hidden in the ice cream truck was cranked up to full power. The windows of every vehicle there shattered. People wailed and covered their ears, but the spaceship remained unaffected.

The boxes reentered the saucer, and the ship's ramp melted back into the craft, sealing the gap in the dome.

On the other side of the country, the president tweeted, "This is all Obama's fault!"

The hoses were reeled in, and the sonic weapon was turned off.

Everyone without earplugs heard a loud ringing for days.

A group of soldiers followed General Finch as he marched to the captives in his net.

"We'll deal with this alien on our terms from now on."

"Take me to your leader!" Pirate's Pet 1 kept squawking.

A soldier wearing thick leather gloves and a flak jacket removed the big blue bird from the net and locked it in a titanium cage.

Agent Orange helped the others.

"Is everyone okay?" he asked.

"I'm fine," said Mrs. Edison.

"Me too." Pamela got up and out of the net with her mom.

"Can you please take us home now?" Mr. Edison said as he got out.

"The crisis isn't over," Orange told him. "We may still need your help."

Soldiers, agents, and vehicles with their shattered windows scattered in every direction like a nest of cockroaches.

As Agent Orange was freeing the last of the Wilsons, a marine rushed up to him.

"The generals want to see you, sir."

Orange turned to the soldier and dropped the empty net to the ground.

"Stay here and protect these civilians."

"Yes, sir!" The marine saluted.

The big agent hustled over to the limo where Admiral Mimsley and the generals were having a heated argument.

"If you hadn't tipped them off, my sound cannon might have worked." Mimsley pointed an accusing finger at Armstrong and Hazard.

"It was our call to make," said Hazard.

"We both agreed it was time to fight," said Armstrong.

"None of that matters. I caught the real alien menace."

General Finch had a smug look on his face. He peered through the limo's broken window at the caged parrot in the back seat.

"Gentlemen!" Agent Orange made sure to look Mimsley and the generals directly in the eyes as he spoke. "What's done is done. We need to move forward."

"Do you think we should build a bigger sound weapon?" Mimsley asked.

"No. I think you should take our avian guest to the Situation Room and consult with the president. I will join you later."

"Where are you going?" Armstrong's foul mood oozed out of every word.

"The energy the boy absorbed may be harmful to him and others. He must be examined," Orange told the generals.

"We're wasting time. Let's go!" Finch climbed into the back of the limo next to his captive.

PEANUT BUTTER AND JELLY SANDWICHES FROM OUTER SPACE!

The other generals and Mimsley grumbled and joined him.

As they drove off, Orange walked back to the civilians.

He released the soldier from guard duty and spoke softly to Mrs. Wilson, who held her son tenderly in her arms.

"There is a medical team nearby. We should take Willys there to make sure the undigester did no lasting damage."

"I'd appreciate that," she said as Willys rubbed his eyes against her shoulder.

"Please, come with me."

Orange led them through the thinning crowd, past a cluster of pine trees to a big white tent.

Dr. Jackson was waiting outside with a team of physicians and nurses. They had been sent to provide medical care in case violence broke out.

"I'm glad to see you," Jackson told Willys while pulling on a pair of gloves. "How are you feeling?"

"I feel like my tummy's turned inside out." Willys wiped his eyes with his forearm. "Why'd you give me all that food?"

"You asked for it. Don't blame the doctor," said his father as they entered the tent.

"I'm sorry you had to go through that." Jackson examined the boy's eyes.

"My eyes don't hurt!"

"Open up." A nurse put a thermometer in Willys's mouth. "He can sit here." She held her hand out toward an examination table.

Mrs. Wilson put her son down.

"Be a good boy, Willys. They'll take care of you."

The nurse checked his pulse and took the thermometer out of his mouth.

"Pulse and temperature are normal."

"Good." Jackson examined the boy's ears with an otoscope, while a technician waved the wand of a Geiger counter all around him and the nurse checked his blood pressure.

"No radiation," the tech announced.

"Check my tummy! That's where it hurts!" A few tears raced down Willys's cheeks.

"We will," said Jackson. He held a stethoscope to the boy's chest. "Cough."

Willys coughed.

Jackson moved it to a different spot on his torso and repeated the process several times.

"His lungs are fine, and I don't hear anything suggesting damage to his internal organs."

The nurse wrote some notes on the boy's chart.

A team of technicians wheeled over a portable MRI unit.

"We're going to run some more tests, just to be safe."

"Do I have to get my blood tested again?" Willys scrunched up his face.

"No, but I need you to lie down and stay still."

The boy was examined with all sorts of high-tech equipment.

It didn't take Jackson long to reach a diagnosis.

"Everything's normal. He should be fine."

"Thank you, Dr. Jackson." Mr. Wilson lifted Willys to his shoulder. "Thank the doctor, son."

"Thanks," Willys mumbled.

Orange led them to a boat, and they headed back, across the river to Government Island.

"I still don't get why Dr. Sasquatch would take the alien," Brad said.

Pamela stared into his eyes.

"Performing a real alien autopsy would make him more famous than actually finding a bigfoot."

"You think he did this just to get attention?" Mrs. Edison asked.

"He's totally nuts, Mom," said Pamela. "Who knows why he did it."

They reached the island and got into a van that was waiting near the dock.

"Situation Room, pronto," Orange told the driver, and they sped off to the secret base.

*****

"Who lives in a pineapple under the sea?" the big agent said.

The captain of the guards nodded, and a soldier opened the Situation Room door.

Admiral Mimsley, the generals, Dr. Baldino, Agent Goldblatt, and the uncaged Pirate's Pet 1 were already in conversation with the president.

"Our agents are checking Harrison's home and the school, but there's no sign of him," Goldblatt reported.

"Keep looking," the agitated chief of state ordered.

"We worked together at NASA," Dr. Baldino said. "He was a close friend of mine."

"He was a hidden enemy!" the president scowled. "He was invisible. An invisible enemy!"

"Goobex 3 must be found!" the parrot squawked as it paced on the long oval table.

"Oh, we will find Goobex 3. Believe me. We will find him no matter where Harrison is hiding him," said the president.

The big bird stopped in its tracks and stared at the commander in chief on the big screen.

"How can the Goobexes trust you? You attacked them."

"That wasn't an attack," he lied. "It was a celebration! We were so happy that little boy didn't really eat Ooby-gooby."

"The Goobexes are telepaths!" The parrot shook its head. "They knew of your plans."

The revelation made most of the people in the room ill at ease.

"Are you a telepath?" Finch asked.

"No, but I know lies when I hear them." The bird stared at the orange-skinned bureaucrat on the screen.

"I'll send five thousand troops to Bend!" the president shouted. "We'll dominate the streets! Believe me, we will find your little Gooby and the so-called doctor who grabbed him."

"That plan is weak!" the bird shrieked.

The president's face turned red.

"I was just getting started. We have the best people in the world working on this."

The big bird strutted around the table, looking at each of those seated around it.

"Gooby-ooby's life is at stake. Why should we have faith in these people?"

"I feel good about it," the president said. "That's all it is. It's just a feeling, you know. I'm a smart guy. I feel good about it, and I've been right a lot."

Willys buried his face deep in his dad's shoulder and said, "I hate Violet's teacher."

"He's not my teacher!" Violet hated being associated with the villain.

"We'll catch the doctor," the president assured the bird. "He's a common criminal! Well, it's not a common crime, but it is a crime all right."

"It's kidnapping," said Goldblatt.

General Hazard twisted one end of his mustache as he pondered the situation.

"He must have left the sandwich as some kind of twisted ransom note, but the boy ate it and threw a monkey wrench into his sick plan."

"We are not going to let this sandwich-napper outsmart us," the president declared.

"He is a scientist." Dr. Baldino nervously tapped a pen on the notepad in front of him. "Perhaps he's taking it to a lab."

"Search the labs!" the parrot shrieked.

"Search every lab in Oregon!" the president shouted.

"Our men can handle that," said Orange.

"Maybe he's still in the forest," Pamela suggested.

"Search the forest!" squawked Pirate's Pet 1.

General Finch bent down and glared into the eyes of the big bird. "I don't take orders from parrots."

"Search the forest!" the president shouted. "We are not going to let this phony doctor get away from us. No way! We are going to catch him, and we are going to catch him bigly!"

"Yes, sir," Admiral Mimsley and the generals said in unison, all saluting.

"Look at them. What an incredible team," the commander in chief boasted. "They're already doing things nobody else could do, and I mean a lot."

"Find Harrison! Find Goobex 3!" Pirate's Pet 1 screeched.

"Go! Go find them!" the president shouted.

"Yes, sir!" Mimsley and the generals all got up to leave.

"Take the children! You need them, bigly!" the big parrot said in the president's voice.

They all turned and stared at Pirate's Pet 1.

The president couldn't decide if the impersonation was a compliment or an insult. "You heard the bird," he said. "Take the kids."

"We can show you where we left the spaceship," said Brad.

"Agent Goldblatt and I will go with them," Orange offered.

"That's good. That's really good. It's tremendous!" the president declared. "I'm putting Agent Orange in charge of searching the forest. I want you to build a human wall in the woods and catch that guy. If he's in the forest, we'll catch him. Believe me. We are going to catch him no matter where he goes. You tell the Goobexes not to worry about their little Ooby-gooby."

"They will be relieved when he is found and grateful," said Pirate's Pet 1.

"Grateful? Hmm." The president rubbed his chin and was momentarily lost in thought. "Go! Go find the alien! I need to talk to this parrot alone."

Everyone rose from the table.

"I can't believe this is happening." Dr. Baldino shook his head. "Dr. Harrison has always been an honest, thoughtful man."

"Maybe teaching high school science changed him," Pamela said derisively.

"The doctor's spiritual journey ain't our problem." Goldblatt headed for the door. "Finding him is, and that means we're going back to Bend."

CHAPTER 17

Operation Get Goobex 3 (Part 1)

The children and their parents followed the agents out of the Situation Room and across the marble floor of the rotunda. They reached a trio of elevators and took one down to the ground floor of the base.

Pamela was relieved they didn't have to face the sniffer dogs on the way out.

Goldblatt summoned a driverless shuttle, and they waited.

The air on the base was charged with tension. People stood straighter and sped up as the generals' orders rippled through the ranks.

Five thousand troops were being mustered for action in Bend. Hundreds of black-suited agents gathered for deployment as well. The hive was abuzz.

The shuttle arrived, and Goldblatt jumped into the front left seat. Brad rushed to claim the other front seat, while the remaining eight people squeezed onto the two bench seats in back.

The shuttle took off like a rocket.

Mr. Edison cursed the contraption as it zigged and zagged its way across the base, dodging jeeps and pedestrians all the way. After dozens of close calls, it reached a bank of elevators and backed into one of them.

"Make sure your seat belt is tight." Goldblatt handed Mr. Edison a motion sickness bag from the front seat.

After the doors closed, the elevator made a familiar grinding sound. It tilted back and rolled down a long, steep diagonal chute. They sped up and over two hillocks going backward. The elevator made a sharp left turn, traveled sideways for five hundred feet, then slowed.

"I hate this place," said Mr. Edison.

"I love it." Brad smiled.

They rolled forward in a gentle arc that turned into a tightening spiral. It felt like they'd been flushed down a giant toilet. They corkscrewed down for a long while.

When the doors opened, they were in the secret subway station. The shuttle drove out of the elevator and up to the front of the train.

"All aboard!" Goldblatt hopped off and was first to get on the railcar.

The Wilsons followed, while Agent Orange stayed back with the Edisons.

"I don't think I can walk. My head's still spinning." Mr. Edison took his wife's hand, and she helped him get out of the shuttle.

"Would you like some help?" Orange asked.

"We've got it." Pamela gave her dad a second shoulder to lean on, and they all boarded the train.

Goldblatt looked at his watch.

"We leave in ten minutes." He smiled at Brad. "Say goodbye to the secret base. You'll never see it again."

Brad frowned as the distant sound of approaching troops filtered onto the train.

The noise grew louder by the minute. It filled the car long before a single man entered.

Soldiers carrying machine guns, grenade launchers, and backpacks full of special equipment poured onto the vehicle. By the time the doors closed, there was hardly room to scratch your nose.

"This, right here, reminds me of a Godzilla movie," said Mr. Edison.

"I hope I don't turn into Godzilla." Willys buried his face in his dad's chest.

"You won't turn into Godzilla. You didn't eat an alien," Violet reminded him.

"You ate a regular sandwich. Dr. Henderson made it," said Pamela.

"I know. I hate that guy." Willys was still worried, and his stomach was still sore.

They got off at FBI headquarters and took an elevator straight to the roof.

Thirty-seven helicopters were waiting there, and many more were on the way.

Agent Orange took his coat off and handed it to Mr. Edison.

"It's like a ride on a big bus," he said as Pamela's dad put on the coat.

Orange pointed to one of the helicopters, and they all headed toward it.

"Gotta love these Black Hawks." Goldblatt boarded the chopper and helped the others climb on.

They all fastened their seat belts, except Orange, who remained standing.

"Take us to Bend," the big man told the pilot. He turned to look Mr. Edison in the eyes. "The danger is over. You're going home, now."

"It's like a *big* party bus." Mr. Edison smiled.

The chopper lifted off the roof and rose into the bright blue sky, soon to be joined by a swarm of similar helicopters.

A great military force was bound for Bend to capture a man who was intimidated by a seven-year-old with a Wiffle bat.

The children knew it was overkill, but this was a military operation. They had no say in the matter.

"Operation Get Goobex 3" had begun.

"Do you think you can find the saucer again?" Orange asked.

"I can!" Willys shouted.

"You've caused enough trouble, young man. You are coming straight home with your father and me." Mrs. Wilson gave him a look that said, "Don't you dare argue."

Pamela looked down at her feet.

"I know the trail pretty well, but I'm not sure if I can find the exact spot."

"I can find it," Willys grumbled.

"You heard your mother," his father said into his ear.

"I think I can find it if we get close enough," Brad told Goldblatt.

"Then Violet can come home with us too," Mrs. Wilson said.

Violet turned to Agent Orange.

"I think I can find it if you take me to the place where we stopped by the creek."

"We should bring them both," Orange told Mrs. Wilson. "I don't have to tell you how important this mission is."

Mrs. Wilson looked at Violet.

"I just hate the thought of my children in the middle of an armed manhunt."

"Don't worry. I'll be safe, and I won't charge you for babysitting Brad."

"Hey!" Brad was insulted.

Their mom was too.

"Fine. Go." Mrs. Wilson brushed her husband's hand off her shoulder and crossed her arms.

Goldblatt and Orange asked the children to describe the trail and the surrounding area. Pamela, Violet, and Brad told them everything they could remember. Willys sat silently, with his arms crossed and an angry scowl on his face, just like his mother.

Time passed quickly. They landed in the street in front of the Wilson's house.

"Anybody who wants to go home, now's your chance," said Goldblatt.

"Let's go, Willys." Mr. Wilson unbuckled the boy and tried to pick him up.

Willys grabbed the seat belt with both hands and refused to let go.

"No! I found the cave! I know where it is!"

"You've had enough excitement," his mother scolded. "You are coming home now!"

"You need to come with me, son." His father pulled his left hand off the belt.

"No! They might need me!" Willys sobbed and kicked his legs in the air.

Mr. Wilson was about to win the struggle when Brad grabbed his brother with both arms.

"He's right!" Brad yelled. "I never would have found the cave without him. I'm not sure I can find it again."

"I can find it!" Willys roared. "I know where it is."

Mr. Wilson reluctantly put his son down.

"Fine. If you're going, then so am I."

Mrs. Wilson was fuming. She stood, hands on hips, with a sour look on her face.

"He's only a baby. Why does he have to go?"

"I'm not a baby!" Willys stared daggers at her.

Violet was still mad about being forced to babysit in the first place.

"You just want an excuse to stay home, don't you? It's not about an armed manhunt. Coming with us is just too much trouble. So go home. I won't miss you. No one will."

Mrs. Wilson's jaw dropped. Her daughter's venomous comments caught her by surprise. After a moment, her expression tightened into a sneer.

"I'm not afraid of a hike," she said. "I'm just trying to protect my family, even if that means trekking through the woods. When will you realize that your father and I are the glue that holds this family together?"

She put Willys in his seat and buckled him in before sitting and fastening her own belt.

"I wish I wore my hiking boots," Mr. Edison told his wife. "We need to shield our daughter from this insanity."

Mrs. Edison took his arm and kissed his cheek.

"It's good that you're coming. You'll all be safe," said Orange.

PEANUT BUTTER AND JELLY SANDWICHES FROM OUTER SPACE!

The "big bus" rose and joined the other helicopters waiting in the sky.

*****

They landed in a grassy field adjacent to the trailhead.

More helicopters landed nearby.

Several more were sent ahead to see if any clues to Harrison's whereabouts could be found. They also searched for places in the forest to land and drop advance troops. They all deposited their passengers and took off to bring more troops to Bend.

The three generals were among the first to arrive. They directed troop movements and aerial surveillance.

Before long, an entire battalion dubbed "Team Hammer" filled the field. As they prepared to head into the woods, Dr. Baldino, Dr. Jackson, Sergeant McGurk, and all ten sniffer dogs joined them.

"Great!" Pamela spat the word out. "What are they doing here?"

"The dogs?" Goldblatt said. "In a place like this, they're our most valuable asset."

"Well, keep them away from me." Pamela folded her arms across her chest and turned her back on the animals.

"I want you to lead the way," said Orange. "Follow the same path you did the day the spaceship was discovered. I'll be right behind you with your parents and friends. The generals and their guards will follow. We'll keep the dogs further back for now. Are you ready?"

Pamela heaved a sigh and started the long hike up the trail.

Over five hundred people followed her down the same shady little path the children had traveled one day before. The troops formed a long, double-file line that seemed to twist endlessly down the trail behind her as she led the way along the creek, through the narrow canyon, deep into the forest. It felt surreal. Everything was the same as the day before, yet everything was different.

Orange and the generals received reports on their radios from the choppers that had gone ahead. They had identified several landing sites scattered throughout the forest. Choppers took turns landing, deploying troops and leaving. The soldiers on the ground used drones for aerial surveillance and to link up with each other in an attempt to form a human wall.

After hiking for nearly an hour, Pamela noticed movement in front of her on the trail. She stopped in her tracks.

"Someone's up ahead," she told Orange.

"They're our people." The big agent strode forward and spoke into a two-way radio. "Team Hammer is approaching your position. Stand down."

They linked up with "Team Grizzly," a group of soldiers who had landed in a nearby meadow.

The children and their parents sat on the smooth stones lining the banks of the creek while the generals and Orange conferred with the Grizzlies.

Pamela felt a twinge of despair.

"I'm not sure if we passed it."

"Don't worry. We can always go back." Her mother hugged her shoulders.

The boys walked a little further up the path. They were anxious to continue the manhunt.

"I wish I had my bat. I'd like to clobber Dr. Suscratch again."

"I wouldn't stop you," said Brad.

"Hey! There's that tree I chopped down!" Willys ran to the ruins of a sapling that had been beaten and stomped to the ground.

Brad turned and tried to peer through the trees. He noticed the top of a hill peeking over the treetops.

"We left the spaceship on that hill."

Brad ran through the trees into the meadow. It was full of soldiers and helicopters.

"Sure looks different," said Willys when he caught up.

The grass and lupine had all been trampled down.

Brad tried to ignore the activity and focus on the landscape.

"Where do you think you're going? You might get shot if you're not careful." Agent Goldblatt stomped up to the boys.

"We found something," Brad said.

"The spaceship's on that hill!" Willys pointed across the field.

"And that tree looks awfully familiar." Brad pointed at the big oak tree on the other side of the field.

"Let's go."

Goldblatt grabbed both boys by the hand, and they crossed the field together.

As they neared the tree, Brad noticed something on the grass below its branches.

"I think I know where we are." He pulled the others toward the empty pillowcase and picked it up.

"This is where we came after the spaceship went crazy."

Willys looked up at the hill. The cave wasn't visible from below, but he spotted an outcropping of stone partially covered by ferns.

"It's up there!" He pointed to the spot.

Goldblatt radioed Orange with the news.

"Stay where you are. I'll join you," Orange radioed back.

The big agent brought the Wilsons, the Edisons, the generals, Dr. Baldino, and Dr. Jackson with him.

Jackson carried a huge load of scientific equipment in a bag on his back.

"Where's the saucer?" Finch asked.

"It's up there by those rocks." Willys pointed up the hill.

Jackson groaned.

"Follow me!" Willys bolted up the path leading to the cave.

Three generals, two agents, two doctors, four adults, and three older children followed the six-year-old up the hill, through prickly bushes, over boulders, and around scattered trees. He reached the sea of ferns and ran through it.

It was the right place. The huckleberry bush and the cave were there, but the saucer was gone.

CHAPTER 18

Operation Get Goobex 3 (Part 2)

A circle of burnt ferns was the only evidence the Goobex spaceship had ever been there.

"That rat Harrison must have taken it." Finch was practically smoldering with anger.

"Another win for the invisible enemy," said General Hazard, with deep concern.

Agent Orange looked over the area surrounding the scorch mark.

"It appears he found a way to control the vessel. If he dragged or rolled it, there would be tracks."

Willys stood at the edge of the circle, deep in thought.

"I got it to fly with a whistle. Maybe he has a flute, like the pied piper."

The thought of the saucer following Harrison as he waltzed through the woods playing a flute gave Pamela a lopsided grin.

"Nothing in here." Goldblatt turned off the powerful flashlight he used to examine the cave.

Dr. Baldino scanned the burnt circle with a device that resembled a squeegee with a digital screen on the handle.

"The energy readings are too weak. I cannot trace it." Baldino turned the device off and put it in Dr. Jackson's bag.

Violet went over all the facts in her mind. There was only one solid clue to follow.

"The last time we saw Harrison, he was going up the path to the hot spring. He said he was looking for bigfoot, but he might have a camp somewhere up the trail."

"Perhaps, but there is no need for speculation. It's time for the dogs." Orange nodded to Goldblatt.

The curly-haired agent pulled his walkie-talkie out of its holster.

"Bring up the hounds. We're giving them the lead."

"Oh, great," Pamela sneered as she spoke. "I've been replaced by dogs."

"Nobody's replacing you." Her dad wrapped his arm around her shoulders and held her next to him as they all headed down the hill.

The ten sniffer dogs and their trainers were waiting on the trail in front of the troops.

"Agent Stanley!" Goldblatt shouted.

"Yes, sir." Stanley came forward. She was a tall muscular blond woman wearing a black suit, sunglasses, and a fedora.

Brad was in love.

"You were at Harrison's house. I assume you brought a scent item for the dogs." Goldblatt held his hand out.

"No. Nobody told me—"

"I got this, Agent Goldblatt." Brad put a hand on Willys shoulder and cocked his head to speak to him.

"Willys, show the dogs where that weirdo was hiding in the bushes." He looked at Goldblatt. "They should be able to pick up his scent there. They might even find a few hairs my brother knocked off his ugly head."

Agent Orange took the boy by the hand.

"I'll go with you."

They led the dogs past the sapling Willys had destroyed to the bush he had battered.

The hounds gave the area a thorough sniffing. Ombre, the miniature poodle, found a plastic bag the doctor had dropped when Willys assaulted him.

It was more than enough for the skilled canines to pick up Harrison's spoor.

Tiny the rottweiler and Sergeant McGurk led the way. The border collie, the Saint Bernard, and the beagle came next with all the smaller dogs behind them.

The generals and their personal guards followed the dogs and their trainers.

"How about a piggyback ride?" Mr. Wilson lifted Willys over his head and let him slide down to his back. He wrapped his son's arms around his neck and held his little legs.

They joined Goldblatt, Orange, and the others in the long line of men once again marching along the creek-side path.

*****

The hike took nearly two and a half hours. The dogs found no clues, but they never lost the scent.

When they reached the hot spring, Tiny pulled Sergeant McGurk to the edge of the steaming pool and sniffed something on the ground. The big dog raised his head high and let out a piercing howl.

The generals jogged over to investigate.

Sergeant McGurk stood at attention and saluted before pointing to several huge muddy footprints leading away from the water.

"Tiny wouldn't howl like that if these were Harrisons," he said.

"Looks like bigfoot prints," Goldblatt told Orange as they approached the generals.

"Holy cow!" Brad was astounded by the huge tracks. "Harrison said he was tracking a Sasquatch, but I thought he was lying."

"Those have got to be fake." Mr. Wilson squatted down and set Willys on his feet.

"Maybe bigfoot took the alien from Dr. Stupid 'cause he thought it was a sandwich." Willys bent down and sniffed one of the footprints. "Yuck! It smells like fish."

Brad pulled a strand of orange hair out of a muddy print and held it up.

"I found some Sasquatch hair. Can I keep it?"

Mr. Edison reached into his pocket and pulled out the motion sickness bag from the shuttle.

"Here. You probably shouldn't be touching that. It's unsanitary."

"Thanks."

Brad took the bag and bagged the hair. He put it in his pocket.

Loud barking sounded atop a rock-faced cliff overlooking the spring. Brutus the chihuahua trotted to the edge with his trainer.

"We found his camp!" the trainer shouted.

The generals rushed to find a footpath up the hill along with their guards, the dogs, and their trainers.

Orange ordered the rest of the troops to surround the hill and look for any trace of Harrison.

He turned and spoke to the Wilsons and Edisons.

"I'm going to inspect the doctor's campsite. You can come with me or stay here with Agent Goldblatt."

"I wanna go!" Willys told him.

"I do too," Pamela said.

"All in favor of going." Mr. Edison raised his hand.

The four children raised their hands in an instant. Mr. Wilson and Mrs. Edison raised theirs two seconds later.

"Fine. We'll all go." Mrs. Wilson stormed up the path the generals took to the hilltop.

Agent Orange followed her, and the rest of the group followed him.

The trail twisted away from the hot spring and past a variety of pine trees and cedar. As they hiked up the hill, the path narrowed and squeezed between thorny berry bushes that grabbed at their clothing and scratched their skin.

"I hope this makes you all happy," Mrs. Wilson said as they reached the top.

The camp was not very impressive. It consisted of a tent, a sleeping bag, a folding chair, a camp stove, a mess kit, a lantern, and some clothing.

"He's not here." General Hazard kicked the chair over. "Dogs would have found him by now."

"They'll find him, all right. It's just a matter of time," said General Armstrong.

"Our time is limited," said General Finch. He grabbed a walkie-talkie from one of his guards and shouted into it, "Launch the rest of the drones! Go infrared now!"

Team Grizzly already had two dozen drones in the air. Team Hammer launched several more. Their collective buzz sounded like a swarm of killer bees as they flew up and over the treetops.

"I've got something here! Get Dr. Baldino!" shouted Harry's trainer from a field of chest-high grass.

"Woof!" the border collie added.

They all rushed to the site.

Hidden in the tall foliage was a circle of burnt grass. It matched the circle of burnt ferns by the cave.

They all crowded around the circle as Dr. Baldino examined it with his squeegee device.

"I've got traceable energy readings!" he shouted. "It left about four hours ago."

"Hmm. That's about the same time the helicopters got here," said Orange.

Brad thought about the muddy footprints.

"Harrison really was trying to catch a bigfoot, but the noise scared it away."

"Bigfoot!" Dr. Baldino scoffed. "There is absolutely no scientific evidence supporting the existence of such a creature."

"Actually, we have good reason to believe bigfoot is very real." Goldblatt had a smug look on his face. "But that's classified information."

"I told you so." Brad grinned at the girls.

"We're still missing something." Violet tried to put the puzzle pieces together in her head. "Maybe Harrison is hunting a bigfoot, but what does Goobex 3 have to do with it?"

Deep in Agent Orange's coat pocket, Cyndi Lauper sang, "Oh, girls, they wanna have fu-un. Oh, girls just wanna have fun." It was Pamela's text ringtone.

He took the phone out and looked at the screen. "It's the Goobexes," he announced.

"They stole my number?" Pamela turned to her mom. "Why do they keep invading my privacy?"

Mrs. Edison shrugged.

"Sometimes even good people do bad things with the best of intentions."

"They say Dr. Harrison is not the only one obsessed with bigfoot. Gooby-ooby had been trying to track one from their ship." Orange handed Pamela's cell phone to Goldblatt.

"Ludicrous!" Dr. Baldino spat on the ground.

"The alien is either working with Harrison or against him." Agent Orange turned to Finch. "Call off the helicopters, general. Harrison and Goobex 3 are hunting the same creature, and the noise is driving it away."

"What about the drones?" Finch asked.

"Keep them above the tree line and avoid forming clusters," Orange told him.

"We still don't have enough men in these woods to form a human wall," General Hazard complained.

"We have all the men we need," said Agent Orange. "We have traceable energy readings and the dogs."

Finch ordered the helicopters to withdraw.

Orange ordered the ground troops positioned throughout the woods to remain as quiet as possible.

"Keep looking for Dr. Harrison and the little spaceship," he said over the radio. "Also, contact me if you see a bigfoot. The doctor and the alien are both hunting it."

The big man turned his attention to the generals.

"We need to split our forces," he told them. "The dogs will lead two teams. One will follow Harrison's trail, and the other will follow bigfoot. A third team will follow the saucer's energy trail."

"I'm on that team," said Finch.

"A marine is ready for any challenge. I'll lead the hunt for bigfoot." General Armstrong grabbed a sniper rifle from one of his men and looked through its scope.

"Then Harrison's all mine. I can't wait to get my hands on that louse." General Hazard rubbed his hands together.

"Agent Goldblatt, I want you to accompany Dr. Baldino. I will go with General Hazard." Orange looked over those gathered on the hilltop.

"In case Harrison returns, I want fifty soldiers to stay here with the pug, the poodle, and the Pekingese."

"These shoes weren't made for hiking. I'm staying here." Mrs. Wilson headed to the folding chair General Hazard had kicked over. She set it up and sat in it.

"You may all stay or come with me, but you must decide now," said Orange.

"I wanna go with Agent Orange." Willys tugged at his father's sleeve.

"I'd like to find the saucer." Brad looked up at Goldblatt. "Can I go with you?"

"Just don't try to sucker me into any more bets."

The girls looked at each other.

"I don't want to chase Bigfoot," Violet said.

"What about Henderson?" Pamela asked.

"Yeah." Violet smiled. "Let's go with Orange."

"I'll go with the girls." Mr. Edison took his wife's hand and kissed it. "You can stay here if you want to."

"I'm going with you. There's only one chair here, and it's occupied."

Mr. Wilson walked to his wife and kissed her forehead.

"I better go with Agent Goldblatt to keep Brad out of trouble."

"Go," said Mrs. Wilson. "I've had enough of this wild-goose chase."

Mr. Wilson joined Brad and Goldblatt as Agent Orange divided the forces.

The rottweiler, Chihuahua, and dachshund led General Armstrong's group of over one hundred marines in search of bigfoot.

The Saint Bernard, beagle, and basset hound led the hunt for Dr. Harrison. Agent Orange and General Hazard shared command of this group, which included Team Grizzly and nearly one hundred men from Team Hammer.

The border collie and his trainer accompanied Dr. Baldino, General Finch, and a force of three hundred men as they tracked the spaceship's energy signature. Goldblatt, Brad, and Mr. Wilson kept pace just behind Finch and his guards as they made their way east through the forest.

The saucer followed no earthbound path, so tracking it wasn't easy. They crossed the creek again and again, climbed over rocky hilltops, and blazed trails around boulders and fallen trees.

After trekking for nearly three hours, they climbed down a hill into a peaceful valley. There was a waterfall nearby and a small pool of bubbling hot water.

Dr. Baldino held his squeegee device over the pool.

"I don't understand this. The spaceship should be right here."

General Finch pushed Baldino aside.

"Maybe it has a cloaking device." He took a rifle from one of the soldiers and waved it over the pool. Nothing was there.

"Another hot spring? That can't be a coincidence," Brad told Goldblatt.

The curly-haired agent pulled out his radio and spoke into it softly.

"General Armstrong. What's your twenty?"

"Forty-four degrees, twenty-two minutes, fifty point one six seven three north by one hundred twenty-two degrees, fourteen minutes, eighteen point nine zero zero two west. We're heading south."

Goldblatt punched the numbers on his special-issue digital watch. It showed a map with Armstrong's location and their own.

"We should pull back and lie low," Goldblatt told Finch.

"Why?" the general asked.

"Armstrong's following the bigfoot, and he's headed this way. It's connected to the hot spring and the saucer somehow."

"So we watch the pool from a distance." Finch nodded his head.

"Position the men south, east, and west in the hills, but leave the north open." Goldblatt turned a knob on his watch, and it turned into a digital compass.

"Do you think Bigfoot is headed to the spring?" Brad asked.

"Yeah," Goldblatt answered. "We'll have it surrounded. Harrison and the alien shouldn't be far behind. When they show, we can wrap things up nice and neat."

CHAPTER 19

Operation Get Goobex 3 (Part 3)

As Finch's force pulled back into the hills, Agent Orange and General Hazard followed Harrison's trail west over a steep hill and down into a wide, wooded valley.

Bessie, the Saint Bernard, sniffed her way along a narrow animal trail until she reached an impassable snarl of fallen trees. She sat.

"He must have climbed over this mess," her trainer said.

"Or he could be hiding in it," said General Hazard.

"We've got that covered, general." The basset hound's trainer, Sergeant Carter, bent down and unleashed her. "Go get him, Reba!"

Reba jogged to the huge knot of deadwood. It was over seventy feet high! Massive tree roots embraced the branches of other dead giants whose wooden corpses formed one massive decomposing heap.

The dog sniffed her way between broken branches and climbed the trunk of a fallen tree. She jumped to another tree trunk and made her way across an obstacle course of branches, roots, and open spaces where she could fall and get trapped or injured. She moved gingerly from tree to tree until she reached the top of the pile, and she sat. There was something white in front of her.

"Keep everyone here," Orange told General Hazard.

The big man climbed up into the tangle of fallen trees as if he were part leopard. He swung around heavy branches and broke off smaller ones. He moved with a grace that matched his strength. He reached Reba in under two minutes.

"Good girl." Orange patted her head and lifted the white object.

"It's his lab coat!" Violet shouted.

Orange nodded and put his finger to his lips.

He radioed General Hazard.

"I can see a trail to the left of this tangle. Take the men south, around the trees. The trail will lead you to a river near the middle of the valley. Go there, and keep it quiet. Reba and I will follow his trail and try to drive him toward you."

Orange picked up Reba and held her with one powerful arm as he descended to the opposite side of the tangle of timber.

Bessie and Frisky, the beagle, led General Hazard's group around the trees toward the middle of the valley.

They had covered nearly a mile before Orange radioed them again.

"Have you reached the river?" he asked.

"No, but we're getting close. I hear water," said Hazard.

"Keep going. Harrison is somewhere between us. Orange out."

Hazard and his men soon reached a spot that looked down on a gentle bend in the river. Their vantage point allowed them to see a vast stretch of the riverbank to the north.

"Binoculars." The general held out his hand.

One of his guards filled the request.

The general scanned the banks of the river with the powerful field glasses.

"There's Agent Orange and the dog. They must be a mile upriver."

He examined the riverbank between Orange and his group. Much of the bank was broad and flat, but in some places, the ground rose up and away from the river, leaving no shoreline at all, just a steep wall of mud or rock.

"I think I see something moving through the trees." Hazard adjusted the focus on the binoculars. "It looks like a scarecrow in camouflage."

"That's him!" said Pamela.

"I have eyes on Harrison," the general radioed Orange. "He's about six hundred yards in front of you."

"Don't lose him. I'll drive him your way," the agent answered.

General Hazard handed the binoculars to one of his guards, and he pointed out Harrison's location.

"Get your eyes on the man, Sergeant Spiro. He's about ten yards from the riverbank. Look for the light glinting off his head. Try to get some drones on him too. I'm taking our men in pursuit."

"Can I come?" Willys asked.

"We all want to see the doctor get his just desserts," said Mrs. Edison.

"Yeah," said Pamela.

"Yeah," Violet agreed.

"You can come if you stay back. Don't get in our way." The general turned and shouted to his troops, "Form up behind me and the beagle! We march in two."

One hundred twenty seconds later, Frisky was leading Hazard's group along a path following the river northeast.

At the same moment, Orange and Reba drove Harrison south from their position. Drones were sent to track the doctor's movements from above as Sergeant Spiro watched him through the binoculars. There seemed to be no way for him to escape.

"He's about two hundred yards from your position," the sergeant radioed.

"I really wanna clobber him again, but don't tell Dad," said Willys.

"He's gone!" Spiro said over the radio.

"What?" Hazard shouted.

"He disappeared into some bushes. We're sending the drones in."

"Double time!" Hazard roared.

The men rushed forward, with Hazard and Frisky in front. As they ran, Spiro radioed again.

"The drones caught him sliding down a grassy slope to a ledge above the water. He's getting on a rope bridge and crossing the river."

General Hazard jogged to the edge of the steep, boulder-studded slope leading down to the water. Less than one hundred yards away, Harrison was nearing the river's opposite shore.

"Fire some warning shots," said Hazard.

Two of his guard fired a volley of bullets in Harrison's direction. The doctor didn't even slow down.

"Go after him!" Hazard bellowed.

Team Grizzly chose a spot to slide down the steep hill. The first group slid into the big rocks and boulders on purpose so they could hold their position and protect others from the dangerous obstacles.

By the time the Grizzlies reached the river, Harrison was already across. A drone buzzed ten feet over his head.

"He's cutting the ropes!" Spiro said on the radio.

Team Grizzly rushed to the rope bridge.

Harrison cut through one hand cable and started on the other.

Violet, Willys, and Pamela heard the sergeant's report as they approached General Hazard. They looked across the river and saw Harrison sawing through the remaining hand cable.

He saw them too. He stopped to give them a self-satisfied smile.

"He's gonna get away," Violet said in despair.

"No!" Willys shouted.

He felt something like a giant burp that finally relieved the lingering pain in his stomach. A crackling sphere of light and energy shot out of Willys's mouth. It flew across the river and struck the doctor right in his gut.

Harrison doubled over in pain. He dropped his knife and struggled to stay on his feet.

The Grizzlies reached the bridge just as Dr. Harrison released a huge stream of vomit.

The undigester had endowed Willys with all its power.

Reba led Agent Orange to the spot where Harrison had slid down to the bridge. Orange picked her up and half ran, half surfed down the slope.

The Grizzlies were everywhere when Orange arrived. He put Reba down and headed for the bridge, but two soldiers barred his path.

"Only two men at a time," said one of the Grizzlies. "That hand cable is holding on by a thread."

The sight of his vomit turning into a pile of macaroni and cheese mixed with canned tuna, two bananas, and a bran muffin was too much for the doctor. The two soldiers on the bridge witnessed him passing out just before the second hand cable broke and they plunged into the middle of the raging river.

Agent Orange removed his shoes and socks.

"My training has prepared me for something like this. I'll get Harrison."

The Grizzlies moved aside as the big man stepped onto the sole remaining rope across the river. Orange moved like a trained circus performer who was used to doing this sort of thing on a unicycle. He reached the opposite bank as quickly as most men could have with both hand cables intact. He picked up Harrison's knife and tossed it aside before stepping around the doctor's undigested meal and picking up the unconscious man.

Sergeant Spiro had abandoned the binoculars and taken control of a drone. He gave General Hazard a running account over his radio.

"Orange is carrying Harrison to the river. He's getting on the rope!"

"Is he crazy?" Hazard watched Orange begin his crossing from his viewpoint on the hill.

Orange had to continually shift the doctor around and twist his own body to stay balanced.

He was forty feet away from a safe return when Harrison woke up.

"What the devil?" Harrison shouted, and he wriggled around in Orange's arms.

Orange tried to catch his balance, but the doctor's resistance made it impossible. They both plunged into the river.

Several of the Grizzlies rushed downstream anticipating an emergency extraction.

None was needed.

Orange had grabbed the rope with one hand and Harrison with the other. He pulled the rope to his chest and hooked it under his arm. This allowed him to hoist Harrison onto his shoulder. He finished the crossing by pulling himself along the rope to dry land.

"We have Harrison," one of the Grizzlies announced on the radio.

"And we have a bigfoot sighting," Goldblatt said on the radio. "It's headed for the hot spring."

"The creature would already be in our hands if you idiots hadn't made so much noise." Harrison was drenched and angry.

"So you're working with Goobex 3. Where is he, doctor?" Orange asked.

"You'll find out soon enough," Harrison answered.

In another part of the forest, bigfoot approached the hot spring and Armstrong's team approached bigfoot.

A drone high overhead gave the marines the creature's exact location, until it clipped a tree branch. The device plummeted to the ground and bounced a few feet in front of the beast. It took one look at the thing and vanished into the trees.

"One of our drones spooked the Sasquatch. We don't know where it went," one of the soldiers reported.

"Congratulations. You messed things up again." Harrison shook his head in disgust as a Grizzly secured his hands behind his back with a zip tie.

"Where is Goobex 3?" Orange peered deeply into the doctor's eyes.

"I don't know. My job was to lead you away from the spring. It's a Sasquatch trap. The alien could be watching it from anywhere."

"Then how are we supposed to find it?" asked Orange.

Harrison had no answer.

*****

General Finch ordered drones to blanket the area and find bigfoot, but the stealthy creature easily avoided them.

Armstrong and his men saw the beast bolt through the woods. They fired at it, but it escaped unscathed. The creature was quick, but the marines had Tiny, Brutus, and Fellah, the dachshund.

"It's on the run," Armstrong radioed as he and his men pursued it through the tall trees.

The dogs raced through the forest. They followed the scent to the stony banks of the river.

Tiny ran to the rock wall below the waterfall. He stood on his hind legs, sniffed as high up the wall as he could get, and howled. He was too big to climb the rocky wall before them, but Brutus and Fellah found little footholds that let them follow the scent further up the face of the craggy slope.

"It's scaling the cliffs below the waterfall," Armstrong said on the radio. "Get some drones here now!"

"We don't need drones," Finch answered. "We have men all over that mountain. Bigfoot's not going anywhere."

Finch's troops above the falls braced themselves for an encounter with the beast. Capturing a Sasquatch wasn't part of their training.

Sweat beaded up on their foreheads as they waited.

"It's a long climb, even for that thing," said one of the soldiers, and they waited some more.

They grew impatient and peeked over the edge of the waterfall. Bigfoot was not there.

Drones were sent to search the cliffs for the beast, but they failed to spot anything.

"It's got to be up there somewhere," Armstrong told Finch on the radio. "I'll send some of my men up, and you send some of yours down on ropes."

"I don't know what that thing is, but it's not a bigfoot," said Dr. Baldino. "There is no such thing."

"Bigfoot is as real as you are, doctor," said Goldblatt. "And frankly, if you aren't willing or able to help us find the Sasquatch or the spaceship—"

The ground started shaking. It felt like a small tremor before a much larger earthquake.

The little hot spring in the once-peaceful valley became a geyser. Plumes of steam and boiling water spouted into the air like a liquid fireworks display.

A disk-shaped mound of mud slowly rose from the water. It flipped over, dumping earth and water back into the pit below it. It flipped again and again, flinging mud and debris everywhere until it looked like a shiny silver sphere.

Brad watched the scene from a hilltop with his dad.

"That's the spaceship," he said.

Crackling bolts of energy surrounded the flipping disk as it rose higher and higher.

Baldino rummaged through Jackson's bag and pulled out a device that looked like a mini satellite dish attached to a gun with a video screen on the side.

"It's going straight up," Baldino said.

"I can see that without a million-dollar gadget," said Finch.

The saucer looked like a big mirror ball gleaming in the sun. The ship reached a predetermined altitude above the treetops, and it stopped.

A few drones got too close to the saucer and suffered complete electronic failure. They crashed.

"Fascinating," said Dr. Baldino.

"It may have a protective force field," Dr. Jackson told General Finch.

"We need to get a closer look at that tech." Finch looked at Baldino. "Do you think a Stinger could bring it down?"

The alien craft began moving northwest like a basketball starting to roll downhill.

"The saucer's headed your way," Goldblatt told Armstrong over his radio.

"I can see that! What the hell's going on?" Armstrong asked.

"We don't know. It just exploded out of the spring," the agent answered.

All eyes were on the little spaceship as it streaked across the sky.

It flew directly over Armstrong's men and vanished into the waterfall!

CHAPTER 20

To Catch a Sasquatch

The marines aimed their weapons at the spot where the saucer disappeared.

"There must be a cave back there," Armstrong said on the radio.

"Keep your eyes on the falls. I'll take a team down from the top." Goldblatt was already on his way.

General Finch, his two guards, Mr. Wilson, Brad, and the doctors followed him up an animal trail along the ridge leading to the top of the waterfall.

Goldblatt paid no attention to them. He changed the frequency on his radio and spoke into it.

"Agent Stanley, meet me at the top of the falls and bring Agent Kirby."

"We'll be there in ten," she answered.

"I'm going down to that cave with you," said Finch.

"Then we need to go too," said one of his guards.

Goldblatt stopped and turned to look at the men.

"This climb is going to be treacherous," he said.

"I've jumped out of airplanes at eighteen thousand feet. Climbing down a rope doesn't scare me." Finch was practically bumping chests with the agent.

"All right. Six people. I can handle that," said the curly-haired agent.

"Can I go?" Brad asked.

"No," said his dad.

"I'm sending four men up," Armstrong radioed. "I'll let you know if they find the cave."

"No live ammo," Goldblatt said into his radio.

"Marines don't carry tranquilizer darts. Armstrong out."

Goldblatt put his radio back in its holster.

"We've got to get to the cave before they do." He turned and jogged up the trail. Brad and his dad followed.

Finch took a radio from one of his guards and spoke into it.

"Lieutenant Moss, I need six lines prepped for a descent. Do it right, and do it right now."

The marines had a healthy head start, but no time was lost preparing the ropes and harnesses. Everything was ready by the time Goldblatt, Finch, and the others reached the top of the waterfall.

"Watch your step and don't cross your lines." Goldblatt checked the straps on his harness and nodded. A team of soldiers began lowering him down the cliff adjacent to the waterfall.

General Finch went next. His guards and the two agents followed, one at a time.

Two soldiers lay on the cliff's edge and watched the descent through binoculars. They reported the climbers' progress to a sergeant. The sergeant radioed Lieutenant Moss, who commanded the troops manning the ropes.

Mr. Wilson pulled his son away from the cliff.

"You're way too close, Brad."

"I wanna see," the boy complained.

"It's not safe." Mr. Wilson released his son several yards from the precipice.

Brad moped and kicked a stray rock. He ambled over to a young soldier sitting on a campstool and holding a portable control console. She looked like a teenager playing a video game. Brad peered over her shoulder. She was operating a drone and aiming its camera at the climbers.

"There's too much mist. You can hardly see anything."

"Watch this."

The soldier hit a button, and the video changed to infrared mode. All six climbers appeared as red figures. So did the four marines climbing up from eighty feet below.

"Can you pull back and look at the waterfall?" Brad asked.

"Why would I do that?"

"Well, when we found the spaceship, there was a flashing blue light on top. That was before my brother ate the sandwich."

Airman Taylor looked up at Brad.

"Gotcha." She turned off the infrared and scanned the side of the waterfall near the climbers. "I don't see anything."

"Wait a second." Brad leaned in close to her and pointed to the upper left corner of the video screen. "What's that?"

The light in that part of the screen fluctuated ever so slightly.

"Could be the mist." She sent her drone a little higher. The changes in the light became more noticeable. She sent it higher and higher still.

"That's it!" Brad shouted. He pointed to a dim blue light flashing at the side of the falls.

Airman Taylor radioed Lieutenant Moss.

"They missed it! They're about twenty feet below the cave."

The lieutenant signaled his men, and they stopped lowering the climbers.

Goldblatt radioed him within a few seconds.

"Why did you stop?"

"You missed the cave, sir. One of our drone pilots spotted it about twenty feet above you."

"Then pull us up. The marines are almost here."

Moss positioned himself about twenty feet behind the men in front of the rope teams.

"Walk it back till you're even with me," he told them.

The men followed their orders, and the climb team was pulled up the rock wall.

Goldblatt was the first to notice the dim blue pulsing light illuminating the mist. He also saw a ledge of stone that marked the cave's entrance. The agent crawled across the stony cliff like a spider. His black suit was drenched by the time he pulled himself up onto the ledge. He helped General Finch climb onto the narrow shelf, and Agent Stanley climbed up next to them.

Goldblatt nodded toward the cave and led the way across the uneven slab of slippery stone. They walked sideways with their backs against the face of the cliff.

"Aah!" Finch slipped and nearly fell.

Stanley grabbed his shoulder and held him in place until he could regain his footing.

"Thank you. You must have great balance," Finch said.

"It's not my balance. It's the shoes," Stanley told him.

The closer they got to the cascade, the wider the ledge grew. It passed behind the wall of water and opened up into a deep cave.

They couldn't see very far inside, but the little flying saucer with its flashing blue dome was resting just a few yards past the cave's mouth.

Finch rushed to it.

Goldblatt pulled out his flashlight, but it was drenched and wouldn't work.

They heard bat wings flapping and other noises coming from deep in the cavern, and something smelled like dead fish rolled up in a moldy carpet.

Finch's guards and Agent Kirby made it to the cave within a couple of minutes.

"Can we have some light, please?" Goldblatt asked.

Agent Kirby, a short thin man known as a gadget specialist pulled a button on the sleeve of his jacket. His suit lit up as if he were a human torch. Everything within two hundred feet was illuminated.

The cave looked like a long tunnel that twisted its way deep into the mountain.

"This must be an ancient lava tube. It could stretch for miles," said Kirby.

"Bigfoot is somewhere in this cavern, and that spaceship wouldn't be here if the alien wasn't after it." Goldblatt took his coat off as he spoke. He shook off some of the water.

"Go get 'em," Finch said. "Me and my men will guard the saucer."

"You'll need a light." Kirby took a pen from his pocket and clicked it twice. The bottom half of the pen opened like an umbrella and became a reflector for dozens of LEDs arrayed around the ink cartridge. It produced a 150-WATT light.

Finch took the light and shined it on the saucer.

"The boys at Skunk Works would love to get their hands on this."

"If we find Goobex 3, maybe his parents will let you borrow it."

Kirby pulled the button on his sleeve again, and his suit went back to normal. Stealth was called for.

All three agents squeezed the right earpiece of their sunglasses three times. The tinted lenses changed to night vision mode.

Goldblatt led the way up the lava tube, in pursuit of an alien in pursuit of a bigfoot.

Finch watched the agents leave.

A few minutes later, he spoke softly into his radio, "Send down the net."

*****

"Agent Orange!" Willys ran to him. "You walked across that rope like Daredevil!"

"Thank you."

The big man had just carried Reba up from the riverbank. He put her down, and she jogged to her trainer.

"I got a superpower too." The boy smiled up at the agent. "I can make people barf."

"Interesting," said Orange.

"I used it on him." Willys scowled and pointed at Dr. Harrison, who had climbed up with the help of the Grizzlies guarding him.

"Keep that child away from me!" Harrison instinctively jerked away from the boy, but the Grizzlies guarding him blocked his retreat.

Agent Orange put a hand in front of Willys as if he were preventing an assault.

"We'll hold him back. Just tell us everything you know about the alien, the bigfoot, and the cave they're in."

"I don't know anything about the cave," said Harrison.

"I'll make him talk." Willys tried to get past Orange's outstretched hand.

"No! Please." Harrison pressed his back into his guards. "Goobex 3 asked for my help. We exchanged emails about tracking a Sasquatch. I didn't know who he was until later."

"You worked at NASA. You know the protocols. Why didn't you contact us?" asked Orange.

"I didn't believe he was an alien! He told me, but when he asked me to meet him in the forest to capture a Sasquatch, I thought it was a practical joke."

"Why did you put a sandwich in the spaceship?" Willys asked.

"The alien asked me to bring the sandwich. It's another reason I thought it was a prank. He was very specific. It had to be wheat bread, creamy peanut butter, and strawberry jelly."

"But why?" asked Willys.

"Goobex 3 was afraid his parents would come for him before he could catch a bigfoot, so he left a dummy to fool them. He never expected anyone else to find the spaceship or the sandwich."

"I need to know more." Orange lifted Willys and cradled him in one arm.

"I don't know any more! Nothing useful." Harrison's Adam's apple bobbed as he gulped nervously.

Agent Orange put Willys down and tried to radio Goldblatt.

There was no reception in the depths of the cave his partner was searching.

He radioed Finch, but he didn't answer.

The agent changed frequencies again and spoke into his walkie-talkie.

"General Armstrong, do you read me?"

"Affirmative," the general answered.

"I can't reach Finch or Goldblatt. Where are they?"

"They're in the cave. Four of my men just got up there. Hell of a climb."

"Do you have radio contact with them?"

"I can only reach Finch. The cave is part of a lava tube. My men are searching it for the alien and the bigfoot like your people. They're too deep for reception."

"I need to know what's going on in that cave," said Orange.

"Well, Finch is on his way out with the saucer. He's tying it up in that super net of his."

"Thank you, general. Orange out."

Agent Orange turned to General Hazard.

"Call in the choppers. We need to move."

*****

The three agents traveled deeper and deeper down the dark cave. They passed over a half-dozen spots where the lava tube forked, but the trail of water droplets and muddy footprints made it easy to choose the right path.

"We're getting close." Kirby kept one eye on his wristwatch scanner as they searched the cave. "I'm getting more heat off the footprints and an anomalous energy reading."

"Stay frosty and keep it quiet," Goldblatt said in a near whisper.

Three hundred seventy-two yards away, Sergeant Saltzman led his band of marines through the cave. His team lit their way with glow sticks.

It took great restraint for some of them not to shoot at the occasional flurry of bats that assailed them.

"Place reminds me of stories my dad told me about Nam," said Saltzman.

"You mean we should watch for booby traps?" another soldier asked with grave concern.

"Just keep your eyes open." The sergeant paused to light a fresh glow stick. "There's no telling what we'll find in this place."

Four hundred thirty-three feet behind the marines, General Finch's guards had finished tying the little spaceship into the super net.

"Bring it up," Finch said into his radio.

His guards guided their prize to the edge of the falls. They stood it up and let it go. Water blasted into the cave when it was pulled up into the waterfall, but it was gone in a matter of seconds.

"It's time to go back up. I have business to take care of." Finch grabbed a harness and began to strap himself in. His men did the same.

*****

Agent Orange, General Hazard, Dr. Harrison, and "the civilians" boarded a Black Hawk bound for the waterfall. A second helicopter was bringing the dogs and their trainers.

"The lava tube may have multiple outlets in the forest. We need to flood the area with our people," Orange told Hazard.

"I have thirty choppers on the way. The Grizzlies can rope drop into the woods if necessary," said the general.

Orange took his wet coat off and handed it to Mr. Edison.

"It's like a big bus," said Pamela's dad as he put the coat on and buckled himself in.

The big whirlybird lifted up above the tree line and headed east.

"We should get there in about twelve minutes, but I can't guarantee a safe landing spot," the pilot said.

"We'll cross that bridge when we get to it."

Orange was the only passenger standing, as usual.

*****

The agents reached a curve in the lava tube. There was something glowing ahead of them.

Goldblatt held his hand up, signaling the others to stop. He held his finger to his lips, and they all inched forward.

A strange sight greeted their eyes. A shallow silver bowl floated in the air emitting a soothing blue light. And standing inside the bowl was Goobex 3.

Unlike his parents, the little Goobex didn't need a levitation device. He had skinny little arms and legs. The alien also had at least one big blue eye. He wore a black patch over the spot where you'd expect to see another. The ridiculous-looking sandwich also wore a pirate hat and held a little wooden sword in one hand and a tiny pistol in the other.

The agents creeped forward in time to see a hairy arm reach out and grab the floating bowl.

"No!" Goldblatt drew his weapon and ran down the tunnel. He stopped ten yards short of the eight-foot-tall Sasquatch because of the creature's stench.

It looked part human and part orangutan. Goobex 3 stood on its shoulder as the beast placed the silver bowl on its head.

The creature convulsed as if jolted by a million volts of electricity. It stood so rigid and upright that the metal bowl on its head pierced the lava rock above it and sent a shower of dirt and debris down its shoulders.

"Should I zap it?" Agent Kirby brandished a small hairbrush with glowing bristles."

Goldblatt held his hand up, calling for restraint.

Goobex 3 opened a panel in the handle of his sword, revealing a series of buttons. He pressed a few, and his sword turned into a small but powerful vacuum cleaner. Gooby-ooby used it to remove the dirt from himself and the bigfoot.

"Let's shed some light on the subject," said Goldblatt.

The agents all turned off their night vision, and Kirby pulled the button that turned him into a human lightbulb.

The alien and the bigfoot shielded their eyes from the bright light with their hands.

"Too bright for you? I've got a dimmer." Kirby loosened the knot in his tie, and the light dimmed.

The four marines burst onto the scene. They had heard Goldblatt's shouts and ran to provide backup. Two of the soldiers took aim and tried to shoot the bigfoot, but Goobex 3 was much quicker than them. He fired his pistol twice, and a red ray enveloped their weapons. The machine guns seemed to freeze in their hands before melting away to nothing.

"There is no need for violence," the bigfoot said to everyone's amazement. "Goobex 3 will gladly return to his parents and I, Pirate's Pet 3, am prepared to go with him."

Goldblatt holstered his weapon.

"Stand down!"

Cyndi Lauper sang in his coat pocket, "Oh, girls, they wanna have fu-un. Oh, girls just wanna have fun." He felt embarrassed as he pulled out Pamela's cell phone and glared at the screen.

"It's your parents," he told Gooby-ooby. "They say you're grounded."

CHAPTER 21

The Maelstrom

Brad and his father watched from the edge of a small field as General Finch supervised the loading of the Goobex saucer onto a helicopter.

"I wonder if the alien's inside. Where do you think they're taking it?" Brad asked.

"I don't know, son. To the base, I guess."

"Yeah. That makes sense." Brad sat in the grass and looked up at the two Black Hawks hovering over the field.

Agent Orange stood in one of them, looking at the scene below.

"I need to get down there," he told the pilot.

"Field's too small for two choppers. There's a clearing about a half mile north."

"That's too far. I'll do a rope drop."

"That's dangerous with a bird on the ground." The pilot looked at the chopper below. "His rotors are spinning."

"I've trained for this," the big man answered. "I want you to keep that copter grounded for ten minutes."

"Roger that," said the pilot.

"When our men get here, I'll send them north to the clearing," said General Hazard.

"Send the hounds with them. I'll take care of business over here." Orange attached a rope to a cable with an eight-inch steel carabiner. He opened the chopper's door and threw the rope out.

"Don't you want a harness or gloves?" the pilot asked.

Orange just gave him a thumbs-up and wrapped the rope around his left leg. He turned and nodded to Willys, Violet, and the Edisons before saluting General Hazard and lowering himself down the rope and out of the helicopter.

*****

Twenty-eight choppers were busy transporting General Hazard's men from the west, and General Armstrong had called for fifteen more to carry his marines to the top of the mountain.

"I'm on the first bird up, and I'm taking the dogs." Armstrong scowled at the waterfall. "If my men don't bag that thing in the cave, I'll nail it when it comes out."

"You really want a bigfoot head on your wall. Don't you, sir?" said one of his guards into his ear.

Armstrong smirked.

"That would be a sight. They'd never let me keep it, though. It'll end up in a museum or zoo or maybe at some...one of the president's resorts. We'll have to settle for bragging rights and a photo."

The choppers carrying the Grizzlies were getting closer. The sound of their engines and swirling rotors swelled until it became a physical presence.

Armstrong was itching to climb onto one of them.

Twenty-eight copters came, and twenty-eight copters went.

The general mumbled some foul words. He stooped to pick up a rock and threw it at a helicopter. It arced through the air and disappeared into the maelstrom created by the plunging waters of the falls.

One of his guards pulled out his walkie-talkie and barked into it, "General Armstrong needs a chopper, now!"

"His birds will be there in five minutes," answered a voice on the radio.

"I won't let that thing get away from me twice." Armstrong retrieved his sniper rifle from the other guard. "Get me some more ammo."

*****

General Finch's guards tugged on the super net to make sure the Goobex saucer was securely fastened to the copter's floor.

"That'll do." Finch checked to make sure the door was locked. "Let's get out of here," he told the pilot.

"That bird isn't giving us much room. I asked the darn rotor-head to pull back, but he won't respond." The pilot craned his neck to get a better look at the copter above him.

Finch marched to the pilot and pulled his headset off. He put it on and flipped a switch on the control panel.

"This is General Finch. I need you to pull back and let my chopper go!"

He flipped the switch again, and a familiar voice blared over a speaker.

"This is General Hazard. The president put Agent Orange in charge of this operation, and he wants you to stay grounded. I urge you to follow the chain of command."

Finch scowled and flipped the switch.

"I have my own orders. You need to back off."

Someone pounded on the helicopter's door.

"Don't open that." Finch pointed to the door.

The pounding got louder and more intense. It shook the helicopter.

The pounding stopped and was replaced by the squeaky sound of twisting metal, blending with the sound of the copter's whirling blades.

Finch's guards drew their weapons as the door slid open.

"Going somewhere?" Agent Orange stood outside the chopper with one hand on the door. His other hand held the exterior door handle, which he had torn off.

*****

Agent Goldblatt took off his coat and held it over his nose and mouth in an effort to block the noxious odor coming from Pirate's Pet 3. He lifted it only long enough to speak.

"Let's head back to the waterfall."

"Leaving through the waterfall is dangerous," said the Sasquatch.

"It would be better than this," grumbled Sergeant Saltzman through his hands, which covered his nose and mouth.

The creature often hid in the caverns and tunnels. It knew them well. Thanks to their telepathic link, Goobex 3 shared this knowledge.

The little alien stood proudly on his pet's shoulder and pointed forward with his little wooden sword.

"There's a place ahead where we can leave the cave. It's much safer," said the shaggy half man. "Follow me." Pirate's Pet 3 turned and walked down the tunnel. His stride was so large, the others had to jog to keep up with him.

Goldblatt pulled Agent Kirby into a position directly behind the beast to illuminate their path and to give himself a little breathing room.

The light from Kirby's suit disturbed the bats hanging from the cave's roof. The bigfoot had to duck to avoid them.

"I hate when those things get stuck in my hair," it said.

As Kirby trotted, he rummaged through his pockets. He found a compact gas mask disguised as a ski cap and put it on his face.

The odd squad followed the bigfoot through the twisting tunnel for nine minutes. It was like following a giant skunk. Most of them were gasping for breath by the time the Sasquatch stopped. It pointed down a side tunnel.

"There it is."

A broad ray of light penetrated the darkness two hundred feet away. It came from a hole in the lava tube left by the roots of a fallen oak tree.

"We better make sure it's safe." Sergeant Saltzman and his men pushed their way in front of the others and ran to the hole.

Squinting through watery eyes, the sergeant wriggled between the roots and crawled out onto his hands and knees. He took a deep breath of fresh air and signaled the next man to come up.

The second marine was bigger than the sergeant. He had a tough time squirming through the broken remnants of the dead tree. It was going to be a tight squeeze for Pirate's Pet 3.

By the time the last two marines climbed out, the bigfoot and the agents were only a few steps from the hole.

"Whoa!" Goldblatt squeezed in front of the bigfoot and held out both of his hands to stop it. "Kirby, you go next. I want you to check for Russian snipers."

Kirby turned his suit light off. He climbed up between the roots and peeped through the hole like a gopher. The agent took his shoes off and placed them outside the cave. He ducked back down and opened his coat, revealing several dangling gadgets. A designer label hid the numerical keypad he used to activate the shoes' radar function. The footwear beeped loudly for thirty-seven seconds. When the noise stopped, the agent looked at a read out on his watch.

"All clear." Kirby climbed out of the hole and put his shoes back on.

"You go next, big guy." Goldblatt stepped aside. "The lady and I will follow."

*****

General Finch scowled at Agent Orange and pointed at the Goobex saucer.

"I'm taking this 'weather balloon' in for analysis."

His guards had their weapons trained on the big man.

"I can't let you do that."

Orange tossed the door handle to Finch.

He caught it.

"I have orders from Citizen One." The general held up his cell phone. A tweet from the president was on it. "I'd love to give our boys a chance to look at that saucer #getgoobex3."

"That is not valid authorization," said Orange.

"No. I got that by text." Finch pulled up a message from the commander in chief, "**If you get your hands on the saucer take it to Area 51.**"

Orange read the message and looked up at the general.

"For the record, I don't like this. You're asking for trouble."

"Orders are orders," Finch answered.

"May I borrow a radio?" Orange held his hand out, and one of the guards gave him a walkie-talkie. He adjusted the frequency and spoke into it, "The bird on the ground has authorization to go."

"I just sent the Grizzlies north to the clearing," General Hazard said over the radio.

"Good. I'll meet you there." Orange returned the radio to the guard.

"Sorry for breaking your helicopter, sir." He saluted General Finch and left the chopper.

As he walked away, he heard the general yelling, "Do you have any duct tape on this crate?"

Orange shook his head. There was no telling how the aliens would react to the theft of Goobex 3's little saucer.

*****

Two Black Hawks had descended to the grassy field below the waterfall. Thirteen others were waiting for space to land. General Armstrong and his guards boarded the first one to touch down, along with the dogs and their trainers.

"Let's go!" the general shouted at the pilot. "If they bag that monster before I get there, I'll never hear the end of it."

The chopper lifted off the ground.

Armstrong stood and pointed his rifle out the open door. He looked through the scope and spotted a raccoon perched in the branches of a tree over two hundred yards away. He squeezed off two shots as the copter rose into the air.

Armstrong smiled when the raccoon fell to the ground.

"Not bad," he said to himself.

*****

The first of the Black Hawks transporting Hazard's men had reached the clearing.

"There's movement down there. I think it's the bigfoot," the pilot reported.

"I want that beast surrounded, pronto," Hazard spoke into a headset. "Have the men fast-rope down."

"If you take me to it, I think I can make it barf," said Willys.

"Let them handle this." Violet put her arm over his shoulder.

"Yeah, you should save your power for emergencies." Pamela patted his leg.

Willys scowled and crossed his arms.

"Well, if bigfoot eats Gooby 3, I'll have to use my superpower to save him."

Violet hugged his shoulder and smiled at him.

"That would be an emergency, but I really hope it doesn't come to that."

*****

Agent Goldblatt was the last to crawl out of the hole. He could hear helicopters approaching.

"We have Goobex 3 and the bigfoot," he said into his radio. "We can wrap this op up and put a ribbon on it."

There was no reply.

Two helicopters landed in the clearing. Ten Grizzlies rushed out of one with their weapons aimed at Pirate's Pet 3. Bessie, Frisky, Reba, and eight more soldiers rushed out of the other.

Sergeant Saltzman and his men stepped into the clearing waving their arms, but the Grizzlies and dogs still rushed forward.

Goobex 3 pointed his pistol at the soldiers as Goldblatt shouted, "Stand down!"

More helicopters came, and Grizzlies began dropping from the trees like a shower of angry pine cones.

Goobex 3 hurriedly opened the control panel on his sword and punched in a code. A small silver disk shot out of the bowl on his pet's head. It stopped several feet above them and flipped over and over, like the Goobex saucer.

"Stand down!" Goldblatt shouted again.

More and more men dropped from the trees.

The bigfoot, the alien, and the agents were quickly surrounded by a circular firing squad.

"Please don't shoot," said the Sasquatch. "Someone could get hurt."

Hearing the creature speak caused most of the men to gasp and lower their weapons.

Agent Stanley stepped in front of it.

"The Sasquatch is with us. He's cooperating and so is the alien."

"General Hazard, we have secured the target," said one of the Grizzlies into his radio.

There was no response. His signal was being jammed.

"Let me see your walkie." Goldblatt took two steps toward the soldiers and stopped. He felt like he had walked into an invisible wall of super-chilled Jell-O. The color drained out of his face. His curly hair uncurled and stood straight up.

"Sorry," said the bigfoot. "Goobex 3 has activated a force field. He regrets not telling you sooner."

Fifty yards away, another helicopter landed in the field. General Hazard, his guards, Willys, Violet, the Edisons, and Dr. Harrison all got out of it. The general marched toward the encircled "target" with the others close behind.

"What in blazes is going on here?" Hazard shouted.

The swarm of soldiers parted like the Red Sea to let the general through. The sight of Pirate's Pet 3 and Gooby-ooby with his hat, sword, and gun made Hazard stop in his tracks.

"Goobex 3 is ready to go home now." The bigfoot's voice was deep and gentle. "Please put your weapons away."

Goldblatt took a step back from the force field. His hair re-curled.

"They're cooperating. I think we can trust 'em," he said.

General Hazard proudly looked over the troops assembled there, and he gave the order, "Stand down!"

The men lowered their weapons.

Goobex 3 punched the buttons on his sword, and the spinning disk flew back into his pet's helmet.

Goldblatt reached his arm out. The force field was gone. He looked over his shoulder at Pirate's Pet 3.

"I'd like to cuff the Sasquatch, but they don't make handcuffs big enough."

Agent Orange, who had sprinted the half mile to the clearing, slowed down and jogged over to Goldblatt. The big man wasn't even winded.

"I assume this is Goobex 3," he said.

"And his new pet." Goldblatt looked at Kirby. "Do you have any kind of restraint we can use on this thing?"

Kirby produced a dog collar and a leash.

"It's electrified, but the collar won't fit unless we put it on its wrist or ankle."

Several choppers hovered above the clearing. A shot rang out from one of them.

The bullet grazed off Pirate's Pet 3's helmet and hit the ground two inches in front of Goldblatt.

Agent Orange lunged forward and tackled the creature. A stream of bullets rained down on his back.

"No!" Willys shouted at the helicopter.

He was horrified by the shooting of his hero. His rage and despair felt like a living thing inside of him. He let it out.

A sphere of crackling energy flew from the boys' mouth faster than a speeding bullet.

It hit General Armstrong.

The general dropped his rifle out of the chopper and doubled over in pain. His men had to grab him to keep him from falling to his death. He disgorged a huge stream of vomit out the open door. It was followed by another and another.

By the time his puke hit the ground, it had undigested into a rare 28-ounce steak, mashed potatoes, string beans, scrambled eggs with sausage, three slices of toast, and a shower of coffee.

"Stand down, damn you!" General Hazard shouted into a radio. There was no reply. "If anyone else fires from a copter, we will shoot back."

The soldiers trained their weapons on the choppers.

Agent Orange rolled off the Sasquatch and rose to his feet, uninjured.

"Glad I wore my Kevlar undershirt today," he said.

"Goobex 3 believes my helmet is causing your communication devices to malfunction." The bigfoot sat up, keeping a wary eye on the copters above.

Gooby-ooby climbed back onto its shoulder and busily typed code into his sword handle.

Willys ran to Agent Orange.

"I clobbered that fink who shot you."

"Yeah. How'd you do that?" Goldblatt asked.

Willys shrugged.

"I got a superpower."

"He's a human undigester," said Pamela.

"Hey, I think I've got something of yours." Goldblatt reached into his coat. He pulled out Pamela's cell phone and gave it to her. "Keep it. I memorized the Goobexes' number."

Gooby-ooby stopped typing.

"Your communications should work now." Pirate's Pet 3 stood up and took shelter under a tree. "Please, tell the people up there to go away."

Gooby-ooby waved his little gun up toward the helicopters as if to say, "Or else."

"Put that weapon away," said Dr. Harrison. "Don't sink to their level."

The alien's eye opened wide. It did a spirited jig and clicked its heels in the air.

"Goobex 3 is happy to see you, doctor," said the bigfoot.

Dr. Harrison could hardly believe he was seeing a live Sasquatch, let alone one who could speak English.

"Astounding," he whispered.

"Please turn around." Pirate's Pet 3 made a circular motion with his massive hand.

Harrison was puzzled by this, but he turned his back to the alien.

Gooby-ooby pointed his gun at him and fired.

PEANUT BUTTER AND JELLY SANDWICHES FROM OUTER SPACE!

The zip tie binding the doctor's hands vanished in a flash of red light.

"Dr. Harrison is our friend. He should not be bound," said the bigfoot.

Hazard raised his radio to his mouth.

"This is General Hazard. Operation Get Goobex 3 is a success. I am ordering all troops to stand down, especially that trigger-happy moron in the helicopter."

"That was General Armstrong," said Orange.

"I know." Hazard smiled.

CHAPTER 22

Connivances and Contrivances (Part 1)

Gooby-ooby surveyed the troops from the Sasquatch's shoulder.

"I've been ordered to bring you to our base," Orange told him. "Your parents' ship is near it. We will travel by helicopter."

He pointed to the whirlybirds in the field.

"Goobex 3 is concerned about my safety." Pirate's Pet 3 looked at the alien tenderly. It was examining the copters through a collapsible telescope. "Before now, only my mother ever cared enough to protect me."

"Aw, they're bonding. Ain't that sweet?" Goldblatt turned to Kirby. "Got anything to deodorize the pirate's pet before he stinks up a chopper?"

Kirby reached into his jacket and pulled out a handful of pine tree air fresheners.

"They're mega strength, but I doubt they'll help much."

"Why don't we just give him a bath?" asked Willys.

General Hazard put a hand on his shoulder.

"It would take a month to wash that stink off."

Everyone moved back when Pirate's Pet 3 lifted his massive arm to sniff his armpit.

The creature shrugged and said, "My friend's saucer can generate an odor-neutralizing field. He will summon it."

The little alien opened the panel in his sword handle and began typing.

"No!" Orange held his hand out. "Your ship is inside one of our helicopters. It's already airborne."

Gooby-ooby put his sword in its scabbard and his gun in its holster. He crossed his pencil-thin arms.

"Where are you taking it?" the bigfoot asked.

"I am not authorized to discuss that," said Orange.

Goobex 3 tried using his telepathy on the big man. The jellylike substance on top of the alien sandwich bubbled as if it were boiling. He tapped his foot on his pet's shoulder. The doughy flesh on his forehead tightened and writhed. It wasn't working.

"Goobex 1 and 2 will be angry with the pirate if he loses his ship." The Sasquatch tilted its head. "It would be best to send it home to the family saucer."

"One of our generals is on that helicopter," Orange argued. "He is important to us. He must not be harmed."

"Goobex 3 would never harm a sentient being!" the bigfoot bellowed. "Your general will probably be safe."

The alien pulled out his little wooden sword, opened the hidden panel, and pressed several buttons. He struck a pose and held up his popsicle-stick-sized weapon. A bright-blue lightning bolt shot out of it and flashed across the sky.

*****

The helicopter was over thirty miles from the waterfall when the bolt rocked it.

The people inside felt like they had flown into a hurricane. The duct-taped door flew wide open, and the Goobex saucer was pulled toward the opening. Waves of energy danced over the surface of the alien craft and penetrated it. The saucer glowed brighter and brighter.

"What the devil?" Finch shouted.

One of his guards got up and leaped onto the saucer in a valiant effort to secure it. His fingers clutched the super net as he sank right through the little spaceship.

There was a bright flash, and it was gone along with the turbulence.

"No! No! No!" Finch unbuckled his seat belt and fell to his knees, pounding his fists on the floor.

"You couldn't know something like this would happen, sir." His other guard stood up and offered Finch a helping hand. "What should I tell the pilot? Do you want to change course?"

Finch looked up at him through angry eyes. He grabbed the detached door handle from the ground and threw it at his face.

*****

The president was golfing when he received the good news from Bend.

He stopped in the middle of the seventh hole to unleash a tweetstorm.

"We found Ooby-gooby and captured a bigfoot! This is a big win for America, very big! We caught Harrison too! The *Enquirer* says he's an alien. The Goobexes stole their little spaceship from us. It was found on American soil, so it's ours! The Sasquatch is American property too! I will not let them steal our bigfoot! I'm the only one who can negotiate with the aliens. No one else can make a deal. No one."

As far as he was concerned, bigfoot was a valuable object. Even a stuffed Sasquatch would draw huge crowds to any of his resorts. That's why he asked General Armstrong to shoot it if he had a chance. A live bigfoot was worth even more!

A worldwide tour would make him much richer than he was already.

Why would he let the Goobexes grab the creature and run?

"If they insist on keeping it, I'll make them pay through the nose," he tweeted.

The greedy narcissist in chief took his golf shoes off and left Mar-a-Lago.

Air Force One was waiting to whisk him to Oregon.

*****

Kirby had strung a dozen air fresheners into a necklace for Pirate's Pet 3, but they only added a touch of pine to the odor instead of concealing it.

"We'll have to provide gas masks to the crew transporting the alien and the Sasquatch," General Hazard told the president on a secure line.

"As long as it's voluntary. They can do it, but they don't have to. I would choose not to. I think wearing a gas mask when I might have to FaceTime with presidents, prime ministers, dictators, kings, queens... I don't know. Somehow, I don't see it for myself. I just don't, but some people may want to and that's okay, but it's only a recommendation."

"Yes, sir." Hazard looked at Pirate's Pet 3. "Gas masks are highly recommended but not mandatory."

"And keep the so-called doctor away from the alien. He could be a threat."

"Goobex 3 swears Harrison is innocent of all charges."

"It could be lying. It lied to its parents. Some very smart people tell me Harrison's a shape-shifting Draculoid who craves blood and Goobex jelly. We should give him a blood test."

"I'll make sure Dr. Baldino does that back at the base."

"I don't think that's smart. I mean, if he is a nasty, jelly-sucking Draculoid, don't you want to know before you bring him onto our beautiful base? I want you to be extra careful."

The general paused briefly.

"Yes, sir."

"You tell Baldino to test Harrison's blood now. See if it's red."

"Of course, sir. Is there anything else?"

"Yes. Have the beast checked for ticks and fleas. I'm coming to Oregon and I want to see it myself, but I don't want Lyme disease."

"Yes, sir."

"I'm holding a rally outside the Goobex saucer, and we need your men for security. I'll teach those aliens about the art of the deal."

The president hung up.

Hazard shook his head and radioed the doctor.

"Baldino, I need you to come to the clearing and bring a med kit."

"Is someone injured?"

"No. It's just something the president requested."

*****

Shivers snaked down Dr. Baldino's back. Visions of an alien autopsy sickened his mind.

Hazard had radioed him as he was walking to the clearing with Dr. Jackson, Mr. Wilson, and Brad to see the alien and the bigfoot.

"Is this something I should be concerned about?" he said into his walkie-talkie.

"Just get here. Hazard out."

Baldino took a deep breath and let it out.

"What do you think he wants?" asked Dr. Jackson.

"God only knows," Baldino mumbled.

*****

Back at Dr. Harrison's campsite, Mrs. Wilson overheard some radio chatter about wrapping things up and returning to FBI headquarters.

"Oh no. I am not going all the way back there." She got up out of the folding chair and stomped over to Private Osborn, Ombre the poodle's trainer. He was talking over his radio.

"I need to talk to Agent Orange," she said. "He's in charge, right?"

"I'm sure he's swamped right now," Osborn told her.

"It's urgent." Mrs. Wilson grabbed his arm and squeezed like a boa constrictor.

"I'll try," said Osborn. He pulled his arm out of her hands and adjusted the frequency on his radio. "Agent Orange, I have Mrs. Wilson here. She says it's urgent that she speak to you."

"I'm listening," Orange answered.

Osborne handed the radio to Mrs. Wilson.

"I have to get back to Bend!" she shouted.

Gary the pug and Teddy the Pekingese barked at her. They didn't like her attitude.

"That shouldn't be a problem," said Orange.

"I've got work to do," Mrs. Wilson grumbled.

"Get on the first chopper out. Tell the pilot to radio me."

"Thank you."

"Your husband and children won't be joining you, though. They're going to the base."

Mrs. Wilson glared at the walkie-talkie.

"Why?"

"Your son is exhibiting side effects from his exposure to the undigester."

"Is he all right?"

"He's fine. We just need to reexamine him."

"Well, Wally can handle it if it's not too serious."

"Understood. Orange out."

"Well, that's a relief."

Mrs. Wilson gave the radio back to Osborn and returned to her spot on the folding chair.

*****

Throughout the forest, soldiers gathered and filed into choppers.

They were tired, but the operation's success put an extra bounce in their steps.

Dr. Baldino gave Dr. Harrison a blood test, while Dr. Jackson rummaged through his bag for the equipment needed to analyze the sample.

Brad and his dad joined Violet, Willys, and the Edisons near Orange and Goldblatt.

"I can't believe you got a superpower and I didn't get to see it." Brad felt like he had been excluded on purpose.

"You missed it twice." Willys held up two fingers.

Mr. Edison put his arm around Mr. Wilson's shoulder.

"I can't imagine raising a super kid will be easy. Let me know if you ever need help."

"Thanks."

"You know, if they're dropping your wife off in Bend, maybe I should take my girls back too."

"It's your choice, Frank, but fifteen seconds on the news with those two and maybe the president, that would give anybody's business a boost." Mr. Wilson smiled and glanced at the Sasquatch and alien with dollar signs in his eyes.

"We should go, Dad." Pamela grabbed her father's arm. "I could take some photos with my phone, but it wouldn't be the same as being on the news."

"No, it wouldn't." Mrs. Edison grabbed his other arm. "The hard part of this fiasco is over. We may as well enjoy some benefits."

For Mr. Edison, resistance was futile. The opportunity was clear and compelling, and he was getting used to flying around in a big bus anyway.

*****

About an hour later, dozens of black-suited agents prepared for the return of the victorious troops at FBI headquarters. They gathered on the roof to usher the soldiers to the elevators leading to the secret subway.

The agents all cheered when the first copters arrived.

Soldiers poured out of the whirlybirds and lined up outside the elevators.

General Hazard, Orange, and Goldblatt left one of the Black Hawks along with several soldiers. They were all wearing gas masks. The Sasquatch exited the chopper last with Goobex 3 on his shoulder.

"The president is on his way to meet you," Hazard told the alien. "We've arranged for your pet to be cleaned and deodorized."

"Goobex 3 only agrees to the cleaning, if he can accompany me."

The Sasquatch noticed the throng of agents and soldiers gawking at him. It made him nervous, so he bent down to their level and growled.

Goldblatt drew his gun and whirled around expecting to spot another sniper.

Orange put a hand on his shoulder.

"Relax, Agent. The only threat here is the possible harm a detox shower may cause the alien."

"A shower?" The shaggy simian shivered and crossed his arms. "I prefer bathing in a hot spring, but my friend is prepared for a shower."

The alien drew his wooden sword and pushed a few of its buttons. A transparent sandwich-sized umbrella sprouted from it.

"Let's get this over with. I can't wait to take this mask off." Hazard headed to the Hazmat tent.

Pirate's Pet 3 followed the general.

Orange and Goldblatt were close behind.

Two men in Hazmat suits met them outside the tent.

"Does the alien need cleaning or just the bigfoot?" one of them asked.

"Just the Sasquatch," said Hazard. "Make sure it doesn't have any fleas or ticks. The president hates ticks."

The men opened the tent's Velcro-sealed flap, and Pirate's Pet 3 entered with Gooby-ooby.

Hazard, Orange, and Goldblatt removed their gas masks as soon as the tent flap was resealed.

"I deserve hazard pay for this," said Goldblatt. "No pun intended."

Agent Stanley rushed over, trailed by Kirby, the Wilsons, and the Edisons.

She held out Pamela's cell phone.

"It's the Goobexes," she said. "They sent us another text."

Orange took the phone from her and read.

"Gooby-ooby cannot tolerate the toxins in your atmosphere much longer. We must insist that he return to our vessel with both of his pets."

"That's not acceptable. The bigfoot doesn't belong to them," said Hazard.

"There's more." Orange paused and looked at the Wilsons and Edisons. "Because of the ordeal the children and their parents have endured, we invite them and Dr. Harrison to tour our spaceship before we leave your solar system."

"Awesome," Brad said, smiling broadly. "Maybe they'll give me a superpower too."

"We need to send a response." Orange began writing a return message.

"Shouldn't you wait for the president's input?" Hazard tried to read the message as the agent wrote it.

Orange finished and read it aloud.

"Goobex 3 is doing fine. He is in no distress. Please be patient." He looked at the general.

"That's good. We need to stall until the president gets here."

Finch and Armstrong stormed to the tent with their guards.

"Where's the alien?" Finch asked. "I have a bone to pick with that little jerk."

"He's in the tent with the Sasquatch, but believe me, you don't want to go in there." Goldblatt shook his head and pinched his nose.

Armstrong glared at Hazard and Orange.

"One of you owes me an explanation and an apology."

"For what?" said Hazard.

"A marine under my command accidentally fired at the beast. He was disabled by an energy weapon. What kind of tricks are you keeping from me?"

"That was me," said Willys with pride. "Your guy shot Agent Orange."

Armstrong gave the boy a puzzled look. Then he smirked.

"You don't expect me to believe this kid has superpowers, do you?"

Hazard and Orange smiled.

"Oh, girls, they wanna have fu-un. Oh, girls just wanna have fun."

Orange looked at Pamela's phone.

"Another text from the Goobexes. It says, 'Thank you for your help. We have established a link with Gooby-ooby and his new pet. We will transport them to our ship.'"

"They will not!" Armstrong tried to grab the phone from Orange, but the big man held it up, out of the general's reach. "Give me that phone!"

Armstrong jumped up and made an unsuccessful second attempt to grab the phone. Orange put a hand on the general's chest and pushed him back.

"I appreciate your input, but I can't let you send the reply."

Armstrong was fighting mad.

"That animal is American property!"

"Let's tell them," said Orange. He lowered the phone and read as he typed. "Goobex 3 belongs with you, but his new pet belongs to the American people."

"Send it," Armstrong barked.

"If the aliens come for bigfoot, I can probly make 'em barf." Willys crossed his arms. He felt like he should be wearing a cape.

Mr. Wilson lifted his young son and held him.

"You need to take it easy with that, champ. I want to make sure it's safe for you."

"I hope they give me super speed," said Brad. "Then I can be a world champion video gamer and a superhero."

The phone buzzed again. Orange looked at it.

"The Goobexes say Pirate's Pet 3 is a sentient being, not a possession. If he belongs to you or your people, he is your slave, and Goobexes oppose all forms of slavery."

"If the bigfoot is sentient, it can make up its own mind," said General Hazard. "It should hear what the president has to offer."

Before Orange could type a single word, people started shouting inside the Hazmat tent. Sparks of blue energy raced in circles around the bigfoot and Goobex 3 who were glowing brighter and brighter. Several technicians left their hoses and instrument panels and headed for the nearest exit.

Finch recognized the intense blue light penetrating the walls of the tent.

"Oh no," he said to himself.

A half second later, the bigfoot and the alien vanished in a flash of light.

CHAPTER 23

Connivances and Contrivances (Part 2)

Agent Orange and the generals phoned the president on a secure line in a conference room.

"The Sasquatch and Goobex 3 are gone," Orange told him in a calm, cool voice.

"Where'd they go?"

"The aliens beamed them to their ship," said General Hazard.

"I knew we couldn't trust those conniving Goobexes," the president declared. "They're thieves and poachers. That's what they are!"

"I've checked with our people at the base. We still have their parrot," said General Finch.

"Why should I care about a parrot?" the bloated bureaucrat shouted. "There are millions of parrots!"

"They want it back," said Finch.

"Why? I don't get it." He paused to think. It didn't take long. "I still don't get it. At least the parrot is something to work with. If those thieving aliens contact you again, transfer them to my phone. I'm taking over. I'll be at the base in three hours. I'm organizing a rally outside their spaceship, and all of you better be there. I won't let them steal our bigfoot."

The pompous bully in chief hung up and called Admiral Mimsley.

*****

Willys sat on the edge of an examination table wearing only his Iron Man underwear.

Dr. Jackson had run an MRI and several tests on the boy before drawing some blood and sticking electrodes to his forehead and all over his body.

"All the baseline readings look normal," Baldino announced. "Now comes the moment of truth. Are you ready to use your power?"

"Sure," Willys answered.

Baldino pointed to a rabbit in a cage.

"Use it on the bunny."

Willys scowled.

"No."

"Why not?" asked Goldblatt, who had escorted the Wilsons and Edisons to Baldino's lab.

"The bunny didn't do nothin' to me. I don't wanna hurt it." Willys crossed his arms and pouted.

The child's display of scruples vexed Dr. Baldino.

"Do you like rats?" he asked.

"No!" Willys scrunched up his face.

Baldino motioned to Dr. Jackson who removed the rabbit and put a caged rat in its place.

Willys clenched his teeth and stretched his arms toward the rat, but nothing happened. After several attempts to stun the rat, the boy lowered his arms and frowned.

"It's not working."

"You yelled the other times," Violet told him. "Try yelling at it."

"I don't like rats!" the boy shouted.

The rat chewed on a food pellet, paying no attention to him.

"You're not trying hard enough," said Brad.

Violet looked her little brother in the eyes.

"You were really angry when you zapped Dr. Harrison. I think you need to get mad."

"But I'm not mad. Why should I be mad?"

Brad rolled his eyes.

"Because it might be the key to your power, stupid."

"I'm not stupid!" Willys glared at his brother.

"Don't yell at me. Yell at the rat!"

"I'm not mad at the rat. I'm mad at you."

Dr. Baldino rubbed his chin and looked at Mr. Wilson.

"Your son's abilities seem to have been temporary, simply a release of residual energy."

Mr. Wilson gave his son a concerned look.

"I'd like to believe that, but can't you run more tests just to be sure?"

"More tests won't help. If he still has powers, they've gone dormant."

Baldino busied himself putting equipment away, while Jackson removed the electrodes from Willys.

"Can I put my clothes on now?" the boy asked.

Brad smirked.

"No. You have to spend the rest of your life in your underpants."

"Shut up!" Willys snapped at him.

"Maybe you should try to zap your brother," Pamela suggested.

"Please don't encourage him," said Mr. Wilson.

"Get your clothes on, kid. We're meeting the president in a couple of hours." Goldblatt looked at his watch. "I'm starving. Is anyone else hungry?"

They all were.

The curly-haired agent led the way to the mess hall, which wasn't far from the lab.

There weren't many people in the hallways or the dining hall. Most of the soldiers who returned from the forest were providing security for the president's rally or helping put up bleachers and related structures.

Brad scanned the stainless-steel serving trays of food in the cafeteria-style eatery.

"Do we have to pay for this?"

"Uncle Sam's picking up the tab," said Goldblatt as he grabbed a plate and headed for the roast beef.

Brad was only a couple of steps behind him.

"I bet none of this stuff is organic." Pamela gave her parents a disapproving look.

Her mother handed her a plate and took one for herself.

"If it's good enough for the soldiers, it's good enough for us."

"I doubt we'll be repeat customers here anyway."

Mr. Edison plucked a plate from the stack, and they all headed for the salad bar.

Everybody got their food, and they sat down together at a long gray plastic table.

"Where are we meeting the president?" Violet asked Goldblatt.

"They've built a bandstand near the spaceship." The agent took a drink of soda and continued talking. "We're meeting him there. He's having a rally to protest the aliens stealing our Sasquatch."

"What makes it 'our' Sasquatch?" Pamela asked.

"It was born in the USA. That means it's ours," said Brad. "Just like the cows this meat came from." He took a big bite of rare roast beef. "Mmm, delicious."

"Ah, there you are," said Admiral Mimsley as he strutted into the room with Agent Orange and the generals.

"We have some things to talk over before the president arrives." General Hazard took a seat next to Mr. Edison.

"What sort of things?" Pamela's dad asked.

Finch sat next to Mrs. Edison. He had a very serious look on his face.

"You do know the Goobexes invited you to tour their ship, don't you?"

The fork full of mashed potatoes never made it to Mr. Wilson's mouth. He put it down on his plate and looked at the men taking seats around the table.

Mimsley sat across from him and smiled.

"Your president sees this as an opportunity for you to serve your country."

"We'd love to get a look inside that saucer," said Finch.

"You want us to spy on the Goobexes?" Pamela couldn't believe her ears.

"You won't be spying, just collecting intelligence," Finch answered.

"Dr. Harrison has already agreed to work with us," said Agent Orange. "He was also invited on the Goobex tour."

"A few threats and he cracked like a nut." General Armstrong smiled wickedly.

"What do you want us to do?" Brad's eyes were wide with excitement.

"Now hold on. We need to think this over," his dad cautioned.

"It won't be anything obvious." Hazard smiled. "You'll just need to wear some special clothing or jewelry."

Brad turned to face his father.

"We have to do it! It's our patriotic duty!"

"Yeah!" Willys agreed.

Violet had her doubts. She didn't think that spying on the aliens was smart or patriotic, but the opportunity to be a real reporter was too tempting to pass up.

"I'll do it, if my dad lets me."

"Girl, are you crazy?" Pamela dropped her fork on the table. "These people are willing to put our lives at risk in order to steal alien technology. Does that sound right to you?"

Mr. Wilson answered for her.

"If my children have the courage to do this, count me in."

"For Pete's sake, Wally." Mr. Edison shook his head.

"If you won't wear the equipment, you can't go on the Goobex tour," Hazard told Pamela's dad.

"The president would appreciate your help," Orange said in his calm, mellifluous voice.

Armstrong, who was sitting next to the agent, leaned in toward the Edisons.

"Know anyone who needs a presidential pardon?"

Mrs. Edison was exasperated.

"We are not going to spy on the aliens!"

"No one should." Pamela stared at her friend.

Violet stared right back.

"It's the story of a lifetime."

"One bad decision can make your life a lot shorter." Pamela turned her face away from Violet.

"Are we still going to meet the president?" Mr. Edison asked.

"No!" the generals and Mimsley answered together.

"He gave us very specific orders," said Orange.

Armstrong stood up.

"If you don't play ball, you get a subway ride to FBI HQ and a bus ticket home."

"Sounds good to me," said Mr. Edison. "Mind if we finish eating first?"

"I'll make the arrangements." Orange stood up next to Armstrong. "Agent Goldblatt will take you to the bus station."

The agent nearly choked on his food.

"I should be at the rally. You might need me."

Finch stood and looked at his watch.

"You might get back in time if you hurry."

Goldblatt wiped his mouth with a napkin and stood up.

"Come on. We've gotta go."

Pamela stood.

"The food here sucks, anyway."

Mr. and Mrs. Edison got up and left with their daughter and Goldblatt.

"I am so disappointed in them." Brad shook his head and took another bite of roast beef.

CHAPTER 24

The Rally

Dozens of people in lab coats poured into the mess hall with laptop computers and metal briefcases.

A tall middle-aged woman with short blond hair sat next to Violet. She had a brush in one hand and something resembling an aluminum lunch box in the other.

"Hello, Violet. I'm Dr. Cooper. I am going to put something in your hair, but first, I want you to put this on." She opened the lunch box and removed a pin featuring a cartoon bigfoot holding a trophy above the words "Hide-and-Seek World Champion."

Violet grinned and pinned it to her T-shirt.

"The pin has a tracking device in it," said Cooper. "We'll know where you are at all times, unless the saucer blocks the signal. That's valuable information in itself."

"Sure. Every detail counts. It's like journalism." Violet watched the scientists tweaking frequencies with their computers in the pursuit of maximum signal strength.

Dr. Cooper brushed Violet's hair back. She took two rectangular "USA" hair clips from her box. They were encrusted with red, white, and blue rhinestones.

"These record sound and radar images. If it gets quiet, I want you to start a conversation."

"I can do that."

Violet looked over at Willys as the clips were being placed in her hair.

A heavyset scientist wearing a tie-dyed T-shirt under his lab coat had removed the boy's shoes. He took a pair of black-and-white patent leather wingtips from his briefcase and held one up.

"This shoe measures radiation." Dr. Begler looked at his reflection on the shiny shoe and stopped to pick at something in his teeth with his pinky finger. "The other one keeps track of electromagnetic energy."

"They look stupid." Willys crossed his arms and pouted as Begler put the shoes on his feet. "Why can't you give me skate shoes with rockets in 'em?"

"Onngh Yanngh! If we had those, I wouldn't be here. I'd be king of the roller derby! Watch out! Here comes the unstoppable Uncle Sam! Yeah, I'd be all over that." Begler chuckled to himself as he tied the laces of Willys's wingtips.

A short but stocky gray-haired man wearing thick glasses sat across from Brad and his dad. He was the oldest scientist in the whole group. His name tag read "Sonny."

He took two bright-red "Make America Great Again" baseball caps out of his briefcase.

"This cap records high-definition video."

He handed the hat to Brad.

"Cool." Brad put it on and smiled.

Sonny offered the other hat to Mr. Wilson.

"Yours records thermal images."

"Repels Democrats too."

Mr. Wilson took the hat, looked at it, and shook his head before putting it on.

"Try to focus on what's in front of you. It works best if you don't look from side to side."

"Do we get guns?" Brad asked.

"No! Of course not. We want the aliens to trust you. We want them to think we trust them too."

Brad gave his dad a puzzled look.

Mr. Wilson shrugged his shoulders.

"What if they find out about our hats?" Brad asked.

Sonny's eyes darted back and forth between Brad and his dad. He hadn't anticipated being questioned, but he felt compelled to give an answer.

"You're not getting a gun!"

Agent Orange returned to the mess hall with an angry, handcuffed Dr. Harrison in his custody.

"You have no reason to treat me like this. I am not a criminal!"

"You're facing a pending charge of conspiring to violate the endangered species act, with an illegal alien." Orange nudged him forward.

A tall thin scientist named Dr. Heimler removed Harrison's glasses. He replaced them with thick black-framed spectacles.

"These lenses match your prescription. The frames register multispectral images."

"In other words, it's an adaptation of technology I developed for NASA." Harrison turned to Orange and held his hands out. "Can you please, at least, remove these?"

"No. The president insists that you remain shackled while you're on *his* base. He claims you're an alien shape-shifter."

Harrison lowered his arms.

"That's insane," he grumbled.

Orange put a reassuring hand on Harrison's shoulder.

"Fortunately, assessing the sanity of the president is not part of my job."

"We're good to go," Dr. Heimler told the big agent.

Orange turned to the Wilsons.

"Are you ready to face the Goobexes again?"

Mr. Wilson looked at each of his children. His chest swelled with pride as he saw the determination in their eyes.

"My family is ready for anything."

The Wilsons rose from the table as the scientists packed up their laptops.

Orange led them to a jeep parked outside the mess hall, and they piled in.

"Take us to the dock, pronto," he told the driver.

"Yes, sir."

The soldier adjusted his rearview mirror and revved the engine.

As they peeled out, their screeching tires echoed through the nearly deserted base. Almost everyone was at the rally providing security, performing special tasks, or acting as seat fillers. The president didn't want a single empty space.

The jeep squealed to a stop next to a scan pad. The driver stuck his arm out of the vehicle and put his thumb on it. The pad flashed blue and then green.

They were bathed in cool sunlight and the scent of pine as the big door in the wall lifted.

Brad turned to Agent Orange as they drove out onto the tree-lined gravel road.

"Can you teach me karate?"

"It would take years of practice."

"I'd rather have a gun." Brad looked down at his hands. "I mean, what if the Goobexes decide to make us their pets? I wanna be able to defend myself. Doesn't that make sense?"

Orange gave the boy a sympathetic look.

"Wanting the ability to defend yourself makes sense, but giving you a gun would not."

The jeep bounced over a fallen sapling, jostling the passengers.

"Whoa! This jeep sure is tough." Mr. Wilson looked at Willys, who was sitting on his lap glaring at his shoes. "Hey, buddy. Do you know who made the first jeeps?"

Brad and Violet both rolled their eyes. They had heard this question many times before.

"Willys–Overland Motors," their brother answered. "People say Willees, but it's really Willys like me."

"Hey, you remembered!" Mr. Wilson bounced his son on his knees.

"I hate these shoes," the boy grumbled.

The jeep soon rolled up to the dock where a patrol boat was waiting.

Orange got out and took a key from his pocket as the other passengers left the vehicle.

"Water looks choppy. I hope you don't get seasick." The big man uncuffed Dr. Harrison and nudged him toward the dock.

Brad and Willys raced to the boat. Brad had a clear advantage, but as they approached the dock, he let Willys surge ahead and win.

"No running on the boat," said Ensign Kroll, who gave each passenger a life vest and helped them climb aboard.

Brad put his vest on and helped Willys with his.

Willys stared at his shoes with a confused look in his eyes.

"These weird shoes must make me faster. I never beat you before."

"Those shoes aren't weird. They're awesome." Brad finished with his brother's vest and patted him on the back.

The boat's skipper, Captain Guettler, gave Orange an extra-large life vest.

"I'll drop you off near the bandstand," he said. "There's quite a crowd."

"Very fine people, I'm sure," Dr. Harrison sneered.

They pulled away from the dock and skipped over the roiling waters of the Columbia River. It was a bumpy ride. Water splashed all around the craft as it defied the river's current and headed upstream.

Despite the noise from the boat's motor, they heard music blaring before they could actually see the gathering of people. "Macho, macho man. I gotta be a macho man."

They rounded the edge of the island and the rally came into view. A huge four-story arc of bleachers had been set up. They were packed with spectators eager to see the president air his grievances with the Goobexes. Some of them wore military gear. Others wore T-shirts bearing racist slogans. One bearded young man wore buckskin pants, a horned helmet, no shirt, face paint, and a skunk skin cape. He waved an eight-foot spear in the air with a MAGA flag tied to it. This self-styled shaman used a megaphone to lead people in chanting, "Skunk ape's ours! Stop the steal! Skunk ape's ours! Stop the steal!"

On the ground level, concession stands capped each end of the big U-shaped structure. Enormous American flags hung on the walls above the booths selling "POTUS versus Aliens" merchandise, deep-fried foods and snacks loaded with sugar, smothered in artificial cheese sauce, or topped with syrups or condiments pumped from gallon-size plastic jugs. All proceeds went to the president's reelection campaign.

A two-hundred-foot-long bandstand had been built on the riverbank near the Goobex saucer. It was festooned with American flags and red, white, and blue bunting.

Governor Brown had just finished her speech about interplanetary cooperation.

There was scattered applause from the crowd, but it was soon drowned out by chants of the president's name.

Hundreds of people pressed against the short steel barricades separating them from the VIP and press area at the front of the stage.

Shouts of "Blue lives matter!" and "Save our troops!" rippled through the masses who ignored orders from the military police struggling to hold them back.

A cluster of reporters and cameramen waited for the president to appear onstage, while others focused on the congregation of rowdy Republicans.

The atmosphere was getting tense when the boat pulled up to a temporary floating dock set up behind the stage.

The passengers removed their vests, and Ensign Kroll helped them climb down to the dock, where General Hazard and two soldiers were waiting.

"The president asked me to take you to the stage and keep an eye on you-know-who."

"We all know who you're talking about," said Harrison. "You can say my name."

"I don't want to say your name." The general pointed to a hastily constructed wooden staircase. "Now haul your carcass up those stairs, and they'll show you where to sit."

Orange led the way, followed by the Wilsons, Dr. Harrison, and General Hazard.

Cameras focused on them as soon as they reached the stage. Two giant video screens presented them individually and as a group as they were escorted to their seats. The crowd cheered their arrival, but the cheers turned to boos when Dr. Harrison appeared on the screen. Chants of "Hang the doc!" swelled to a thunderous roar. Someone near the barricade waved a crude, handmade gibbet in the air with a peanut butter and jelly sandwich hanging from it.

"Very fine people indeed," Harrison said under his breath as he sat down.

Rudy Giuliani strutted onto the stage. Sweat dripped down his balding head and soaked his freshly dyed hair, resulting in an unsightly seepage of black liquid running down his cheeks and both sides of his neck. He went directly to the podium in the center of the stage and adjusted the microphone.

"The aliens in that ship want to steal our Sasquatch."

The crowd booed.

"Are we going to let them steal our Sasquatch?"

"No!" the crowd roared.

"Your president will fight like hell to save our Sasquatch. Are you willing to fight?"

The crowd exploded in shouts of "Yes!" "Hell, yes!" and "Fight like hell! Fight like hell!"

"The president is a reasonable man." Rudy pulled a handkerchief from his pocket and smeared the black stain on the left side of his face. "He's willing to negotiate with the aliens, but if they don't respect us, there's no deal and it's gonna be trial by combat!"

The spectators trumpeted their approval by echoing the phrase, "Trial by combat!"

All along the barricade soldiers called for reinforcements to hold back the mob.

"It's my pleasure to introduce the president of the United States!"

Rudy stepped down from the podium and crossed the stage to greet the commander in chief.

The president swaggered onstage, waving to the crowd. He shook Rudy's hand and proceeded to the podium.

"Well, thank you very much. This is incredible." He smiled and adjusted the microphone. "The media will not show the magnitude of this crowd. Even I, when I looked, I saw thousands of people here.

But you don't see the hundreds of thousands of people behind you in the woods because they don't want to show you that."

Violet looked out into the woods and saw only about a hundred people, mostly soldiers.

"I want the fake news media to recognize what's really happening out here because these people are not going to take it any longer," the president continued. "They came from all over the world and from all over our country. I've never seen anything like it. I just want to see how they cover this. The media is the biggest problem we have as far as I'm concerned, single biggest problem. The fake news and the big tech and maybe the aliens. I'm honest, and I just again want to thank you. It's a great honor to have this kind of crowd and to be before you and hundreds of thousands of American patriots in the woods who are committed to the honesty and integrity of our glorious republic.

"All of us here today do not want to see our Sasquatch stolen by emboldened radical-left aliens, which is what they're doing. We will never give up. We will never concede. It doesn't happen. You don't concede when there's theft involved. Our country has had enough! We will not take it anymore, and that's what this is all about. We will stop the steal! And by the way, does anybody believe the Sasquatch chose to go with the aliens? Does anybody believe that? They're using mind control. His vote was rigged. It's a disgrace! There's never been anything like this."

The crowd applauded and chanted, "Fight! Fight! Fight!"

"If the aliens do the right thing, we win bigfoot's vote. They call it Sasquatch, but I call it bigfoot, and he was defrauded. All they have to do is let bigfoot rectify his vote and he stays with us and you are the happiest people. In the history of this country, we've never seen an election so corrupt. One person, one vote, right? Well, there was only one vote, and the Goobexes told bigfoot who to vote for. What does he know about voting? He doesn't know. You can go all the way back, and you'll never see an election so corrupt. The aliens need to know that America is blessed with elections. All over the world, they talk about our elections. Now the world says the aliens decide if we have free and fair elections."

The angry spectators booed with all their might.

"All we're asking for is to rectify the Sasquatch vote. If bigfoot votes to stay on planet Earth, that will make me so happy. Will that make you happy?"

The crowd erupted with cheers and applause.

"And if bigfoot wants to go with the aliens, that's fine, but we need to get something in return. We deserve compensation. It's not like there's a million of these creatures running all over the place. Bigfoot is a valuable natural resource. There's no telling how much damage stealing just one from the forest will cause the rest of the bigfeet. They call them Sasquatches, but I call them bigfeet. I hope the aliens are listening. If they're watching the fake news, they're probably not seeing any of this. You can bet on that."

Violet cringed as the crowd booed and chanted, "Fake news! Fake news! Fake news!"

The president smiled, waved, and pointed at people in the crowd.

"And we fight. We fight like hell. And if you don't fight like hell, you're not going to have a country anymore. The aliens need to pay a price for stealing our bigfoot. It's a big price! I mean really big. I hope they can hear me. I hope they see this enormous crowd. It shows that we have truth and justice on our side. We have a deep and enduring love for America in our hearts. We love our country. And we will stop the steal! Stop the steal! Stop the steal!"

The crowd picked up the chant. It shook the ground and echoed through the bleachers.

Soldiers were forced to use truncheons and pepper spray in an attempt to keep spectators from breaching the barricades.

A few responded by spraying the soldiers with bear spray.

Others joined forces to wrestle truncheons, helmets, and tactical gear away from the embattled perimeter guards.

It looked like a bloodbath was inevitable when the crowd was illuminated by a flashing green light. It came from the spaceship's dome. As the light grew brighter, it distracted the frenzied mob. By the time the light changed to blue and then yellow, everyone was watching. The crowd gasped as the colors cycled faster and faster. The light turned red and grew brighter still!

There was a blinding flash and a long rectangular strip of metal melted away from the ship, forming a ramp that ended onstage, next to the podium.

Dozens of cameras were trained on the narrow opening in the saucer caused by the ramp's creation.

"Something's coming out of the spaceship," one reporter said into her microphone. "It's one of those little black boxes."

"The crowd seems to have quieted down for the moment," her partner said as he searched his pocket for something to wipe his sweaty brow.

The box rolled down the ramp and stopped six yards from the podium. A familiar T-shaped metallic gadget sprouted from it. It produced a loud, baritone, robotic voice.

"Greetings, Mr. President of the United States of planet Earth. We apologize for any trouble we have caused. We will gladly negotiate with you regarding the future of Pirate's Pet 3. Do you accept?"

A smug smile spread across the president's artificially tanned face.

"Yes. Of course, I accept! I'll negotiate with you anytime anywhere."

"Agreed. You may join the humans invited to tour our ship. We will discuss the future of Pirate's Pet 3 there. Please, follow our robo-box."

The device rolled about six feet up the ramp and stopped.

The president signaled for the Wilsons and Dr. Harrison to be brought to the podium. Then he pointed to the crowd and spoke into the microphone.

"I'm going to walk up that ramp, and I love that ramp between us and the Goobexes. I'm going into that spaceship with the kind of pride and boldness and love of America that we need to take back our bigfoot! I'm not just president of the United States. I am king of the deal!"

The president winked and waved to the crowd as he strode to the robo-box.

Two Secret Service agents escorted the Wilsons and Dr. Harrison to the president's side.

"These are my bodyguards. I want them to come with me," said the arrogant aristocrat.

A green light flashed from the bottom of the box, and it resumed its ascent of the ramp.

Brad scowled as they walked up the ramp. He felt the sting of deep hypocrisy. He was defenseless, while the Secret Service agents got to bring their guns.

CHAPTER 25

King of the Deal

Pirate's Pet 3 greeted them when they reached the top of the ramp.

Gooby-ooby stood proudly on his shoulder. He had removed his eye patch, revealing a bright-green twin to his big blue eye. His pistol was holstered on his left side, and his little sword was sheathed on his right.

"Goobex 3 is excited to show you our home," said the deodorized bigfoot. "I have my own hot spring and grotto."

"I can give you a thousand grottoes," the president boasted.

The shaggy half man stared at him.

"Will you protect me from men with guns?"

The vainglorious head of state returned the creature's stare.

"Of course, I will. If you stay with me, I'll protect you like you wouldn't believe."

The Sasquatch bared his teeth and growled softly.

Gooby-ooby tapped his little sword against his pet's helmet, and the Sasquatch regained his composure. He snorted and spoke in a gruff voice.

"Follow me."

The bigfoot set a pace that challenged even the adults.

They hustled through a long, spiral corridor full of odd machinery and doorways of different shapes and sizes.

Brad remembered being told his hat worked best if he looked straight ahead, but looking straight ahead was totally unnatural.

Willys puzzled over why his new super shoes failed to help him keep up with the others. He had to race at his father's side while his dad held his hand tightly.

Mr. Wilson was tempted to pick his son up and carry him, but he was afraid it might interfere with whatever the shoes were supposed to do.

The floor seemed to absorb the sound of their footsteps, and the speed of their trek through the long hallway made conversation difficult.

The only sound was the huffing and puffing of people struggling to keep up.

Violet took a deep breath and looked up at the alien on the bigfoot's shoulder.

"Where's Pirate's Pet 2?" she blurted out.

The Sasquatch slowed slightly.

"She is on her nest. Pirate's Pet 1 is over three hundred years old, but he will soon be a father."

"Astounding," Dr. Harrison said to himself. "I hope you know how much I respect your people and their remarkable technology."

"This isn't remarkable," the bigfoot said, humbly. "This craft was used for nearly a thousand Earth years before the Goobexes acquired it."

"We're negotiating on a used spaceship? I can't believe this. Where's the respect?"

The president was getting tired. He squeezed one of his guards by the shoulder.

"Can we slow down?" the guard said. "You're tough to keep up with."

The bigfoot stopped.

"Certainly. I will take smaller steps."

He shuffled forward very slowly.

The president gave both his guards an annoyed look. He motioned to one of them and pointed at the Sasquatch.

The guard cautiously stepped up to the bigfoot and put his hand in the middle of its hairy back.

"Can you walk, maybe half your normal speed?"

The Sasquatch snarled softly and looked down at him.

The guard took a step backward. He instinctively threw his arms back to shield his boss.

Pirate's Pet 3 leaned down and spoke close to his face. The creature's fur no longer stank, but its breath had the odor of rotting fish guts.

"I'll do my best to set a pace more comfortable for you and your friends."

The wide-eyed guard coughed into his hands the instant the Sasquatch turned away. He had to be nudged forward when their parade through the ship continued.

"Are there any more Goobexes on this crate?" The president's eyes darted all around the hall.

"No. Just Gooby-ooby and his parental units."

"Good. We only have to deal with three of 'em."

"What's that?" Willys pointed at a glass wall. It was the flat face of a huge hemisphere containing blue liquid and orbs of various colors that drifted up and down, bumping into each other and sometimes merging into larger orbs.

The Sasquatch stopped and gazed at the wall.

"The Goobexes call it a lava lamp. I love it."

Brad's hat was starting to feel warm. He wiped the sweat from his forehead.

"I love playing video games. Do you know what they are?"

Pirate's Pet 3 looked down at the boy.

"The Goobexes know all about your video games. The ways sentient creatures entertain themselves can be very revealing."

The petulant potentate pointed at Gooby-ooby.

"I hope you don't buy all the garbage those Hollywood, liberal, big tech, video game, fake news people shovel out."

"The Goobexes are not fans of Hollywood films, and Gooby-ooby prefers adaptive holographic adventures to your video games."

"Good," the president said with a little swagger.

There was a metal door at the end of the hallway. It lifted into the ceiling when they approached it.

"This will take us to the Goobexes," said Pirate's Pet 3.

They entered a cylindrical shaft that rose hundreds of feet to the top of the saucer.

"This ship is awfully large for just the three of you," Dr. Harrison said as he looked up at the multitude of doorways, marking the different levels of the ship.

"The Goobexes often transport delegations from other galaxies to Goobex Prime. They need a large vessel."

The words had barely left the bigfoot's mouth when they were all embraced by a broad beam of light from above. It felt like the air around them had thickened into a liquid.

They floated up off the floor.

Brad tried to speak, but it was like trying to talk under water. He could barely hear himself say, "Whoa!"

When they reached the middle of the shaft, the air below their feet crystalized into a glass-like substance. The light faded, and they found themselves standing on a transparent floor.

A door in the shaft opened into another spiral hallway.

"Almost there," said Pirate's Pet 3 as he walked to the door.

They followed the Sasquatch to a nearby room, and it announced, "This is the central nexus."

A large round table sprouted from the floor the instant Pirate's Pet 3 entered the room. One Sasquatch-sized and eight human-sized swivel chairs grew out of the floor next.

The Goobexes were observing and telekinetically operating a wide variety of monitors and control panels from their egg-shaped flying pods. They were three times the size of Gooby-ooby but far from the ten-foot-tall holographs the Wilsons had seen earlier.

The aliens flew over to the table, and Goobex 1's pod spoke in a deep voice.

"Please be seated. We will come to terms first and conduct your tour later."

The president took a seat next to the bigfoot.

His guards sat next to him.

"I don't know why you let that Draculoid jelly sucker onto your ship." The ridiculous leader of the Republicans pointed at Dr. Harrison.

"There is no such thing as a Draculoid." The robotic voice produced by Goobex 2's pod was feminine and gentle.

"That's not what the *Enquirer* says."

Pirate's Pet 3 sniffed the president's head.

"The doctor is as human as you. You all smell alike."

"Okay, big guy. If that's what you say." He looked at his guards. "One thing I learned in television, you never argue with the star, and this guy, he's a star."

The guards nodded in agreement.

The president swiveled his chair to face the Sasquatch.

"You know, these alien sandwiches can give you a grotto on a spaceship, but I can offer you more, much more. You can have mansions and limousines, hot tubs and forest chalets, as much as you can eat, any food you like. In fact, if there's anything you want, I'll make sure you get it. You want a female bigfoot? I'll set up a reality show on TV, and we'll find your perfect mate. We'll make tons of money doing it. You'll be the most famous couple on the planet!"

Pirate's Pet 3 looked down at him with sad eyes.

"You cannot buy love or friendship."

"Friendship? People are crazy about you. They love you, and it's going to get even better. When you have money, everyone wants to be your friend, and believe me, you are going to make truckloads of money. I mean it! Boatloads!" The president put his hand on the bigfoot's knee. "Stick with me and you'll be rich beyond your wildest dreams. You'll be so happy. I'll be happy. The whole planet will be happy."

Pirate's Pet 3 took a deep breath and let it out.

"You asked for a revote. I am ready," said the Sasquatch.

"Not with that thing on your head." The angry orange politician pounded his fists on the table and pointed at the Goobexes. "You're brainwashing him!"

"I cannot speak without my helmet."

"I can't trust the words you say when you wear it."

The bigfoot glared at the president menacingly until Goobyooby once again tapped on his helmet with his little sword.

The little alien offered a solution telepathically.

"I will remove my helmet and clap for the Goobexes or stomp my feet to stay with the humans."

"No deal. I want you to clap for us humans," said the president.

Pirate's Pet 3 snarled softly as he stared at him.

"Agreed." He removed his silvery helmet.

The Sasquatch was no longer connected to the thoughts of Gooby-ooby. He was momentarily disoriented.

"Clap your hands to stay with us on Mother Earth. We'll take care of you." The conniving chief executive nodded and clapped his hands as if trying to entertain an infant. He turned and glared at his guards. "Clap your hands and smile." He turned back to the bigfoot, grinning and clapping. "Clap your hands. You'll be the happiest bigfoot ever and the richest. Come on. You can do it."

Pirate's Pet 3 looked at the chubby, orange-haired man and stomped his foot.

"He didn't mean that. It was just a nervous tic. Come on, friend, clap your hands." The president smiled and clapped his hands up in the air near the bigfoot.

Pirate's Pet 3 stomped his other foot. He stomped both feet again and again, at least seven times before he put his helmet back on.

"The Goobexes are my friends! I vote to go with them."

The president shook his head and swiveled his chair to face the aliens.

"Well, that is going to cost you. Creatures like this are very rare. I can't let you snatch endangered species out of our forests without paying for them."

Goobex 1 flew closer to the president.

"We will negotiate a fee, but first, you must release Pirate's Pet 1 as a sign of good faith."

The president leaned closer to Goobex 1.

"You've gotta give something to get something. So what are you willing to give?"

"What are you asking for?" asked Goobex 2 through her pod.

"Hmm." The self-satisfied leader of the USA leaned back in his chair. "Why don't we start with a personal force field. In fact, I want the tech to make force fields for myself and all my people."

"Done," said Goobex 1.

The president gave his guards a double thumbs-up sign. One of them pulled out a walkie-talkie and spoke into it.

"This is Agent Cole. Do you read me?"

The radio crackled to life, and a staticky voice answered.

"We read you loud and clear."

"Eagle One has authorized the release of the big blue bird."

"Roger that," said the voice on the radio. "I'll send word to the base."

"Let's not wait for the parrot. I don't know why you care so much about it anyway." Eagle One pointed at Pirate's Pet 3. "This guy's worth a million parrots. I'm not gonna let him go for a lousy force field. You'll have to pony up a lot more than that."

"Are you serious?" asked Dr. Harrison.

The president swiveled toward Harrison with daggers in his eyes.

"Yes, I'm serious, so shut up! You're not part of this negotiation!" He turned to face the Goobexes. "I want him out of here now!"

"But he is our guest," said Goobex 2.

"This is unanticipated," Goobex 1 chimed in. "We've been told this human is our friend."

Pirate's Pet 3 stood, and Goobex 3 spoke through him.

"He is our friend. We will take him and the other humans to see our ship while you haggle."

The president looked up at the powerful creature. "Thanks, big guy. I appreciate that. Man, I wish you were staying with us. I could use a…a helper like you." He smiled.

The bigfoot shared a mental link with Goobex 3, and the Goobexes could not help reading the hateful honcho's thoughts. Cartoonish images of a Sasquatch tearing the limbs off people he considered rivals or enemies scrolled through the creature's head.

"I will never be your helper."

Gooby-ooby raised his arms signaling his guests to stand.

Dr. Harrison rose from his swivel chair, which immediately melted back into the floor.

"Whoa! That's way cool." Brad jumped off his chair and watched it melt.

"Way cool," Willys echoed.

He stood, along with his dad and his sister.

They all watched their chairs melt away.

"Not bad for a used spaceship," said Mr. Wilson.

Goobex 3 pointed to the door.

"Please follow me." The Sasquatch turned and walked through the doorway with the Wilsons and Dr. Harrison keeping pace.

There was no door to close behind them, but the walls flowed together and the opening vanished.

The president looked at his guards and nodded.

"Way cool. But you know what's cooler?" He swiveled to face his alien hosts. "Antigravity!"

"That technology can be very dangerous in the wrong hands," said Goobex 2.

"The United States is the right hands. We stand for truth and justice. We would only use it to build walls and maybe to help Space Force get into space."

"We are not authorized to give you this technology. It could be used to destroy entire cities," said Goobex 1.

"I'm not going to destroy any cities. I'm a builder. What do you think? I'm crazy? I'm not crazy." The president turned to his guards. "Do I look crazy to you?"

"No, sir," both guards answered and shook their heads.

"See, I'm not crazy. That bigfoot is a rare and precious commodity. We need to get something for it."

"It is a sentient being," Goobex 2 replied.

"It's still rare and precious. You can't expect to get it for nothing, and I want antigravity."

"My mate and I need to confer," said Goobex 2.

"Sure, go ahead." The president gestured with one hand and swiveled to face his guards. "So what else do you think I should ask for? Maybe they can give me something to sweep the forests so California won't have another fire season like it had in 2018."

The guards nodded their approval of the idea.

"Nah. I should ask for something bigger. Screw the forest."

The president swiveled to face the Goobexes.

They were having a heated telepathic discussion. The jellylike substance that pulsed at the sides of their bready skin was glowing. It shifted about and little ripples crossed its surface.

"Can we get going here? Being president is a tough job. I'm a very busy man."

The Goobexes did not respond.

The president swiveled to face his guards.

"Are you hungry? I'm getting hungry." He swiveled back toward the aliens. "So what are you waiting for? Pirate's Pet 4 to hatch?"

"We will give you an antigravity device to examine," said Goobex 1.

"Now we're getting somewhere." The shady aristocrat smiled and rubbed his hands together. "I understand you can travel to other galaxies. That's amazing. I wish my people could do that."

"If you would like to visit other galaxies, we can take you," Goobex 2 answered without hesitation. "However, giving your people the ability to do so is forbidden."

"Forbidden by who?"

"By the highest authority in my galaxy," Goobex 1 answered loudly.

"Okay! Fine!" The president held his hands up in surrender and leaned back, away from the Goobexes. "We'll figure out space travel on our own, but you still have to throw in something to sweeten the deal. That bigfoot is extremely valuable. I can't let it go for force fields and antigravity."

"What more do you want?" asked Goobex 2.

"Let's see." The president knit his brows and rubbed his chin. "Can you turn things into gold?"

"No," said Goobex 1.

"How about silver?"

"No," said Goobex 2.

A three-foot-wide circular hole opened up in the wall where the door had been. One of the guards saw this and stood with his hand on his gun, prepared to draw.

Pirate's Pet 1 flew through the hole and circled the room. He squawked and then spoke in the president's voice.

"If we find Ooby-gooby, his folks will owe me bigly, right?"

"I never said that!" The president pounded his fists on the table.

The versatile piece of furniture produced a T-shaped perch, and the parrot landed on it.

"I'm relieved to be home. I was afraid I'd miss the hatching of my chicks."

The president pointed at the parrot. "Don't blame me for that. We didn't know you were expecting. How could we? I didn't know. Congratulations, by the way."

Pirate's Pet 1 tilted his head to the left and examined the president's face. Then he tilted his head to the right and continued, as if the change in perspective made a difference.

"The Goobexes are weary of negotiating," the big bird said. "They will grant one more request."

"Well." The president rubbed his chin again. "That little kid got a superpower. He can make people vomit."

"The undigester had an unexpected effect on him." Pirate's Pet 1 paced on his perch. "Do you want to share his abilities?"

"No, but I want a superpower," said the president. "Can you give me super strength?"

"No," the bird answered.

"Super speed?"

"No."

"I don't need to be invulnerable if I have a force field." The president smiled. "How about invisibility. I think I'd like that. Yeah, I would like that. Can you do that for me?"

"The Goobexes can do that." The big blue parrot bobbed his head up and down several times and then stood very straight. "They will make your clothes invisible," he squawked.

The president fingered his lapel.

"So my clothes will turn invisible, and since I'm wearing them, I'll be invisible too. Right?"

Pirate's Pet 1 hopped off his perch and strolled up to him.

"Your clothes will become invisible at your command."

The president looked puzzled.

"So I say a secret code word and my clothes will turn me invisible?"

"Your clothes will become invisible, yes," Goobex 1 answered.

"Code words are the preferred method," said Goobex 2.

"Great!" The president grinned at his guards. "I want my code word to be 'God bless America.' When I say those words, boom, I've got the suit of invisibility." His expression soured. "Hey, what about my head?"

"We will give you a hat to turn your head invisible," Goobex 1 told him.

"Perfect. Make it a MAGA hat. It's the only kind I wear."

"I'm sorry. We only have the template for one style of hat," said Goobex 2.

"Do we have a deal?" Pirate's Pet 1 asked.

"Sure. Why not?"

The president stuck his hand out toward the parrot.

When he realized the bird could not shake his hand, he extended it toward the Goobexes, who had no arms or legs.

He put his hand down and said, "You Goobexes drive a hard bargain, but I think this worked out for both of us."

The aliens flew back to the ship's controls.

Pirate's Pet 1 hopped back onto his perch.

"The Goobexes must prepare for their departure. They have much work to do."

The president crossed his arms and scowled.

"Well, I'm not leaving till I get my force field, antigravity device, and magic hat."

"Those things are on their way."

The parrot turned its back to the president and began grooming his feathers.

"Good." The president looked at his watch. "I might still get in a round of golf."

The tabletop near him began to bubble. He backed away from it, and his guards both stood.

Agent Cole drew his gun and pointed it at a bubble that kept growing larger and larger.

"What's this?" the orange-skinned oaf shouted.

Pirate's Pet 1 turned his head around to look at the president and the bubble.

"Your gifts are growing inside it."

The bubble grew to nearly three feet in diameter, then melted away.

Inside were a large sombrero, a duplicate of Gooby-ooby's little wooden sword, and a shiny silver disk.

"What the hell is this?" The president scowled.

"Those items contain the technology agreed upon and more. Is there anything else you want?" asked the parrot.

"Well." He thought about it for a few seconds before addressing the aliens. "If you ever want to, you know, take a vacation, you're welcome to stay at any of my resort hotels. You'll be my personal guests."

A bright-blue light encompassed the president and his guards. Sparks of energy raced in spirals around them. They seemed frozen in space and time and then they were gone.

CHAPTER 26

The End?

The Goobex ship projected a blue light onto the stage. The leader of the United States and his guards materialized within it.

The heavyset head of state held the alien sombrero in one hand and the tiny wooden sword and silver disk in the other. He smiled at his guards and strode to the podium to address the crowd.

"The Goobexes have refused to release our bigfoot."

The crowd booed.

"They were supposed to give me force fields and antigravity, but all I got was this!"

He held up the sombrero and the other alien gifts.

The items were shown up close on the giant video screens.

His supporters hurled threats at the Goobex ship.

"It's up to us to confront this egregious assault on our democracy. Because we'll never take back our bigfoot with weakness. You have to show strength, and you have to be strong. We demand that the aliens do the right thing."

The crowd repeatedly shouted the president's name.

He held up his right hand to quiet them.

"I fought like hell for our bigfoot, but those aliens knew exactly what they were doing. They're ruthless, and it's time that somebody did something about it. Sure, they let the creature vote, but it was hypnotized! If it wasn't, it would understand everything we can offer and that would be enough to give us a big, beautiful victory. Make no mistake, the bigfoot's vote was stolen from you, from me, and from our country."

The booing was soon supplanted by chants of "Toast the sandwiches!"

"We will not be intimidated into accepting the hoaxes and lies the Goobexes are trying to force us to believe. And fraud breaks up everything, doesn't it? When you catch somebody in a fraud, you're allowed to go by very different rules. We must ensure that such outrageous fraud never happens again."

The applause and shouting was nearly deafening. The president waved and pointed at his followers as he waited for them to quiet down.

"Despite everything we've been through, looking out all over this country and seeing fantastic crowds. Although this, I think, is our all-time record. I think you have 250,000 people. Two hundred fifty thousand! Looking out at all the amazing patriots here today, I have never been more confident in our nation's future. And after this, we're going to walk up that ramp." The president pointed to the narrow ramp leading up to the Goobex ship.

"I know that everyone here will soon be marching up that ramp to peacefully and patriotically make your voices heard. As this enormous crowd shows, we have truth and justice on our side. We have a deep and enduring love for America in our hearts. We love our country and our bigfoot. We have overwhelming pride in this great country, and we have it deep in our souls. Together, we are determined to defend and preserve government of the people, by the people, and for the people, and that includes bigfeet. And we fight. We fight like hell. And if you don't fight like hell, you're not going to have a country anymore. The aliens will come back and take everything.

"And I say this despite all that's happened. The best is yet to come. So we're going to walk up that ramp and stop the steal. And I'll be right there with you. So let's walk up that ramp together.

"Thank you all for being here. This is incredible."

The president smiled at his guards and winked.

"God bless you and God bless America."

With those words, his suit vanished.

The crowd gasped to see his corpulent body clad only in shoes, socks, red tie, and boxer shorts printed with fake $1,000 bills with his face on them.

He smiled, unaware of his appearance. The overconfident oaf put on the sombrero and his head vanished.

Several people in the crowd fainted. Others shrieked in horror.

A murmur spread through the crowd, inflaming the anger of everyone who heard it. "The aliens did this. They murdered the president! The aliens murdered the president!"

The angry throng burst through the barricades and headed for the stage.

Agent Cole rushed to the president and grabbed him by his arm.

"We have to get out of here, sir."

The president resisted.

"Why? This is going beautifully. I want to see this."

"It's too dangerous," Cole warned.

"No, it isn't. I'm invisible."

Cole shook his head. He took his coat off and offered it to the commander in chief.

"Your head is invisible, sir, and your suit."

The president looked down at his body. He grabbed the coat and struggled to put it on over his invisible clothing as Cole led him backstage, away from the rampaging horde.

"Those freaking sandwiches are going to pay for this! God bless America. God bless America!" The code word did not work in reverse.

When they reached the backstage area, the president removed his sombrero and stomped on it.

The riotous crowd stormed past the soldiers and security guards. They climbed onto the stage and rushed up the ramp to the Goobex ship. The lucky ones fell into the river on the way.

When the rioters reached the ship's entrance, they encountered a protective force field. There was nowhere for the people in front to go. They could get crushed by the mob or go down into the chilly water below. Yet the impassioned mass of the president's supporters advanced like lemmings, determined to have their revenge on the aliens.

"Thank God you're alive," Admiral Mimsley said when he saw the president with his head in place.

"Once I get out of here, we're hitting that spaceship with our hammers," the vindictive narcissist snarled.

Mimsley blinked several times and took a half step backward.

"But all those people on the ramp."

"What about 'em? No one cares about them. They're losers and suckers. We'll say the aliens did it."

"The children are still on the ship!" The admiral gave him an angry glare.

"So what? They'll be remembered as American martyrs! I hate losing the bigfoot. It's worth a fortune, but it's a traitor to our planet. Besides, we can't let aliens humiliate the president of the United States. What kind of message would that send?"

Mimsley puffed his chest out and stood straight and tall.

"I cannot condone the use of our weapon against American citizens."

"Fine." The president grabbed a walkie-talkie from one of Mimsley's men. "I'll do it myself." He turned to Cole. "Get me out of here."

His guards ushered him through the crush of people to the floating dock behind the stage.

Several boats were engaged in rescuing people from the river, but one was waiting for the commander in chief and his guests. Two soldiers guarding the vessel were detaining a man whose face was completely smeared with a black substance, until they realized it was Rudy Giuliani.

Mimsley followed the president and his guards as they approached the boat.

"There must be another way. Call off the crowd. Then we'll attack."

"It's too late for that." The shameless bully climbed onto the boat with a hand from his guards.

Mimsley tried to follow him, but the president held his hand up to block him.

"No. No. No. I don't reward disloyalty. You are staying here."

The blood drained from the admiral's face.

Cole untied the boat and climbed aboard.

"Get us out of here!" the president yelled.

The boat pulled away from the dock, nearly hitting several people struggling to swim to shore.

Mimsley turned to one of his men.

"Get me to a vehicle. We need to get as far from this place as possible."

The admiral and his men struggled against the masses pouring onto the bandstand.

They were getting nowhere until Agent Orange made his way to them.

"Admiral!" Orange put his hand on Mimsley's shoulder. "Looks like you could use some help."

"Only if you can get us out of here!"

Orange's height allowed him to see over the crowd. He quickly determined where the nearest exit was. He bent down slightly to speak to Mimsley and his men.

"Follow me."

Orange plowed his way through the sea of humanity. Mimsley and his men followed, but even with the powerful agent leading the way, it took over ten minutes to reach the concession stands.

By then, the president was halfway to the base and he issued the order, "Fire up the hammers and crush those aliens!"

The giant American flags hanging above the stands fell to the ground, revealing two enormous arrays of sound cannons. They dwarfed the one that had been hidden in the ice cream truck. Mimsley had been hard at work supervising their construction, while the generals searched for Dr. Harrison and Goobex 3.

"Oh no," he murmured.

Behind him, unnoticed by the people crushing each other to reach the ramp, a little flying saucer flew out of the top of the Goobex ship.

The "hammers" unleashed an unthinkable barrage of sonic energy, but the little spaceship blocked the attack.

The mountain-crushing waves of sound were deflected far up into the air, which began to shimmer and shake. The atomic integrity of everything in the path of the sound tsunami was weakened creating a cascade effect.

Hundreds of feet above the makeshift stadium the fabric of space-time was torn asunder. A shimmering crack appeared in the sky.

On the other side, in roughly eighty-two million BC, a hungry pterosaur peered through the strange hole in the air and spotted a large gathering of tasty-looking mammals. It flew toward the rift, anxious to feast.

Agent Orange scanned the area around him and saw the skunk shaman's spear abandoned on the ground. He lifted it and tore off the MAGA flag.

"I'll try to take out the power," he told Mimsley.

Orange made his way to the concession stand and slid inside over the counter. The plainclothes agents manning the booth stepped aside and let him pass.

He hoped to find a single power line to pierce, but the device was riddled with them, twisting in and out of it. The big agent followed the many power chords to a common point, the generator. It was over seventy-five yards away.

Orange took careful aim and hurled the spear. The long iron shaft flew across the field more like a bullet than an arrow. It sank into the power plant, which immediately produced a shower of sparks. Smoke billowed out of it, and a series of explosions rocked the machine. It burst into flames.

Orange had succeeded in taking out one of the two super weapons, but the other was not affected.

The rift in the sky shrank, but the flying dinosaur had nearly reached it.

The dome of the little flying saucer melted away, and Goobyooby jumped out in full pirate regalia. He fired his little pistol at the prehistoric creature.

It dodged the blast and was forced to circle back for another attempt.

Gooby-ooby aimed his gun at the remaining sonic weapon and fired.

The "hammer" grew white hot. Within twenty seconds, it was melting into an amorphous lump.

The pterosaur's head emerged from the rift just before it closed, resulting in instant decapitation. The creature's cranium fell into the bleachers and bounced over the seats.

More people fainted.

"Thank God," said Admiral Mimsley.

Gooby-ooby doffed his pirate hat and took a bow.

The saucer's dome rematerialized, and the little craft returned to the Goobex ship.

*****

The Wilsons and Dr. Harrison watched in horror as the aliens monitored the chaos outside their ship.

The telepathic Goobexes were prepared for the sonic weapons, but they were also disappointed that the humans chose to use them.

"Your leader did this," said Pirate's Pet 3. "He is a maniac!"

"I didn't vote for him." Mr. Wilson removed his MAGA hat and threw it on the floor.

"No, you didn't," said Goobex 1 through his pod. "Many humans are peaceful, but they often follow selfish, corrupt, power-hungry demagogues."

Dr. Harrison shook his head and put his glasses in a shirt pocket.

"It's a tale as old as time."

"Yes." Goobex 2's pod flew closer to the doctor. "It is a recurring story that threatens the very existence of your species."

"When can I take these shoes off?" Willys asked his dad. "They're squishin' my feet."

"I'm not sure," his dad mumbled.

"They're just shoes," said Pirate's Pet 1. "Your spy equipment has been neutralized."

"Good." Brad took his cap off and tossed it on the floor. "I was afraid that stinkin' hat would electrocute me."

"I was worried about these things causing brain cancer." Violet took the USA pins out of her hair and laid them on the big round table.

Willys was struggling with the laces of his right shoe when a hole opened in the wall and a familiar little saucer flew in.

It landed on the table, and Gooby-ooby stepped out.

Willys forgot about his shoe and gawked at the little alien with admiration.

"I'm so glad you're safe." Pirate's Pet 3 held his hand out.

Gooby-ooby climbed up the Sasquatch's arm and onto its shoulder.

"We are terribly sorry for the trouble our offspring has caused," said Goobex 2.

Dr. Harrison smiled at Gooby-ooby.

"Goobex 3 has been less troublesome than my fellow humans. Besides, he risked his life to save us from our own weapons."

"That is irrelevant." Goobex 1 flew to his son. "You must promise to never again leave this ship without our knowledge and permission."

"He just wanted a new friend," Pirate's Pet 3 spoke in a strangely gentle voice. "You didn't give him time."

Goobex 2 joined her spouse, hovering inches from Gooby-ooby.

"There is no excuse. You have compromised our mission."

"What mission?" Violet asked.

"You don't have to tell us," Dr. Harrison advised them.

"There is nothing for us to hide," said Goobex 1.

"Good, I'd like to know why aliens keep coming to planet Earth." Brad was keen to fill in the blanks left by ancient alien theories.

"We are here to observe your progress," Goobex 2 told them.

Pirate's Pet 1 hopped off his perch and strutted across the table.

"Goobexes have been visiting our planet for thousands of years, once every century. They hope that one day, earthlings will be ready to join the Intergalactic Alliance of Nonviolent Sentients."

"My people are hardly nonviolent," said Harrison.

"Any real newspaper will confirm that," Violet agreed.

"It is the sad truth," said Goobex 2. "Until the human race learns to settle disputes and distribute resources without resorting to violence, you will not be allowed to join the vast intergalactic community of sentient beings."

"Due to the violent nature of your people, we must ensure that our technology is not put to ill use." Goobex 1 flew back to his place near the saucer's controls.

Vibrations shook the ship, and the ramp outside melted back into the dome. The people attempting to lay siege to the craft were dumped into the river below as the enormous disk began flipping.

"For everyone's sake, no one on Earth can be allowed to remember our visit. We must engage our fail-safe device." Goobex 2 flew to her partner's side.

The vibrations grew stronger.

The saucer rose through the clouds. Soon, it was orbiting planet Earth.

"Should I try to make 'em barf?" Willys asked.

Dr. Harrison put a hand on his shoulder.

"No. The Goobexes are right. Our people aren't ready for them or their technology."

Mr. Wilson knelt down so he could speak to his son eye to eye.

"The doctor has a good point. It's better if no one remembers this, especially if your powers come back."

Pirate's Pet 1 hopped over to them.

"Your son's abilities will return. In time, they may expand. He could become the most powerful human in history."

"Yes!" Willys pumped his fist.

Mr. Wilson sat his son on his knee and removed the shiny shoes from the boy's feet.

From orbit, they could see an intense beam of energy from the ship strike the planet. A thin plasma that looked like the ghost of grape jelly quickly covered the entire surface of the globe and spread into space.

"What are you doing?" Harrison asked.

"Creating a temporal anomaly," said Pirate's Pet 3.

"It will affect everything in your solar system except us," Goobex 2 told them. "We are shielded by Goobex technology."

Around the world, the flow of time was reversed. It was as if the aliens had hit a cosmic rewind button. Drowned people flew out of the river and ran backward down a nonexistent ramp before attending the rally in reverse and driving home backward.

In roughly eighty-two million BC, a pterosaur's life was spared. The rift in time never happened.

Sound cannons were uninvented.

Digestive juices were pumped back into the guts of countless soldiers.

Driverless shuttles, subway cars, and helicopters retraced their travels with or without the original number of passengers.

The process took only two hours.

As she watched the plasma slowly melt away, Violet thought about what it would take to join the Goobex alliance. Warfare, poverty, pollution, greed, and cruelty were all huge obstacles. If only the aliens could make those things melt away like their purple plasma.

"I wish there was an easy way to change things," she mused. "But as Martin Luther King said, 'I refuse to accept the view that mankind is so tragically bound to the starless midnight of racism and war that the bright daybreak of peace and brotherhood can never become a reality.'"

Dr Harrison smiled at her. "A little consideration, a little thought for others, makes all the difference."

"Is that quote from the Dalai Lama?" Violet asked.

"No," he answered. "It is from Eeyore in *Winnie-the-Pooh*."

"The process is complete," Goobex 1 announced. "You are the only humans who know the truth. Is there anything we can do to thank you?"

"No. We cannot give you superpowers," Pirate's Pet 1 answered the unasked question.

"Rats!" Brad was extremely disappointed.

"We are in position for your return to Earth. Your planet has traveled forty-eight hours into the past," Goobex 2 informed them.

The Wilsons exchanged glances.

Pirate's Pet 3 gave Dr. Harrison a bone-bruising hug.

"Gooby-ooby and I want to thank you for your help."

"Please, don't squeeze so tightly." The doctor looked up at the creature after it released him. "Now that I know the truth, continuing my search for your kind seems pointless."

"Maybe not. My people could teach you a lot about living in peace," said Pirate's Pet 3. "I have a whole community of cousins up in Canada. They've got a great foot doctor named Paul something."

Goobex 2 flew over to the humans.

"It is time for you to go."

Dr. Harrison nodded to the alien.

"Is there some way we can reach you in case we need your help or advice?"

"Yes," Goobex 2 replied. "We have left the means to communicate—"

Before the alien could finish her sentence, the humans were bathed in blue light and they were transported to a shady little trail in the forest.

Mr. Wilson picked up his shoeless son and put him up on his shoulders.

"Sorry, doc. I guess we'll never know about that communication device."

"No, we won't. Very unfortunate." Harrison clasped his hands behind his back and looked down at his feet.

Violet took off her bigfoot pin and offered it to the doctor.

He looked at it before taking it and pinning it to his shirt.

"I can't wait to see if Mom's memory was really erased," Violet said.

Her dad smiled.

"She doesn't forget much, does she?"

"I guess she won't remember my BB gun," said Brad.

"Or my superpower," Willys added.

"Or that she still owes me for babysitting." Violet kicked a pine cone off the trail.

As they hiked to town, Mr. Wilson tried to solve a puzzle involving time travel.

"I don't know if we've gone back to before I order the pizzas, but if you'd like to join us for dinner, I'd be honored to have you as our guest, doctor."

Harrison shook his head. "No, thank you. My sour disposition would make me bad company."

Violet had lost the greatest story in history, but she had her whole life ahead of her. Dr. Harrison's sacrifice was much greater. Instead of being vindicated as a risk-taker, willing to face scorn, ridicule, and even political persecution in the name of scientific discovery, everyone would think of him as a loser and a crackpot again.

Brad reached into his pocket and pulled out a plastic barf bag.

"Here," he offered it to Harrison. "I found this in a Sasquatch track by the hot spring."

The doctor took the bag and examined its contents.

"Thank you. This could be very helpful."

"Maybe I can write about it in our school paper." Violet smiled at him.

"Good luck with that." Harrison put the bag in his pocket. "By the way, I think you should call it *Sky View True News*."

"Why didn't I think of that?" Violet thumped her forehead with the palm of her hand.

Willys looked up at the doctor with mixed feelings.

"Your sandwich was good," he said. "But I don't ever want another one."

EPILOGUE

The next few days were fairly normal.

Violet canceled her hike with Pamela, but they had a very productive meeting while Brad and Willys took a well-deserved nap.

Dr. Harrison traded in his truck and moved to Kamloops, British Columbia, where his search for bigfoot continued.

Mrs. Wilson was the only member of her family who couldn't fathom why her son had a sudden aversion to peanut butter and jelly sandwiches. She knew something had happened, but what concerned her most was the newfound respect between Violet and Brad. Those two had grown closer for some reason, and she wanted to know why.

It seemed like most of the weirdness was behind them as the new school year approached, but that was before the COVID-19 pandemic, among other things.

I don't expect you to believe this story.

It seems too strange to be real, but that doesn't change the truth.

In a reality touching our own, you saw the Goobex spaceship on television. You heard General Hazard deliver the president's proclamation of our peaceful intentions as tanks and soldiers aimed their guns at the alien craft. You watched the news reports as Willys was subjected to the undigester and as the president's rally turned into a riot.

If not for the time-warping effects of a thin purple plasma, another you would recall seeing the president's head disappear as he stood onstage in his underwear. Even in our own universe, you would have a gut feeling that bigfoot is real and that our planet has been visited by strange creatures from another galaxy.

But in the world where these things happened, the timeline was rewritten. The memories of what happened were erased. It was an act of benevolence, compliments of the Goobexes, the peanut butter and jelly sandwiches from outer space.

The End

If we are to teach real peace in this world, and if we are to carry on a real war against war, we shall have to begin with the children.

—Mahatma Gandhi

ABOUT THE AUTHOR

I. S. Noah grew up with his four siblings in Los Angeles in the 1960s. In his early years, camping trips with Boy Scout Troop 13, watching classic television sitcoms, and collecting comic books were his favorite activities. He studied playwriting at UC Santa Barbara before earning an MFA in dramatic art at UC Davis in 1985. After graduating, he worked as a production assistant on the television show *Falcon Crest* for several seasons. His creative skills were next employed in creating scripted lesson plans and fun math materials for the nonprofit Mike's Math Club program through which he taught inner-city schoolchildren for twenty years.

He now lives in Marin County, where he loves hiking among the giant redwoods and praying for sanity and peace in the world.

Printed in the USA
CPSIA information can be obtained
at www.ICGtesting.com
CBHW072330020624
9360CB00003B/7